D0211558

The Floating Girl

Also by Sujata Massey

The Flower Master
Zen Attitude
The Salaryman's Wife

The
Floating Girl

Sujata Massey

HarperCollins*Publishers*

THE FLOATING GIRL. Copyright © 2000 by Sujata Massey. All rights reserved. Printed in the United States of America. No part of this book may be used or reproduced in any manner whatsoever without written permission except in the case of brief quotations embodied in critical articles and reviews. For information address HarperCollins Publishers Inc., 10 East 53rd Street, New York, NY 10022. ·

HarperCollins books may be purchased for educational, business, or sales promotional use. For information please write: Special Markets Department, HarperCollins Publishers Inc., 10 East 53rd Street, New York, NY 10022.

FIRST EDITION

Designed by William Ruoto

Printed on acid-free paper

Library of Congress Cataloging-in-Publication Data has been applied for.

ISBN 0-06-019229-1

00 01 02 03 04 ❖/RRD 10 9 8 7 6 5 4 3 2 1

Acknowledgments

I thank sincerely the friends who introduced me to Japanese animation and made writing this book a pleasure: J.D. Considine, of Baltimore, and Akemi Narita and her daughter, Aki, of Yokohama. I am also indebted to each eagle eye belonging to dear friends in my two local writers' critique groups, as well as Susanne Trowbridge, Manami Amanai, and Chris Belton, the Tokyo-based novelist and translator. To my agents, Ellen Geiger and Dave Barbor, at Curtis Brown, and my friends at HarperCollins, especially Carolyn Marino, Betsy Areddy, Robin Stamm, and Gene Mydlowski, thanks once again for your flexibility, kindness, and good ideas.

Much of this book was written while I was staying in India, and I benefited from the loving support of my relatives, especially the ones who were with me—Rekha Banerjee, Hemantika Puri, and Padamaben and A.V. Parikh. Also, thanks to the ones who kept things going at home: Claire and Karin Banerjee, Subir Banerjee and Manju Parikh, and Sam, Harriot, Alex, and Don Massey. I also am indebted to the staff at Parikh Steel Calcutta, especially Jawaharlal Joshi and Neelam Mishra, who let my muse run rampant on their computers. To Pia

Massey, my new daughter, thank you for being so much fun. To Rose Anne Ullrich, Jingkun Zhu, and Tamara Clark, thanks for making it possible for me to write. To my husband, Tony Massey, who got me safely back into the United States: You are the best.

The Floating Girl

Cast of Characters

REI SHIMURA: Japanese-American antiques maven moonlighting as a columnist

ALEC TAMPOLE: Australian-born entertainment editor at the *Gaijin Times*, Tokyo's monthly for foreigners

RIKA FUCHIDA: Showa College student working as an entertainment-section intern at the *Gaijin Times*

MR. SANNO: Owner of the *Gaijin Times* and Sanno Advertising

TAKEO KAYAMA: Temporarily unemployed flower-arranging teacher turned home renovator. He has a twin sister, Natsumi Kayama, and a father, Masanobu Kayama, who is headmaster of the Kayama School of Ikebana.

KUNIO TAKAHASHI: Amateur artist of the *Showa Story* comic strip

Marcellus: Senegalese immigrant who works as a hawker and dancer at Show a Boy nightclub

Chiyo: Mama-san of Show a Boy

Nicky Larsen: Showa College student who falls in love with Japanese amateur animation and the dancing life

Seiko Hattori: Showa College student who shares Nicky's passion for amateur animation

Lieutenant Hata: Rei's confidant in the Tokyo Metropolitan Police

Hiroko Shima: Managing editor of the *Mars Girl* comic strip published by the mainstream publisher Dayo Comics

Manami Oida: Head artist for the *Mars Girl* comic strip

Tsutomu "Tom" Shimura: Rei's cousin, an emergency-room attending physician at St. Luke's International Hospital

The Fish: A businessman who swims with the sharks

The Hedgehog: A rabid animation fan

Plus a colorful array of beauticians, journalists, animation fans, and others who dream of turning staid Tokyo into a more animated city.

1

"Is the pain killing you? Shall I stop?"

I shook my head because the pain had eased temporarily. Miss Kumiko sighed and stroked more sticky warmth over my inner thigh—a deceptively pleasant sensation. I knew that six more inches needed to be cleared. The aesthetician pressed a strip of cotton over my thigh, and I sucked in my breath as she began to pull.

"Oh!" I gasped as she yanked at least a hundred hairs from their follicles.

"Japanese women don't like to cry out," Miss Kumiko said brightly. "Not even when delivering babies. When my niece was born, my sister was silent. At moments of severe pain, she bit a handkerchief. Would you like a handkerchief?"

"No, thank you, and this is hardly childbirth. It's a bikini wax!" Damn my American half for making the process necessary. If I'd been fully Japanese, I would have inherited the hairless gene. But I was a *hafu* or *hanbunjin* or *konketsujin* or whatever name Miss Kumiko secretly used for mixed-race people. It was my own stupid vanity that had brought me into Power Princess Spa before the start of the July beach season. I had one final business appointment that afternoon, and then a drive the next day to the beach. But first I had to get through the pain.

"Madam, it is not that I mind, but the manicurist in the next cubicle has problems," Miss Kumiko whispered. "Surprise screams from customers can cause her to lose rhythm."

"Maybe there's a reason your customers scream," I said.

"*Ja*, we are all done!" Miss Kumiko made a series of light slaps against my groin. This was kinkier than I'd expected, but then again, this was my first experience with waxing in Tokyo. I would live and learn.

I put on my skirt and limped out to the stylish black-and-white reception area.

"Rei Shimura?" The salon's bleached-blond receptionist called me up to her stylish chrome desk.

"Yes?" I continued at my slow pace, thighs sticking together because of a few remnants of wax.

"We have two kinds of bikini wax, large and small," she announced so clearly that some of the other customers in the waiting area looked up from their magazines. "When we spoke on the phone, we thought you were a typical Japanese, so we quoted you the price for a small wax. However, Miss Kumiko reports that you required the large wax. Therefore the fee is a bit higher: six thousand yen. Is that fine?"

The entire reception room seemed to be leaning close to hear my embarrassed answer.

"Fine," I said glumly. With an exchange rate of about 100 yen to the dollar, making the price of hair removal about $60, more than twice the going rate in the United States. I paid up, thinking the only silver lining was that Miss Kumiko wouldn't require a tip. This was Japan, where you never paid extra for good service. It was expected.

I walk this uneasy line between pleasure and pain—and understanding and confusion—almost daily. Four years ago, I emigrated from San Francisco to Tokyo seeking a job working with Japanese antiques. Nobody would hire me, so I had to establish my own business. It's been a struggle at times, but I'm proud to say that at last I've leaped over the poverty line. Miss Kumiko would not think of asking me to find her an antique chest, but plenty of older, wealthy Japanese have done that. Even in an economic downturn, I'd had some very lucky breaks.

As I struggled out of the Power Princess Spa, I was headed toward my latest lucky spot: the *Gaijin Times*, an English-language magazine aimed at foreigners living in Tokyo. Its editor in chief, an ambitious young woman journalist called Whitney Talbot, had hunted me down after she'd read my article on ceramics for a Japanese antiques magazine. Whitney had asked me to write similar articles with, as she put it, "an element of street sass." I was apprehensive, but when she named a price for a monthly column, I decided I had to try. My first article was a guide to haggling for antiques at the weekend flea markets held at Tokyo's Shinto shrines. It was supposed to be a do-it-yourself article, but my phone started ringing off the hook with insecure foreigners willing to pay me to haggle for them. It had become very good business.

I put away my quick rush of pride as I entered the narrow sliver of a building that was home to the Sanno Advertising Agency and the *Gaijin Times*. I rode the elevator up to the third-floor hall, where everything was painted a dull beige.

Throbbing music coming from speakers stationed on either side of the *Gaijin Times* office door was the first indicator that the magazine was striving to break free from a beige mold. Inside were chocolate-colored walls, chocolate brown tables, and a gray lump lying across the chocolate-and-strawberry print carpet.

I drew closer to the lump to identify it. Alec Tampole, an Australian who edited the magazine's copious nightclub listings, was stretched out on the floor, arms angled out from his side in an A shape, his knees curled snugly against his chest.

"What's wrong?" I asked, hurrying over.

"I'm doing some Pilates exercises. I forgot you were coming in today, Rye." He pushed his legs over his head in a move that looked like the yoga plow.

"My name is actually pronounced 'ray.' As in Sugar Ray," I said, striving for a pop music reference that he would understand.

"Come closer so I can hear you over the music." Alec slowly lowered his legs, grunting with exertion.

I stood as close to his ear as possible and shouted the correct pronunciation.

He laughed. "Right, Rye. Had an accident coming over?"

"No. What do you mean? Is something going on outside?"

"That's not the kind of accident I'm talking about. What's that gunk on your knickers?"

"You bastard!" I realized belatedly that the music maven had been angling himself for a perfect view up my skirt. I leaped away from him.

"Heh heh. Had a hot wax for a hot date, eh?" As he swung his hips over his head once again, I kicked his large, khaki-clad behind. His anguished yelp was music to my ears as I left the reception area, heading into the tiny warren of offices and my next assignment.

2

"Where's Whitney?" I aimed my question at Rika Fuchida, the magazine's college intern, who was standing with bare feet on Alec's desk taping up the edge of a Cibo Matto poster that had come loose. I was surprised Alec wasn't in the room watching Rika. Her skirt was shorter than mine.

"Oh, hello, Rei-san!" Rika was Japanese, so she had no trouble with my name. "Didn't you hear that Whitney-san is not here anymore?"

"No. Is she working from home?" I glanced at my watch. I had to be somewhere else in two hours, but I really had wanted to see the *Gaijin Times* editor for approval of my next column topic. I was proposing a do-it-yourself piece on how to buy and refinish a *tansu* chest for less than a thousand dollars.

Rika shook her head so vigorously that her trendy short pigtails bounced. "Whitney quit."

"Oh, no!" I was aghast.

Alec leaned in the doorway and joined our conversation. "She took a job at the *Asian Wall Street Journal*. Going on to greener pastures, heh heh. Good thing for all of us that she did a bunk. This magazine needs to be more culturally connected.

Whitney spoke the language, but she didn't know much about the pulse of modern Japan."

"If the *Journal* hired her, somebody obviously thinks she's good," I said. From what I'd heard about her Yale education and journalism experience, Whitney was almost over qualified for the *Gajin Times*.

"Mr. Sanno, the magazine's owner, is sitting in on the story meeting today. He's the one who's going to select the new editor." Alec looked as if he would explode with excitement. "Don't get any ideas about showing off during the meeting. I saw your resume. The only journalism experience you've had prior to this is the *Johns Hopkins University News-Letter*."

"I'm not interested in the editor's job," I replied coolly. His mention of the magazine owner had made me nervous— would Mr. Sanno even want to keep me on as a columnist? I was very grateful for the publicity that the *Gaijin Times* column had given my business. My net earnings were 20 percent higher since I'd started being published.

"It's almost time for the meeting," Rika said. "May I pause in your office redecoration, Alec-san, in order to serve the coffee?"

"I'll help you," I offered, not wanting to stand next to Alec for a minute longer. It was only when Rika and I were placing small glasses of iced coffee on wooden coasters around the conference table that I realized how foolish my move had been. I was acting like an obsequious office lady. This was not the way to reinforce my stature as a columnist to the magazine's owner.

I wondered what Mr. Sanno was thinking when he took the seat of power at the end of the battered steel table. The magazine's staff of six full-time editorial employees was a motley assortment of young people who perfectly reflected patterns of immigration to fin de siècle Japan. There was Joey Hirota, the half-Taiwanese, half-Japanese restaurant critic; Norton

Jones, a fresh Columbia University graduate who covered national politics; Toshi Ueda, a recent Waseda University graduate who was the photo editor; my friend Karen Anderson, a former model who had put on weight and now wrote about fashion trends; the repulsive Alec, who did the music and entertainment listings; and Rika Fuchida, Alec's intern assistant. The gang wore faux- and genuine vintage patterned polyester, double knit and jersey. Earrings swung from multiple holes, and heavy rings and bangles clattered against the table whenever anyone reached for their coffee. There was an undeniable odor of tobacco hanging over the group and a ratio of one ashtray per person on the table, although nobody was smoking yet, perhaps in deference to the magazine's owner.

Mr. Sanno appeared about forty years old, but instead of the gray or navy suit that was de rigueur with men his age, he was wearing a flashy green suit with wide lapels. He sat at the end of the table flipping through a large ring binder filled with pages of spreadsheets. Numbers, I thought, tensing up. I suspected that he would talk about what had proven profitable in the past, and how we would need to change.

"Thank you for allowing me to join your regular story meeting. You are kind to let me intrude into your busy day." Mr. Sanno's voice was surprisingly high. I wondered if this was because he found speaking English a strain. He spoke at the level of someone who did business on a daily basis with English speakers, but he didn't have the fluency of Japanese who had lived or studied overseas.

"Hey, no worries! I'd like to see a lot more of you," Alec said in his brash Australian way, and I sensed a stiffening around the table. Alec was trying to turn his role as de facto editor into a permanent promotion.

"Thank you, Mr. Tampon," Mr. Sanno said, smoothly botching the pronunciation of Alec's surname. I didn't hide my smile. "We shall all miss the leadership of Miss Whitney Talbot. However, as we frequently say in Japan and China, the kanji character for *crisis* is made from those for two words: *danger* and *opportunity*. Our challenging time offers a great chance to move forward, to create a larger circulation for *Gaijin Times*."

I stopped smiling. Mr. Sanno was talking about numbers even sooner than I'd expected.

"You may know that the *Gaijin Times* is the only magazine that Sanno Advertising owns. Perhaps you would like to understand why we created this magazine." He glanced around the table. "Because we own the *Gaijin Times*, we can run advertisements on its pages for free. Of course, we charge our clients the cost of our advertising services, and they agree that it is a fair system. If we have a Mexican restaurant as a client, we run an ad for the spot, and in the same issue, Joey Hirota gives it a good review."

"Mr. Sanno, if I might say a few words, the magazine is more than an advertising circular. I report stories on the banking crisis, the *yakuza*, the future of the Diet," Norton interjected.

Norton didn't know the right etiquette for a conversation with a Japanese boss. I exchanged quick unhappy looks with Toshi and Rika. Joey Hirota was still staring down in his lap, as if he'd been horribly embarrassed to be revealed as having written phony reviews. I should have figured out the reason for the review scam long ago. Personally, I never took much stock in anyone who thought you could buy a decent chimichanga in Tokyo.

"With changes in the economy, however, our loyal advertisers have less money to spend. To keep the magazine alive, we need more subscriptions."

I did know that the business of being a working foreigner in Tokyo had gotten tough. Salaries for English teachers, bar hostesses, and the like had dropped precipitously in the last few years. Young *gaijin* were deeply skeptical of the length of time that they could make a living in Tokyo, which made the prospect of their paying 6,000 yen up front for twelve issues of a magazine unlikely.

"I agree that we need to up our subscriber list," Alec chimed in. "We have to increase page space for music and clubs, things that remind *gaijin* kids of the stuff they left behind. A cover with the Beastie Boys or Mariah Carey would sell far more than one with a Japanese person on it. Get it?"

"I see your point," Toshi Ueda, the photographer, said. No Japanese person would blatantly tell another person he was wrong, but I had a sense that Toshi had something up his sleeve. "Speaking of musical culture, it is interesting that the Namie Amuro cover sold more than any other issue to date."

"Yes. Sales of that issue prove that Japanese idol singers appeal to foreigners. Foreigners come to Japan because they admire our popular culture!" Mr. Sanno's mild voice had become vehement, proving to me that Alec's brash, anti-Japanese comment had annoyed him.

I saw my chance to make a gentle comment to help my own cause along. "I agree. Another aspect of Japanese culture that foreigners love is Japanese antiques. Even if budgets are small, people are still enthusiastically buying vintage Japanese furniture."

"What about original Japanese fashion?" Karen chimed in. "Why don't we point out some of the local designers who aren't yet in the department stores and are thus less expensive?"

"So many good ideas." Mr. Sanno rubbed his smooth chin. "In this case, I have looked at the Japanese publishing market for guidance. Can you identify the single largest-selling category of book in Japan today?"

"Business," Norton said with a yawn.

Mr. Sanno shook his head.

"Pornography," Alec said with a sneer.

"No, I'm afraid it's something rather more innocent in its nature."

Rika raised her hand. When Mr. Sanno nodded at her, she said timidly, "*Manga?*"

He smiled expansively. "That's right. Forty percent of all written material sold in Japan is comics. Will the young lady please tell me her name? I'm afraid we haven't met."

"Rika Fuchida. I'm just the intern here from Showa College—"

"A fine school. I am a graduate." Mr. Sanno twinkled at her. "Do they still have the *manga* club?"

"Oh, yes. I'm a member."

Mr. Sanno flipped open the binder he'd been perusing and read from it.

"As Rika-chan could probably tell you, there are several English-language magazines aimed at fans of Japanese anima-tion. But there has not yet been an English-language *manga* that instructs foreigners about life in Japan."

Was he going to turn *Gaijin Times* into a comic book? No wonder Whitney had quit. Every face at the table was neutral. I could only imagine that the others were as shocked as I.

"When do you anticipate the change happening?" Toshi croaked. I imagined he was pondering what role his artsy black-and-white photographs could have in a comic maga-zine.

"Since most of the three future issues' articles and art are already completed—yes, Miss Talbot was very efficient—that must not go to waste. However, I would like to see at least two articles in next month's issue that explore the idea of *manga*. We will also put out a call for cartoonists to audition their work, and begin running two or three different comic stories per issue. It's now July, so let's see . . . a full *manga*-format issue by December would be reasonable. With the hard work of everyone, it could happen. Joey will write his restaurant reviews as a comic strip—imagine the possibilities! The reader will not only read about what the food is like, but see it. Likewise for you, Miss Karen. Photographs don't work anymore."

"What do you mean?" Karen sounded confused.

"If a dress is not flattering to a woman, the real-life appearance"—Mr. Sanno gestured to Karen's muumuulike black dress—"makes it look bad. Likewise, photographs tell the true story, which can make the retailer upset. A cartoon illustration, on the other hand, can make any dress look truly lovely."

I felt strange, as if I were hovering over the table and witnessing the beginning of a disaster. Karen felt bad enough about her weight gain, which Mr. Sanno was cruelly pointing out. What would happen to the rest of us, and to the publication? The *Gaijin Times* had never been a prizewinning publication, but it had done a decent job imparting crucial lifestyle information to foreigners. I'd used the *Gaijin Times* to search for apartments and jobs when I'd arrived. Come to think of it, I'd learned about the waxing specialists at Power Princess Spa after reading an article Karen had written in last month's issue. Could all that be scrapped for wasp-waisted, big-eyed androids carrying guns?

"I assume you'll bring in a new editor." Joey sounded glum. "One who is expert in comical matters."

"We Japanese always believe in promoting from within," Mr. Sanno said. "I am certain that one of you could easily rise to shine in the transition. We will decide on some projects for all of us today, and that will keep us busy before I select the editor."

There was a long silence, and I imagined everyone was trying to think of projects.

"I've heard there is an American scholar who is an expert on comic books aimed at salarymen. I could explore the changing ethos of work in Japan through *manga*," Norton suggested. "Toshi could take pictures of salarymen reading comic books on the subway to go with the story."

"The photos can be used as a basis for *manga* sketches," Mr. Sanno said. "If the salarymen are ugly, the drawing can make them look better. In my opinion, there have been too many ugly people in the magazine lately."

Mr. Sanno was not exactly a Japanese version of Hugh Grant, but of course, nobody could say that.

"Well, that salaryman idea takes care of Norton and Toshi. But what about Karen-chan?"

Mr. Sanno was calling all the women in the room by the suffix *-chan*, which means "little." I could tell that Karen thought it was demeaning, because her pale skin flushed. She spoke rapidly, another sign he'd rattled her.

"I was writing a story about fall cocktail dresses worn by some of the top bar hostesses in town. I will call a fashion illustrator who can sketch the clothes on the girls. They're very, very attractive," she added, as if to head off further comments on ugliness versus beauty.

"What about sketching the clothes on well-known cartoon characters?" Rika, the intern, ventured.

"It might not be legal. Betty and Veronica are probably copyrighted," I said swiftly, to avoid having Mr. Sanno slap Karen with an impossible assignment.

"Actually, it's different here," Rika replied. "Japanese *manga* publishers don't really care if amateur artists copy the figures. What the amateurs sell is called *doujinshi,* and when those *doujinshi* comics sell, it is believed to create publicity for the original series."

"Rika-chan is right." Mr. Sanno nodded at Rika, who promptly hung her head and mumbled how worthless she was. It was a perfect Japanese etiquette moment that I would have appreciated if Mr. Sanno had not swiftly turned his gimlet gaze to me. "Rei-chan, I know that you are only a part-time employee, but you will be a part of the transformation. Your column relates to antiques and fine arts, so you will have many possibilities."

"I know very little about *manga*," I said stiffly. "My background is in Japanese decorative arts."

"*Manga* are today's most important art form," Mr. Sanno said. "Can't you write that in your column?"

A battle raged inside me. I wanted to walk away from this stupid fantasy comic book of Mr. Sanno's, but I didn't want to give up seeing the phrase REI SHIMURA ANTIQUES in fourteen-point type once a month. I spoke carefully. "My goal is to help the *Gaijin Times* be the best that it can be. That is why I would be willing to resign if my writing doesn't fit the new format."

"Are you hoping to be fired, Rei?" Alec asked. I was really beginning to hate him.

"I know what you can do, Rei-san!" Rika offered. "Since you are a serious person, you can write a serious article about the history and artistic significance of *manga*. If you can present *manga* in a worthwhile light, the readers will become prepared for the switch to the new format."

"That's right, Miss Fuchida! Please help with Miss Shimura's assignment."

Rika, sitting across from me in her short pleated skirt, knee socks, and braids, still looked more like a junior-high-school student than a senior at Showa College. But at that moment I, and probably every other staffer in the room, could imagine what form she would emerge into as surely as Clark Kent transformed himself into Superman: She'd be Rika Fuchida, *Gaijin Times*'s youngest-ever editor in chief.

3

"Jealousy is a sin," I muttered into my arm on Saturday afternoon.

"What's that? I can barely hear you over the waves." Takeo Kayama was rubbing some sort of superorganic sunblock on my back. Up and down, back and forth—his fingers, rough from gardening, created a pleasant abrasive sensation on my skin.

"I'm jealous of the student intern at the *Gaijin Times*," I said in a louder voice. "Rika Fuchida was a glorified gofer until yesterday, when she turned out to have the equivalent of a Ph.D. in cartoon history! It's all so suspicious. She started working at the magazine just a few months ago. There was nothing on her resume about her knowledge of animation. It surfaces at just the right time, in front of the right person. I wonder if she knew in advance what was going to happen to the magazine."

"Whatever the situation, you should feel glad for her," Takeo said. "You've had your own share of lucky breaks. As have I."

"That's true." I counted Takeo Kayama as one of my blessings. In the few months that I'd known him, he'd brought a considerable amount of fresh air and sun into my life. It was an ironic union, because I was struggling to become an upwardly mobile capitalist while Takeo was on a downward slide, forgoing a management role in his family's prosperous flower-arranging school to plant his own organic seedlings.

"Are they paying you as much as usual for the story?" Takeo asked, putting the cap back on the tube of sunblock. We were on Isshiki Beach in Hayama, a seaside town an hour south of Tokyo where Takeo's family had a summer house. Ping-Pong balls and Frisbees were in the air along with the excited squeals of a few hundred schoolchildren on their brief summer vacation.

"Mr. Sanno became so thrilled about Rika's idea that he asked me to write something longer than I usually do. He even said to me later that he'd pay me more for it. He really wants some kind of article that gives *manga* credibility."

A toddler stumbled by, kicking up clods of dark brown sand. I readjusted the sun umbrella we'd rented for 5,000 yen, and reminded myself that the dirty-looking sand was that way for geological reasons. Isshiki Beach was supposed to be one of the cleanest beaches in the Tokyo area because of the proximity of the emperor's summer villa. However, there was an ominous trickle coursing through the sand from the beach's sole outhouse-style lavatory.

"You don't have to do it, but I think you'd have a good time," Takeo said, resuming the discussion of my potential assignment. "All you have to do is read comic books for a few days, then sit down at the computer and type out your impressions of the comics versus what you know about wood-block prints."

"There are two problems with that," I said. "The first one is that I know the wood-block artists are going to be far superior in terms of artistry and social relevance. It's a foregone conclusion, and one Mr. Sanno won't want to hear. The second problem is one that you know well. I can't read much Japanese." I knew that *manga* for elementary-school children were written in the phonetic *hiragana* and *katakana* alphabets that I knew well, but adult *manga* were written almost completely in kanji, the vast system of pictographic symbols for words that had originated in China. At the beach snack shop, I'd paged through a magazine called *Morning* and found it almost indecipherable.

"Hmmm, maybe this will get you to finally learn to read." Takeo continued to massage my back.

I was a nearly fluent speaker but was stymied at reading and writing—a great embarrassment for me. The only way to fix it was to seriously study kanji for a few hours a day, but at the end of the day, after having pounded the pavements of Tokyo look-ing for antiques and suitable homes for them to enter, all I wanted to do was read escapist English-language fiction.

Takeo looked at me serenely. His complexion had tanned to copper from his work as a gardener, work that was extremely unusual for a man with his background, but something he'd chosen to do to get away from his father's dictatorial ways. Takeo was only twenty-eight, but several months of labor under the sun had already carved a few lines around his eyes and built lean muscles that were noticeable as he crouched over me in nothing more than his black swimming trunks.

"You know how hard reading is for me," I began.

"You always say that," Takeo told me in a voice as warm as the day. "Just as I should be practicing English but have given up because you're so good at speaking Japanese. But I don't live in America, and you live here. I'll help you learn to read. We'll work on the *manga* together."

"But this should be a time for you to relax," I said, feeling grateful but a little bit disappointed at the same time. I had hoped that this would be a special weekend for us to figure out where our relationship was really headed. Hence the no-telephone-contact-until-Monday message I'd left with my answering service. Hence the cooler I had packed with my most delectable home cooking. Hence the bikini wax.

As I lay in my twisted position, trying to sense Takeo's feelings, a Ping-Pong ball smacked the center of his forehead. I gasped as a young man wearing a semiobscene red nylon thong jogged over to retrieve the ball. He apologized with a flurry of bows and darted off, his muscular buttocks gleaming under a sheen of oil. It was amazing how young Japanese men had so little modesty about their nether regions. In a stark contrast, most of the beach's females wore maillots, regarding their stomachs as an X-rated region. I was the only one in a Speedo bikini. It had been my bathing suit of choice for the last ten years because it kept my tummy in firm check and the top had straps that couldn't be pulled down by waves.

"Would you like to go for a swim?"

"Actually, I can't swim very far," I said. When Takeo looked puzzled, I said, "I swim, but you'll see I'm rather clumsy. My best stroke is the sidestroke. Obviously, I'm not going to be able to make it as far as the buoys, if that's where you want to go."

Takeo smiled at me. "We don't have to swim anywhere. A lot of people are just hanging around."

I looked and saw what he meant. Many of the people in the water seemed to be floating in place, playing Ping-Pong, or just standing together, conversing.

"Our things will be safe on the beach?" I asked, gesturing toward my beach bag, which held the comics and a little money.

"Of course. This is Japan!" Takeo laughed and set off in a sprint for the water. I caught up just as he entered the water. It was gloriously warm, almost bathlike; I sidestroked for fifty meters behind his crawl before becoming a little bit tired.

"I'm going to have to stop," I called, stretching my legs downward to check the depth. It was about four and a half feet deep. I wondered how far out the drop-off was.

Takeo swam back to me with a few quick strokes. He dove under the surface, grabbed me by the waist, and pulled me down for an underwater kiss.

I came up sputtering and laughing. With our heads out of water, we kissed some more. We had only recently become lovers, so there was a playful quality to our time together.

"I like your bathing suit," he said, slipping his hand into my bikini bottom.

"You wouldn't dare," I said.

"Wouldn't I?" With a flick of his fingers, my pants were off and dangling over his wrist.

"Wow," I said, casting a glance around us. Nobody seemed to be looking. I'd heard about the Japanese enthusiasm for public sex. Of course, was this public? Nobody could really see what was going on underneath the waves. Something soft fluttered across my inner thighs—was it a fish, or Takeo? I wrapped my legs around his waist, feeling my body temperature rise. I wanted to do this.

"Just relax," Takeo murmured, bending over me. I did.

As wave after wave of pleasure swept over me, I wasn't afraid to moan, knowing the surf was covering the sound of my voice. But when we were through and had both caught our breaths, a problem presented itself. Sometime during our wild wigglings my bikini bottom had gotten loose from Takeo's arm and floated away. Now I was bottomless, and could go in one of two directions—either suicidally into the heart of Tokyo Bay, or back toward the hundreds of families picnicking on the sand. The irony of my recent bikini wax struck me—I'd appear as immaculately groomed as a men's magazine centerfold if I had to show myself.

"It's quite simple, really," Takeo said in between guffaws. "You just stay in the water. I'll go out and buy a bikini at a beach shop. I'll swim back to you with it. You can dress underwater."

"No!" I laughed back just as merrily. "How can you possibly find a bikini that resembles the American one that I'm wearing? It's a better idea that you give me your swimming trunks. At least they match my top, and the boy-leg look is in. I'll go out and buy you some new trunks. Do you really want the same style? I think one of the vendors on the beach is selling thongs. One-size-fits-all okay with you?"

"Do you mean what you're saying?" His eyes were huge and horrified.

"Do you wear a different size?" I asked mischievously.

"Rei, you're being impossible! If you leave me here without my bathing trunks, I'll be completely naked. It is safer that you remain half dressed and concealed by the water than leave me with nothing at all. What if someone discovers me and reports me to the police?"

"That's not logical at all!" My mirth was starting to fade.

"Look! Do you see those boys over there? What are they playing with?"

I looked, and indeed there were a couple of elementary-school-age boys about twenty feet away lounging on water rafts. One of them was fashioning a kind of mask out of my bikini bottom, using the leg holes for eyes.

"This is just . . . too bizarre," I said.

Takeo swam over to them quickly and started talking. I couldn't hear a word of his explanation, but I saw the boy's mouth moving and he rather reluctantly handed over the bottoms to Takeo.

"Thanks. Now they'll know they're mine, won't they?" I grumbled when Takeo had swum back to me with my bikini bottom.

"The weird thing is, when the bikini washed up against their raft, they didn't think it was a bikini bottom. They thought it was a Batman mask."

"Crazed by comics," I said.

"Exactly. I let them remain in their state of ignorance."

"I guess this must be a message to me," I said.

"Oh?"

"I shouldn't look down on comics. They've saved my reputation."

4

Two hours later we were sprawled across Takeo's futon, surrounded by comics. As I lay watching Takeo read aloud to me,
I found it hard to keep my pencil moving, dutifully translating
the words into English and writing them down. My attention
kept wandering over his golden brown back and down to his
loose-fitting drawstring pants.

Takeo, showing samurai toughness, was intent on finishing
the translations first. His voice droned softly.

"In a central Tokyo hospital on New Year's Day not so many
years ago, a baby girl was born. The baby had laughing green
eyes and black corkscrew locks that were quite unusual, so her
loving family named her Mezurashiko, 'rare and special
child.'

"Because Mezurashiko did not resemble a typical Japanese
child, the neighbors were convinced that she was the result of
an illegitimate union between her mother and an alien worker.
Poor Mezurashiko was bullied all the way through high
school. Little did anyone know that Mezurashiko's father
really was an alien—a handsome Martian who had left his
spaceship and slipped through an apartment building win-

dow on one of Tokyo's hottest nights to plunder the innocent sleeping body of Mezurashiko's mother. This alien's genes passed to little Mezurashiko, who became capable of incredible feats. When she matured, Mezurashiko decided it was time to make use of some of her powers."

I jotted down the translation, my thoughts somewhere else. If I had powers, I would have transformed the space around us. The Kayama house was a classic seaside villa built in the 1920s; rare because it hadn't been torn down, but sad because of the state into which it had fallen. Many tiles were missing from the charmingly arched roof, and on the inside, there were water-stained walls and tatami mats that housed a zoo of insects. Takeo had been living here almost all summer. I didn't know how he did it. Sure, I could see bits of his work here and there—a bathroom with new plumbing, and patches on walls that were going to be repainted. I had to admit that he was working hard. At least his futon was new and had nice cotton sheets on it. But he needed serious decorating help, given that the walls were covered by posters of endangered animals and martial artists that had to be relics of Takeo's boyhood, and the floor was covered with stacks of magazines.

I returned my attention to the two-hundred-page volume of *Mars Girl*. It was a far cry from the concise, colorful comic books I'd read in the United States. In *Mars Girl*, there was tremendous emphasis on facial expressions but very little attention given to drawing the background of the scenes. In that way, contemporary Japanese comics were also very different from the painstakingly etched wood-block print illustrations of the previous century. Of course, an artist couldn't do much in a black-and-white box two and a half inches long by four inches wide. *Manga* were artistically compromised from the start.

"I don't think *Mars Girl* is worthy of review," I said.

"Just as you thought *Ogre Slayer, Ah! My Goddess,* and *Tokyo Babylon* weren't worthy," Takeo said, throwing back his head back and taking in the last few drops of a can of Asahi Super Dry Beer.

"Your translations showed me that these comics have far stronger stories than they do art," I said. "However, I don't want to write about the improbable adventures of aliens mixing with the Japanese. That theme is so hackneyed it's in half the comics that we've already surveyed. And if I see another schoolgirl being raped, I'm going to throw up."

"But I mostly bought you *shoujo manga*, girls' comics, because I didn't think you'd like the violent ones!"

"The rape of an innocent sleeping woman isn't violent?" I put down the notebook in which I'd written Takeo's translations.

Takeo shrugged. "The *manga* aimed at women sometimes have themes that are very dark. But if the readers didn't want to read about such things, the stories would change."

"It makes me wonder what women want." I got up and stretched, looking out the floor-to-ceiling windows toward the garden and, beyond it, the sea. Because the house was situated high on a cliff, I could see all the way down to the sand, where a man was tossing a ball into the ocean for his dog to retrieve.

I felt pressure on the back of my neck and realized it was Takeo's lips. I stayed in place, watching the man and dog play, enjoying the sensation of the kiss.

"Is this what you want?" Takeo asked softly.

I rested my head on his shoulder, and I thought. I had known Takeo as a friend and now a lover for a few months. I had to admit that I thought about him when we were together, but not a lot when I was alone. This was our first full weekend together. I wanted it to go well.

"I want to succeed at this article. And I want to be with you," I said, still looking out of the window. "But you know, that underwater thing that happened . . . well, I'd never done anything like that before. I don't think I'd try it again."

"It was a fantasy." He turned me so that I could see his face. "I'd had it for a long time—ever since I was a teenager, really. Thank you for indulging me."

"Well, maybe you can return the favor." I smiled at him. "I have a fantasy, too."

"Oh, yes?"

"It involves a bed with clean cotton sheets. Air conditioner set on low. And a door that locks."

I slept better that night than I had in ages, lulled to sleep by the sound of waves. We'd turned off the air conditioner some-time in the middle of the night, and the cool breeze blowing in from the screened windows felt wonderful at 6 A.M. I slid out of bed, pausing to rearrange the covers over Takeo's long, lean body.

As I dressed for the run, I contemplated the last hour we'd spent awake, making love. Takeo had revealed himself to be passionate and skilled, capable of bringing forth feelings from me that had been locked up tightly for a long time. I'd spent the past year mourning the loss of my last boyfriend, a Scottish lawyer who had simply gotten tired of Japan and moved on, expecting me to go wherever he did. I wouldn't go—I loved Hugh, but I loathed the idea of being his depen-dent. Soon enough, his letters to me dropped off, and I heard he'd started a liaison with another woman. Still, as angry as I was with Hugh, I thought about him constantly.

I'd told myself that the best thing for me was to find a Japanese boyfriend, someone who obviously wanted to stay in the country. Takeo had not seemed interested in me when we first met months earlier at the Kayama School, but as we got to know each other, sparks began to fly.

Could I love Takeo? I asked myself as I unlatched the house's handsome wooden sliding doors and went out into the splendid morning for my run. When I was with Takeo, I enjoyed him thoroughly. But when I was at work, I forgot about him. Not that there were other men around that drew my attention—I thought with repulsion of Alec Tampole at the *Gaijin Times*. Over the last several months, work and pleasure had become sharply separated for me. When I worked as an antiques shopper or arts writer, it consumed all my energy.

I finished stretching and started off in a slow jog down the bumpy beach road into the heart of the village of Hayama. I ran past the wall guarding the emperor's summer villa from prying eyes. A group of stone-faced policemen were standing guard next to a dark gray police bus, a vehicle ready to cart off anyone who threatened the monarchy.

The imperial family was not at the villa that weekend— Takeo said that we'd have hit massive traffic delays if they had been there.

"I saw the emperor and crown prince walking on the beach when I was seven," Takeo had said to me. "My father told me that we should walk away so they wouldn't be embarrassed by having to see us. He said they wanted privacy. But I waved really hard, and the crown prince waved back. So I was glad, even though my father made me go to bed without dinner that night."

Takeo had disobeyed his father and been punished. I wondered what his father would think if he knew his son and I had become lovers. I'd first met Masanobu Kayama, just as I'd met Takeo, after a murder of a teacher at the Kayama School in the spring. The crime had been solved, but with that came a number of embarrassing discoveries, some of which pertained to Mr. Kayama's private life. I'd not told these things to Takeo, seeing no point in driving the father and son further apart.

I turned my mind firmly toward Project *Manga*, as I had begun to identify my *Gaijin Times* assignment. I would stay true to Mr. Sanno's desire to discuss the aesthetics of comic books, while offering the kind of straightforward shopping advice for which I was known. Perhaps Japanese comic books were collectible. I knew that in the United States, old comics could sell for thousands of dollars. To learn about the comics market in Japan, I would probably have to move from common convenience shops such as the one where Takeo had found popular girls' comics for me and into specialty stores and flea markets.

The beach road had narrowed, slowing the traffic of convertibles, buses, and family cars. I continued on, my sights set on the Morito Shrine, which signs told me was only five hundred meters ahead. I ran smoothly past a hodgepodge of tiny houses and beach shops and through a tall red gate leading to the religious haven.

Shinto shrines are places where Japanese people go for blessings upon birth and marriage, and to make prayers to their ancestors. My own pilgrimages to Shinto shrines were usually on Sundays, when flea markets were held on their grounds in Tokyo. I found that along with looking at antiques, I loved the shrines for their great jolts of color. I liked the crisp red-orange paint that decorated the gates and trim on the shrine buildings, and I was always thrilled to see the occasional priest walking the grounds in stiff, skirted habits of turquoise and purple.

This morning, it was early enough that the priests and worshipers weren't around. My Asics running shoes crunching on gravel were the only sounds as I walked past the weathered wooden stands tied with small strips of white paper, unlucky fortunes that shrine visitors had received and then abandoned in order to protect themselves. It was going to be a clear, beautiful day; I could stare straight across the bay to see the top of Mount Fuji, usually shrouded by cloud cover.

Seeing Fuji-san was a good omen, I decided. Project Manga would go well. Standing here, surrounded by old stone and wood and the waves, I felt it in my bones.

5

I was stretched out on the living room's worn tatami mats icing my knees when Takeo wandered in, dressed in a pair of wrinkled cream linen drawstring pants and a T-shirt that read SAVE JAPAN'S DOLPHINS FROM THE CRUEL TUNA FISHERMEN.

"Are you always such an early riser? And what happened to your knees?" he asked, dropping a kiss on my head.

"I run in the mornings because it's cooler, and I use ice so the muscles don't get inflamed. Sleep well?"

"Great, thanks to you. The best dream that I remember was that I was Batman and you were Mars Girl and we had to conceive a baby superhero to defeat all forces of evil."

"Um, I hope this isn't a way of telling me that the condom broke," I said, feeling a little bit shaky. I took great stock in dreams.

Takeo laughed. "It didn't. Where do you want to have breakfast after our shower?"

"How about here? Is there bread for toast?" I loved the thick, square slices of slightly sweet white bread that were sold everywhere.

"I thought it would be nice to have breakfast outdoors. There's a European patisserie about two kilometers down the beach road that has the bonus of a specialty *manga* shop nearby. You could buy some more beach reading there."

"Good idea," I said. I wasn't thinking so much about reading as talking to the sales staff who worked there about the collectibles market.

Breakfast passed companionably; I was pleased to be able to buy the *Japan Times* on the street in a setting so far from Tokyo. There actually were a number of foreigners around—Italians, Americans, and Australians savoring café au lait and croissants near our table. Afterward we dodged traffic to cross the beach road to Animagine, the comic store that Takeo had mentioned. On the door, the store name was written in English and Japanese, with the *-gine* part of the name illustrated with the Japanese kanji character for *person*, which was pronounced "jin." It was a contrived, cutesy play on words, but easy enough for a child—or someone like me—to understand.

Animagine stood out from the mostly weather-beaten shops along the beach, a small, ferroconcrete box of a building painted a vibrant purple, with automatic doors that slid open as you approached. I was enveloped by frigid air-conditioning and the sixties girl sound of Puffy.

The popular duo had recorded the theme song for a television *anime* program, I learned from a product display in the front of the store. I hadn't realized that recording superstars would be willing to lend their energies to animation. Takeo ambled through the shop, bouncing a little to the beat—he loved lighthearted, sugary Japanese pop music, while I preferred Japanese artists with a darker, harder sound, such as Cornelius.

The store was filled with low bookcases packed solidly with comic books. Even though all the *manga* I'd seen were printed in black and white, their covers were a riot of colors—the cover was where the artist spent his energy. Maybe it was going to be not the interior of the comic books that was the collectible part, but the cover. I wandered through the rows of magazines, passing comics featuring schoolgirls, baseball players, aliens in outer space, clowning babies, fuzzy animals, and samurai.

I was taken aback by the shoppers' behavior in the store. Why was a sweet-looking fourteen-year-old girl reading *Neon Genesis Evangelion,* a comic book with a cover featuring robots? A samurai comic was in the hands of a woman my age, and a twenty-year-old man had his nose stuck in a comic book about schoolgirls.

I evaluated the store's staff, two young, shaggy-looking people of indeterminate gender, wearing baggy overalls with loose T-shirts underneath. When I got closer, I saw lipstick on one whom I decided had to be female.

"I hope that you can help me," I began. "My name is Rei Shimura, and I'm writing an article for the *Gaijin Times* about *manga.*"

"The owner should answer," her shaggy male companion said, approaching from behind. "He's based in Tokyo."

"I'm really interested in asking about shoppers in this particular store," I said, dreading the thought of a sit-down interview with a businessman similar to Mr. Sanno. "I want to know what the word on the street is about collectible magazines."

"Collectible?" The boy rolled the word around in his mouth. "You mean, the magazines that people are buying these days? There's something for everyone's taste. What do you like?"

"I'm not shopping for myself," I said patiently. "I want to learn which of the older *manga* are valuable collector's items, and which of the new ones might be valuable in the future."

"*Manga* aren't valuable," the boy said slowly, as if talking to an idiot. "They only cost two hundred to a thousand yen, maximum. There are some special issues and anthologies, full color all the way through, that go for up to six thousand yen. Would you like to see some of those?"

"No, thank you," I said, frustration growing. I probably was using the wrong words. "I need to learn about the comics that rise in value. You know, the ones that young people save and then sell to collectors later on to make a profit."

"Nobody saves comics." The young salesman shook his head. "People throw them away once they've been read. They're cheap goods, *neh*?"

"Surely some people save comics. How else would you have auctions of valuable comics of the past?"

"That might happens in America, but not here," he said. "In Japan, people don't have room to store comics. The only people who might keep comic books of a particular series around their apartments are the fans who draw *doujinshi*, and that's just because they're using the comic books as a model."

"I'm afraid that I don't know what *doujinshi* are," I said, even though Rika had mentioned them at the *Gaijin Times*. I wanted to hear an expert interpretation.

"*Doujinshi* are limited-issue comic books created by amateur artists." The young woman, looking a trace defiantly at her colleague, spoke up. "They use mainstream comic characters but give them new adventures. Within *doujinshi*, there are two camps: parody and original. Which are you interested in?" she asked.

"Could you explain them to me?" I was becoming intrigued.

She nodded, looking very serious. "Parody *manga* are stories that are directly inspired by popular *manga* series. There is nothing unusual about them. Original ones might feature the same characters as *manga*, but not always. They are more creative."

"Original sounds more interesting to me."

The salesgirl bit her lip. "Unfortunately, the *doujinshi* are all wrapped in plastic, so you can't look at them in the store. It's because the *doujinshi* artists want you to buy the comics."

I got the hint. I'd been talking and talking, without offering any payment. "I'd like to see a good number of them, and out of that, I'm sure to buy several."

The girl gave her male colleague a questioning look, and he nodded.

"Okay. In this case, you can open some of the plastic covers, but not all. And you'll have to seal them up in plastic once she's done."

Feeling annoyed by how bossy the young man was being toward his colleague, I followed the girl down an aisle of Sailor Moon backpacks. Takeo was hunkered down on the floor, reading the last of his newspaper.

"Having fun?" he asked when I went by.

"Don't know yet," I said. Since the Animagine staff wouldn't let me open the plastic shielding every one, I decided to evaluate the covers and set the best ones aside. This was more like being an art and antiques buyer—no reading ability required.

The first thing that I noticed about the *doujinshi* that the girl handed me was that they were more expensive than regular comics, and so slender that they would take less than the proverbial ten minutes to read. However, the covers were printed in color on glossy cardboard. They had the look of special editions, not mass productions.

I settled down on a stool to evaluate the magazines she'd handed me. Some of the covers offered obvious clues to what lay inside. I didn't bother opening the comic with a cover featuring Sailor Moon on the toilet. The same went for the comic that showed the blue-haired girl pilot from *Neon Genesis Evangelion* caught in a clinch with a barely adolescent boy.

The artists creating these comics strove very carefully to match the originals, which was not that hard when the original drawings were quite simple. Looking at the covers made me feel wistful. Were opportunities for artists so limited that the best path to recognition was imitation? I could guess that these self-published works didn't make much money.

I set aside a book titled *Up and Up, Original June Comics*.

"Ah, June comics! You like love stories between boys," the clerk said with some amusement.

"Well, I'm certainly not against them," I said, striving to stay cool. This was an exciting development in what I'd assumed was a conservative social world. I set aside a few more comics, and paused when I came to one featuring the Mars Girl character.

"I like this *doujinshi*," the clerk said. "The stories are very different from the regular *Mars Girl* series. It's called *Showa Story*."

"How clever," I said, admiring yet another Japanese-English double entendre. The group's name reflected the comic's historic background: the era starting in 1926 that was known as the reign of the late Emperor Showa, more commonly referred to in the West as Emperor Hirohito. Another reading was that the title referred to comics showing stories instead of telling them.

"I'm ready to look," I said.

Back at the sales counter, the clerk used a razor blade to slit open the edge of each magazine's plastic cover. She pulled the slim booklets out as if they were the rarest treasures. I got a kick out of watching the process, and I made a show of wiping my hands with a tissue before touching the materials.

The love story between boys didn't have more than a kiss and embrace in it—I figured the drama had to be in the dialogue box, the drawings were so uninteresting. In general, I was finding that the enticing covers surrounded black-and-white pages drawn with average skill.

The *Showa Story* comic was decorated by a wide-eyed Mars Girl. I'd noticed she was holding a parasol with a pattern that was popular in the first half of the prewar period. That detail had sparked my interest.

To my delight, I found the drawings inside were in color and exquisitely detailed, with great attention given to the background in each frame. Japanese houses and streets were drawn with a style similar to vintage wood-block prints. The clothing and architectural details revealed that the amateur artist had placed Mars Girl in 1930s Japan. To my amazement, the colors were right on target for that period, and even the paper the comic was printed on had a luxurious feel—it was the silky, glossy stock typically used for art books. This was just a comic book, I reminded myself. The story had Mars Girl time-traveling back to 1930s Japan, swapping her sleek blue bodysuit for the figure-hiding robes of a Buddhist nun. Her assignment was to pose as a nun at a Buddhist temple where a corrupt priest was swindling money from donations collected by the nuns. Mars Girl discovered the priest was spending the money at decadent dance halls in the big city, so to catch him, she camouflaged herself as a paid dancer. After dancing the tango and dodging the evil priest's knife, she saved the money for the temple and made sure the priest was locked up in prison.

"Do you have more *Showa Story* comics?" I asked, glancing again at the cover. The issue date was January 2000. The price was 1,500 yen, almost $15. Steep indeed, but given the cost of the paper and color copying, I imagined there was very little profit for the artists.

"That's the only one we carry. I'm so sorry," the girl said. "I asked about getting more the last time a circle member came in, but he said they were having problems with the printer and had a limited print run." She paused. "Actually, you might be able to get some back issues if you went to a *manga* convention. Comiket, the biggest one in the country, isn't till August, but there's a smaller convention called Comiko taking place in Zushi next weekend."

I took the flyer the salesgirl handed me and gave her the *Showa Story* comic I wanted to buy. One thing she'd said puzzled me. "What's a circle?"

"The kids who put together *doujinshi* call themselves a circle. It's a more creative and friendly word."

"So the comic might be the work of several artists?"

"That's right," the salesgirl said. "Maybe you can meet the rest of them."

I was already imagining a cross between the Velvet Underground and the Bloomsbury Group. I wouldn't be able to write about antiques, but I could comment on the historical significance of artistic circles. The story was starting to interest me.

"Do you have any contact information for the circle?" I asked.

She yawned, covering her mouth with fingernails painted with tiny Doraemon decals. "The mailing address is given inside the cover, isn't it?"

I looked. "Sure. But with the deadline, I don't have time to write letters. Do you perhaps have a phone number the circle member might have left behind?"

Takeo had come up behind us, and I was surprised to see him carrying a shopping basket containing a few magazines. I peeked at them and couldn't hide my giggle. They were *manga* devoted to the subjects of gardening and agriculture.

"Kayama-san." The male clerk who had been so obnoxious ducked his head in a bow. "We haven't seen you or your sister in quite a while. How are you?"

"Fine, and how are you, Murano-san?" Takeo answered formally.

"May I have the circle's phone number?" I asked again. Now that there was a customer behind me, I thought the clerk, apparently named Murano, would be more likely to settle the issue.

"I suppose that's okay." Murano scratched the beginning of a goatee and said to the girl who had helped me, "Michiko, why don't you check the inventory record and see what you find?"

As Murano and Takeo chatted idly about surf conditions, the salesgirl rummaged around in the back. She came back with a Tokyo phone number lightly penciled onto *Ogre Slayer* stationery.

"The artist's name is Kunio Takahashi. This is the phone number he left for us."

"You've been really helpful," I said, taking Takeo's magazines from him and placing them with the Mars Girl *doujinshi* on top of the counter. "I'll add these to my purchase. How much do I owe you?"

"Never mind," Takeo said, moving to take his magazines back.

"No, I insist." The total of five comics came to less than 4,000 yen, which was a little less than $40, significantly more than most customers were spending. In the time I'd been in the shop I noticed that many customers had come in to read comics for a half hour or so, and then left without buying anything.

"You're good at getting what you want," Takeo said when we were outside.

"Your timing helped me. It was only because you were waiting behind me that they gave me the phone number." I started walking back on the beach road toward a telephone booth I'd seen. Takeo followed behind me, because the sidewalk was too narrow to walk side by side.

"I doubt it," Takeo said from behind me. "Actually, I dislike Murano, that fellow who sold you the magazines. When we were teenagers, he thought he was the greatest surfer on earth and bullied anyone else who wanted to share the waters. It doesn't surprise me that Murano would wind up with an easy job near the beach. And he's such a gossip. Probably everyone in town is going to know you stayed with me."

"Why is that a problem?"

"I'm supposed to be renovating the house, not entertaining in it. My father would be embarrassed to hear that a guest stayed while the house was in a bad condition."

It was such a Japanese excuse. So typical, in fact, that I was deeply suspicious. Takeo had taken me out to a highly public breakfast spot. What was his problem now?

"If you don't want me to stay with you, I won't," I said. "I've been enjoying the weekend, but I could easily go home. We could stage a big good-bye fight at the train station if you wanted that to get back to your family as well."

Takeo caught up with me and put his hand on my arm, forcing me to stop and look at him. "I wouldn't want anything like that," he said. "I'm sorry for the way I sounded. It's hard to understand what it's like to be part of an uptight clan. You're lucky, Rei."

"If you think I'm so lucky, I'll put your opinion to the test," I said, smiling at him. "Let's see if Kunio Takahashi answers his telephone."

6

The mechanical-sounding operator's voice told me that the telephone number I'd dialed for Kunio Takahashi was no longer in service. Worrying that perhaps the salesgirl had written the number incorrectly, I dialed information and asked for a number that corresponded with the magazine's masthead address. I was given the same dead number.

It's rare to get an out-of-service message in Japan, because people who move or need to change phone numbers usually sell the old number. The phone numbers are bought and traded by individuals, not by the telephone company. For example, I'd bought my home telephone and fax numbers from my ex-boyfriend Hugh when he moved from Japan. I paid him exactly what he'd bought the telephone numbers for: about five hundred dollars per number. A telephone number was a low-level investment of sorts. In the four years I'd lived in Japan, I'd seen telephone numbers sold for sums anywhere from the mid-$500s to $800.

I couldn't understand why the *Showa Story* telephone number was no longer valid. There had to be some kind of breakdown in phone service. It was irritating, because I'd have to try to track the group down through the street address. In Japan, where streets didn't have names, that would be hard work.

"Nobody's forcing you to write about *Showa Story*," Takeo had said when I told him that I'd hit a stumbling block. "You have time to go back to Animagine and find some easily accessible *doujinshi* artists."

I shook my head. "I'm a reasonable person. If a client asks me to find an original wood-block print of Hiroshige's *Wave*, I tell them why I can't do it. There was a limited printing of the woodblock made in 1842, and all those are now in the hands of serious collectors and museums. None in antiques shops, none on the street." I paused. "This comic book in question was printed seven months ago. It should not be an impossible feat to find the people who created it, especially since we live in the same city."

"How much energy do you want to put into something that is a side job for you?"

"That column accounts for a third of my monthly income," I said. "Probably more, if you count the added business I get."

"You won't get any added business out of a story on comics. If anyone gets the business, it will be Animagine and all the other *manga* shops in Japan."

"Why are you being so moody about the project, when yesterday you wanted to help me?" I mused aloud.

"I still want to help. Unfortunately, I don't have as much time as I'd like. I've got to get up on the roof and fix some tiles this afternoon."

"Okay. I'll just nip back to Tokyo to check on something. I'll bring back something nice for a late dinner."

I was thinking of the savory pork-stuffed *shumai* dumplings sold in to-go boxes at Yokohama Station, my transfer point for the train into west Tokyo. *Shumai* were the only lapse in my vegetarian diet.

"But we still have leftovers," Takeo, who was recycling-crazy, protested. "There are six courses in the refrigerator already. Why don't we eat that?"

"Fine." I ended the conversation by sprinting across the street to catch the approaching bus marked for Zushi Station. If I had known how late I'd get back that night, I would have acted differently: kissed Takeo good-bye or, at the very least, told him to eat the most perishable foods first. But how was I to know?

Shibuya is the kind of neighborhood that is best to avoid if you're over twenty. Not because the teenagers would beat you up—crippled by their twelve-inch platform shoes, that would be an impossibility—but because their attention was not on the cars or pedestrians in their path, but on small plastic objects straight out of a science fiction comic book. The teens were holding "pocket bell" beepers, cellular phones, and a kind of walkie-talkie carefully tuned to frequencies that allowed them to broadcast to other owners of the same gadget. With a walkie-talkie in hand, a person could send a signal to unknown others indicating a particular mood and willingness to get together. The abundance of coffee shops and rent-by-the-hour love hotels in the Shibuya side streets made any eighteen-year-old's dream a possibility.

It was in this epicenter of teenage lust that *Showa Story* had listed its office address. The artists were all probably very young, I thought gloomily as I went to the police box to ask where 6-7-22 Shibuya was located. The fact there were very few street names in Tokyo made my life an endless series of visits to the police.

The policeman on duty didn't know the building in question, but from the numbers he guessed that it was on the same street as the Yamato Building, a low-rise building a few blocks away that housed an Italian restaurant and various boutiques catering to teenagers. That was enough information for me to proceed, and I crossed the big intersection and proceeded behind the Tokyu department store into a street jam-packed with clothing stores and parlors where one could play pachinko, a game similar to pinball that made a deafening racket. The Yamato Building had a sign identifying it as 6-7-22 Shibuya. The *Showa Story* office had to be inside.

A quick scan of the building's registry showed the tenants included the Italian restaurant, and numerous sneaker and blue jeans boutiques, but no *Showa Story*.

I decided to comb through the businesses on either side of the street, and found that a majority were boutiques, restaurants, and bars. There was a short, run-down-looking office building that seemed the most likely, but it contained a travel agency, a fax machine repair shop, and a language school.

Showa Story had to be somewhere, but I was getting dizzy in the midafternoon heat. I needed to cool off and rest my feet, which were getting blisters from the rubber thongs that I had stupidly worn into the city. I decamped into a coffee shop, and when I had refueled with an iced coffee, I asked the waitress about the *manga* circle.

"Show a Story?" She pronounced the name as if it were three words and not two.

"That's right. They design comic books and supposedly work in this area. That's all I know."

"Ah. I think I know where they are, but the name of their business is slightly different. It is called Show a Boy."

"I'm afraid that's not what is written on the magazine. See?" I showed her the inside page, which listed the circle's name and address.

"Yes, that address is located halfway down the street, attached to the Yamato Building. Look for a green door with a doorman outside."

"I can't believe I missed it."

"The hawker might not have been outside, so how would you know?" the waitress said.

"What kind of doorman is he? I wonder if I can get in."

The waitress laughed. "Definitely. It's a women's club, and it's a lot of fun. As they all say, everyone should see a foreign *chin-chin* once."

The waitress, talking in an extremely vulgar way about the male anatomy, obviously had mistaken me for a Japanese-born person. Ordinarily I would have been pleased by this, but this time I was embarrassed. A strip bar featuring foreign men? Show a boy, indeed.

It seemed unlikely that this Show a Boy establishment had anything to do with the *Showa Story* circle, but as the waitress had pointed out, the address was correct. And the iced coffee ricocheting through my system was enough to give me the jolt to check it out.

As I walked toward Show a Boy, I chided myself for having missed it the first time around. The name of the establishment was engraved on a small brass plaque next to a glossy green door decorated with the silhouette of a man tipping a top hat. A couple of high-school girls in uniforms, the skirts hitched up high and the socks puddled around the ankles, had stopped to talk to a tall, handsome man with skin the color of the coffee I'd been drinking. The man handed the girls a leaflet, and I saw them look at each other, hesitate, and giggle a bit. When the girls went inside, I took that as my cue to approach him.

As I came near, the hawker waved as if I were an old friend of his. I couldn't keep my eyes off his outfit—shiny athletic pants worn with suspenders over a bare torso. Ex-military, I guessed, eyeing a tattoo of the rising sun on his biceps.

"*Konnichi wa. Boyzu ga suki ka?*" he greeted me in melodious Japanese, telling me good afternoon, and following it up with "Do you like boys?"

I imagined this was one of the few Japanese phrases he knew, but to test him, I answered back in rapid-fire Japanese, "I prefer men wearing Hugo Boss suits."

To my surprise, the man whipped off his mirrored sunglasses to take a better look at me.

"*Chérie*, you are a live one," he answered in English, but it wasn't American-sounding English: it was English spoken with a French accent, and a hint of something else.

"Where are you from?" I asked smiling.

"Senegal, but please hush," the man whispered. "I am supposed to be a rape *artiste* from Los Angeles."

"Don't you mean *rap?*" I asked. "The way you said it could lead to trouble—"

"Not in this country! I am violated twice a night—three or four times on Friday and Saturday! The schedule is exhausting. Please look."

I took the pamphlet that he had been waving at me. It was printed in Japanese and English. *Come dance with a stranger! Show a Boy, established 1993. Explore the culture of international dance with our talented boys. Please wet your seat at dancing of your choice. Choose from Cowboy Time, Handyman Special, Flamenco Love, Windsor Naughty, and Black Magic. Our guarantee is authentic foreign boys only. Membership available to lady customer of all nations.*

"*Je m'appelle Marcellus,*" the man said. "I am the Black Magic dancer. My first show is at six tonight, during happy hour. Lifetime membership to Show a Boy is just fifteen thousand yen, with the bottle-keep system. A special introductory rate of five thousand yen includes a drink ticket and one evening's admission. Other services require an additional charge."

Other services indeed. I asked, "How bad does it get in there?"

"How bad do you wanna be?" Marcellus leered at me.

I shouldn't have asked him such a leading question. I said in my most businesslike way, "My name is Rei Shimura, and

I'm writing an article for a monthly called the *Gaijin Times*. I'm trying to track down a comic book circle called *Showa Story* that is based somewhere in this neighborhood. Their *manga*'s name is similar to Show a Boy, don't you think?"

"These *artistes* are foreign boys?" Marcellus raised an eyebrow that looked as if it had been waxed by Miss Kumiko.

"No. Well, actually, I don't know the sex and nationality of everyone in the group. I'm assuming they're Japanese."

"A Japanese man would not be allowed to dance," Marcellus said firmly. "Our customers desire to escape their everyday existence. Nobody wants to see a dancer who reminds them of the salaryman who works in the same office. Our boys are surreal."

I shook my head. "The man I seek is an artist. Someone who works with a pen, not a—"

"Penis," Marcellus finished. "I can reassure you that our dance program is only risqué, not obscene. We keep the G-string on."

"Gee. That makes me feel better."

Marcellus burst out in peals of laughter. "I look forward to dancing for you, Miss Shimura. However, I must beg you to slip into something a little more comfortable before you enter our club. No denim allowed, except of course on the cowboy dancer."

"That's okay, because I'm not interested. Male dancing isn't my cup of tea. I was looking for an artist." I smiled at Marcellus, so that he wouldn't take offense that I was turning down my opportunity to see the Black Magic performance.

"Ah, but you do not know until you try. Tell me more about these comic book people whom you are seeking. Do you have a name?"

"Just one. Kunio Takahashi," I said, and watched his eyebrows rise again.

"Oh, he's not a dancer."

"But you know who he is," I said quickly. "How is that?"

"He painted the walls when the place opened. He's not around anymore. Our *mama-san* was the one who talked to him most."

He was talking about the club's female manager. It was customary for hostesses or hosts to call their boss *mama*. "What is your *mama*'s name? And is she here tonight?"

"Yes, but Chiyo-san is rather . . . difficult. I don't know how far you'll get without giving her something. She's that type of person."

"Too bad." I didn't have more than a few thousand yen and a credit card in my shorts pocket, and I wasn't interested in handing over either. "Perhaps I'll mention this place in the article. That's like free advertising."

Marcellus nodded. "That might be attractive to our *mama*. I'll say you were on our guest list. No payment to get in, but as I've told you, you cannot enter wearing jeans."

"You're sure that if I go away now, I'll still have a chance to get in? Even if you're not at the door?"

"*Chérie*, you have my guarantee. And that's not jives."

7

Too impatient to go all the way to my apartment in northeast Tokyo to change out of my T-shirt and shorts, I decided to make a quick purchase at Tokyu, the massive department store that anchored Shibuya Station. I could hear the rumble of trains as I rode the escalators up to the juniors' floor. Tokyu was cheaper than Sogo, Mitsukoshi, and Isetan, and it also took credit cards.

I rarely let myself buy new clothes, so this would have felt like a treat if I hadn't had such a small amount of time to browse. I went straight to the junior boutique called Nice Claup. The clothing brand had recently changed its name to this unusual moniker after it got wind that the brand's original name, Nice Clap, had unfortunate connotations.

I found a fashionable red-and-purple floral rayon dress that flowed almost to the ankle, minimizing the impact of my thong sandals. Marcellus hadn't commented on my footwear, and I hoped that it would escape the *mama-san*'s notice. The idea that women going out on the town to relax and ogle men had to meet a dress code struck me as rather silly. Or, as Marcellus would say, surreal.

I had the salesgirl cut off the price tag so that I could pay her and leave the store without changing clothes. My shorts and T-shirt went into a Nice Claup shopping bag. Since I'd found clothes so fast, I decided I could spare the time for a five-minute Shiseido makeover on the ground floor. I emerged smelling and looking like a rose, all for less than 9,000 yen. It was a good deal.

Marcellus was not in sight when I made it back to the sidewalk outside Show a Boy. I looked at my watch and saw the time was close to six o'clock. How the afternoon had zipped by; Marcellus was probably inside performing. There was a new hawker outside now, a Germanic-looking blond in lederhosen. He opened the door for a small stream of office ladies in pastel suits. Their show of unity made me realize that it was going to look rather eccentric to enter the strip club by myself.

After taking a deep breath and forcing a phony smile on my face, I told the lederhosen boy that I was on the guest list; he said, "*Ja wohl,*" and held the door open for me.

Show a Boy was dominated by a short, elevated runway decorated with spotlights and poles. The runway itself was surrounded by small tables draped with damask tablecloths, and small but comfortable-looking dark velvet club chairs. Most of the tables were already taken by females ranging in age from the schoolgirls, some of whom were sipping canned soft drinks, to women my mother's age with balloon glasses of cognac. The majority, though, were women within ten years of my age and were wearing fashionable suits and dresses. They clinked wineglasses together, screeched with laughter, and shouted greetings to friends coming in the door. They were loose, loud, and behaving in a way that would make people look askance in any office or home.

"Madam, may I inquire as to whether you are a member?" A blue-eyed blond man wearing a tuxedo without a shirt underneath—this was obviously the club's trademark—addressed me in polite Japanese.

I shook my head. "Marcellus said it would be all right for me to come in. I need to talk to the *mama-san*."

"So you're the one. Marcellus told us. I am Nicky, your host." Nicky's gaze was warm. So this was how they turned normal women into quivering masses.

"That's nice, Nicky-san, I just need to—" I stopped talking abruptly, catching sight of the wall behind his head. The whole expanse, about twenty feet long and ten feet high, was covered by a mural. The colors were jewel tones that played off the club's burgundy carpet and emerald green tablecloths, so you could see the mural had been planned as an interior design feature, and its content certainly was perfect for this crowd. The first illustration was of a man and woman dressed in 1920s fashions clinking martini glasses together. The second illustration was of a couple dancing, the woman bent all the way back over a man's arm in a tango position. The final picture was of a woman lifting her evening dress to expose a thigh, while a man knelt before her, fixing her stocking to a garter.

"Do you like the art?" Nicky murmured in my ear. He must have caught on to something Western about me, because he had switched to English with a midwestern twang. Ordinarily, this fact would have puzzled me, but I was too caught up in what was some of the most wonderful modern artwork I'd ever seen in Tokyo. The extravagant painting on the wall was obviously the work of the *Showa Story* circle. The exquisitely detailed dance hall background, the sweeping lines of the figures, and the emotion in the faces were familiar to me from the *manga* I'd seen. I hadn't thought that a comic book artist, used to cramming a lot of detail in a small square box, could enlarge his work so successfully.

"I love it," I said, somehow finding my voice. "I think I know who the artist was."

"Oh, it wasn't anybody famous. Just our house painter," Nicky said.

"One person alone?" I asked.

He nodded. "The boy you want to speak to Chiyo-san about, isn't it? Let me take you to her."

How could the club's guests not be spellbound by the walls? I thought crossly as we circled the perimeter of the room, heading toward a polished mahogany bar in the back. A dance show had started, with Marcellus on the stage. He was dressed head to toe in an Oakland Raiders football uniform, doing a series of football-inspired poses while he lip-synched to "White Lines." It seemed especially bizarre to see a dance such as this in front of the beautiful, nostalgic illustrations of courtship that Kunio Takahashi had painted.

The bar area was illuminated by a hanging Tiffany-style colored glass lamp, and in the small circle of light that was cast on the wooden counter, I saw a woman's hand. The hand was fairly plump, but the nails were dragon-lady long and painted a dark purple. I squinted in the darkness to try to make out the woman who went with the hand, but she was faster on the draw than I was.

"So the schoolteacher comes back." The *mama-san*'s voice was rough but not unfriendly.

"I'm not a teacher anymore." Now I recognized the woman Marcellus had called Chiyo. I'd last seen her almost two years before, in a hostess club on the west side of Shinjuku Station. She'd used a different name then. Struggling to maintain my cool, I said, "I write about art and antiques these days. I see that your business has changed as well."

"Yes, with today's economic hardships, men have less money to spend on hostess bars. So I changed my focus. No matter what happens in Japan, women always have disposable income. We changed everything! And the name I'm using now is Chiyo. Don't forget it."

I could understand why Chiyo wouldn't use her old name. In her previous incarnation, she'd gotten in trouble with the law. I'd been peripherally involved with that situation, and that was the reason for her coolness.

"Chiyo-san, may I buy a drink for you?" I asked, settling down on the only stool at the bar that was not taken. Girls were everywhere, flipping back their hair, checking their friends' teeth for lipstick, buying huge, colorful cocktails with umbrellas in them. The club's fleet of foreign waiters were attired in tight gym shorts, with T-shirts flipped back over their shoulders to reveal their bare chests.

The *mama-san* leaned toward me, coming into the light. Her forty-something face was puffy, and there was a telltale redness to her nose. Either she had spent some time at the beach, or she'd become a hard drinker.

"We have a fine selection of Spanish sherries. Lady customers prefer sherry over whisky," she purred, taking down two glasses and tipping a golden brown liquid into both. It looked as if I was going to have to drink on an empty stomach, and I didn't like that.

"Do you have any snacks here?" I asked.

She raised her eyebrows. "We offer yogurt. Chocolate mousse torte. Strawberry tarts. Crackers with cheese."

"Girl food." I smiled at the irony. "Would it be too much trouble if I ordered some crackers and cheese?"

"No trouble at all." She reached below the counter and tossed out a couple of packs of vending-machine-style cheese crackers. I had been hoping for a plate of water biscuits with a selection of real cheeses, perhaps some properly aged Stilton and Brie, but that was clearly not on the menu.

"*Itadakimasu.*" I uttered the traditional Japanese grace as I pulled the plastic off the crackers. I was starved.

"Marcellus was quite charmed by you." Chiyo lifted her glass of sherry to the underside of her pug nose and sniffed deeply. "After he explained your situation, I agreed to speak to you."

A tipsy girl in a green-and-pink checked suit bumped up against the bar. "Excuse me, but it's my friend's prewedding party. We promised her the Cowboy Time dance, and I hear that Cowboy-san is sick! I don't believe it—he was in the best of health two nights ago! Could you call him to come in?"

Chiyo smiled tightly. "Cowboy is having some surgical work done, so I assure you it would not be in your interest to see him. Aren't you enjoying the Black Magic dance?"

"We wanted Cowboy-san because he has the rope," the girl whined.

Chiyo nodded thoughtfully. "Ah, so you wanted to tie them together. Don't worry, just wait for the Windsor Naughty dance. That dancer carries a necktie, and if you point at your friend, he will carry out special instructions. Of course, there is an added fee for that personal service."

"Put it on my bill. Thank you very much!" The girl beamed.

"Is that kind of thing legal in Shibuya?" I asked when the girl had gone back to her seat. The audience began a rhythmic clapping, urging the dancer on.

"Completely. I don't take chances anymore. So, what about this magazine you're writing for, the *Gaijin Times*?" Chiyo's hard eyes, dressed up with thick liner and mascara, did not leave me. "Are you going to report on the club?"

"Well, my chief interest is in the artist who painted your mural."

"You could mention the décor, but don't forget to mention the dancing! We need more paying customers."

I glanced over my shoulder at the crowd and saw that it had become standing room only. Marcellus was unlacing his tight football pants, swiveling his hips for the cheering ladies. I looked away, embarrassed not by the sight of him but by how crudely the women were reacting. Did he think we were all like that?

"Sure. I'd be happy to do that in exchange for some information about Kunio."

Chiyo drank some sherry and said, "Kunio was a part-time employee who worked for me when we opened."

"Just as a painter?" I asked.

"Yes. He came in to see me when I was renovating the building for my grand opening last winter. He said that he lived nearby but was going to have to move. He said he would provide labor in exchange for continuing to receive mail at this address; he didn't have much money. I asked what kind of work he did, and he said he was an artist. I said to him, 'Good, you paint the interior for me and provide touch-ups if needed, and you can have mail privileges.'"

"You were willing to help a stranger that way?" I asked. Chiyo had never seemed warmhearted.

Chiyo smiled in a supercilious sort of way. "Have you seen the boy?"

"No. I have heard he's handsome—"

"He's gorgeous. I would have paid him to dance, even though he's Japanese. We could have said he was a Chinese or Thai boy, if necessary. But he didn't want to dance! He said that he had no rhythm." Chiyo snorted, as if this were the most ridiculous thing in the world.

"How old is he?" I asked.

"He is twenty-two, the age of good whisky," Chiyo said. "He graduated this spring from college—I know this because he showed me his diploma, as if that would make me more likely to be willing to continue to allow him use of the mailbox." Chiyo rolled her eyes. "He looks like a young Toshiro Mifune. Who wouldn't share space with Toshiro?"

Toshiro Mifune was the late star of many great 1960s films, especially those by Akira Kurosawa

"You mean he's got that samurai hairstyle?" I asked.

Chiyo laughed. "No, no. His hair is actually dyed a red-brown, like many of the kids are doing. He wears it falling into his eyes like some English movie star. But I think of Toshiro Mifune because Kunio likes to wear old Japanese clothes. Suits from the Showa period. That's how he appeared the first time I saw him."

"He dresses like that when he paints?"

"Ah, for that he wore very little. The heat, you know. Shorts and a T-shirt with some kind of *manga* character on it."

"Mars Girl?" I asked.

"I don't keep track of that silliness," Chiyo said. "His painting costume was an irritation because some of my dancers, well, they kept too much of an eye on him. He is attractive to men as well as women."

"He captured the idea of seduction perfectly." I stole another glance at the painted wall, which was practically pulsating with color and emotion. The work was a bit like that of the Japanese artist Hashiguchi Goyou merged with the style of the French painter Balthus, both of whom created extraordinarily haunting pictures of women, children, and the social landscape. In Kunio's mural, the young artist had captured the beauty and decadence of modern young life in Japan just before the war changed everything.

Chiyo snorted. "I think the wall looks good, but I was worried for a while. I thought the Japanese people he pictured there might draw attention away from my theme of foreign dancers."

"Your foreign dancers seem to be getting enough attention," I said dryly. I could barely see Marcellus, due to the three girls who had jumped up from the audience to dance around him. Now I knew why he had used the word *rape*—he looked in danger of losing the athletic cup that barely covered his privates.

"I am counting on you to write a positive article about my club," Chiyo said, following my gaze.

"I have to submit everything I write for approval to the editor," I said, feeling uneasy. "They want the focus of the article to be on *manga*."

"Well, do what you must to mention my club, *neh?*"

"First I'll need to meet Kunio," I said pointedly. "The information you've given is helpful, but I've got to see the man and speak to him one-on-one."

"Normally that would be easy. He comes here daily to pick up his mail, but he hasn't been in today. The last time I saw him was about three days ago."

"Do you think he left town?" I asked. "The phone number for his company has been disconnected."

Chiyo shook her head. "No, he would never leave without telling me. And besides, he just recently came back from a trip to his parents' hometown. He came in that morning—the time I mentioned, a few days ago—with a box of souvenir sweets from there. He said that he was tired of travel and was going to stay in Tokyo for the rest of the summer, concentrating on his art."

"So maybe he's in some kind of artistic retreat at his apartment?" I put down my empty sherry glass with a feeling of regret. "I still don't understand why, if he's got an apartment, he wanted to use your address."

Chiyo's attention was elsewhere. I followed her line of vision and saw that one of the schoolgirls had knocked over her orange soda and was frantically trying to mop it up.

"Nicky," Chiyo barked, snapping her fingers, and the handsome host in the shirtless tuxedo who had been hovering within a discreet distance of us went to clean up the table.

On the stage, Marcellus had been replaced by a dark-haired man who was a younger, better-looking version of Prince Charles. He was wearing country tweeds, minus a shirt, of course, although he was swinging a necktie. This had to be Windsor Naughty. It was amazing, this little world I had stumbled upon, where men danced, served, and courted women. Strangely enough, I had stopped feeling guilty about looking at the dancers. With the warmth of the sherry, a strange sense of entitlement had flooded me.

"Have another drink. My treat," Chiyo said, as if sensing my mood.

"It's getting kind of late." It was after seven o'clock. I thought guiltily that Takeo was waiting for me while I drank surrounded by half-clothed men.

"Very well," Chiyo said. "If you give me your phone number, I can have Kunio call you when he finally comes in."

Ordinarily I would have been quick to give my number, but I hesitated.

Chiyo had taken personal information about me in the past and used it to try to hurt me. I thought we were on the same side now, but I couldn't be sure.

"Could you have him call this number?" I wrote down the phone number for Takeo's beach house. Chiyo raised her sharp eyebrows when she saw the area code.

"So you're a country girl now," she said.

"That's right," I said, wondering whether I'd be able to make the next train departing Shibuya Station. I was eager to get out of there and tell Takeo what I had learned.

8

I missed the express train, so I had to take one that made numerous local stops, trying my patience. I attempted to telephone Takeo from the train platform to tell him to expect me in about two hours' time, but he didn't pick up. His answering machine did. I listened to the recording of his voice telling callers to leave a message, and found myself comparing Takeo's cool tone to the breathy warmth of the men working at Chiyo's club.

Marcellus and Nicky's solicitous air had to do with the money they were being paid. I supposed it was natural. I'd behaved cordially to Chiyo, a woman I disliked intensely, because I needed something from her. Now I wondered if I should have asked her for more—to give a more complicated message to Kunio, to tell him that if he called me, I could help him start making money from his art. From the moment I'd seen his mural, I knew Kunio Takahashi's historic interpretations deserved a major art exhibition. I could represent his work, selling it for him all over Japan and perhaps even getting commissions for him to do similar large-scale paintings in restaurants and office buildings.

Was it a conflict of interest for me to first write about his work and then represent it?

If I had been working for a real magazine, undoubtedly. But the *Gaijin Times* had its editorial and advertising interests in a hopeless jumble. Mr. Sanno would probably be thrilled if my story turned Kunio into a prominent, profitable artist. Of course, there was a chance that Kunio already had a gallery owner or art dealer behind him. I thought not, since he was so poor that he didn't have a mailing address.

I reminded myself that even if he was unrepresented, Kunio might not want to work with me. Artists were supposed to be temperamental. I dealt with works created by people who were long in the grave, so I hadn't had to negotiate with any of them. It would be a new experience.

There was no point in worrying about questions that couldn't be answered yet. I opened the *Showa Story* comic that I'd carried with me from the beach. Takeo hadn't translated it for me yet, so I had to rely chiefly on the artwork to tell me the story. This particular comic began in the year 2000 with a teenage Mars Girl, in a red jumpsuit, beaming herself out of an uncomfortable situation with schoolyard bullies and into outer space. After successfully undergoing training on her home planet, Mars Girl traveled back to Earth in a space capsule loaded with various weapons, including a pretty amulet worn around her neck. At this point, being able to read the dialog boxes would have helped, since I couldn't understand the exact power of the amulet. I was able to understand that Mars Girl's space capsule hit some turbulence on her return trip to Earth, and she was sent back to the 1930s. There was no school, just a private house. I could tell that the artist was saying both the house and school occupied the same location because the same address, 1-2-8 Nezu, was written in the corner of each illustration.

1-2-8 Nezu. The 1 in the address referred to the first *chome*, or section, of a neighborhood in old-town inner-city Tokyo; 2

signified the block, and 8 the house number. Nezu was close to Yanaka, the pint-sized neighborhood filled with artisan sweet-makers and Buddhist temples where I lived.

Kunio was clever to use Nezu as the setting. Nezu and Yanaka had not been bombed during World War II, and there were still plenty of old houses standing. He could use real houses as a model for those painstakingly drawn in his comic book. In this case, he was saying that an elementary school stood on the ground where a house had once been. As far as I knew, Nezu had one elementary school, and it was in a different *chome*.

Comic books were fiction. Kunio could place schools wherever he wanted. But the insistence on street numbers intrigued me. I paged deeper into the story, watching Mars Girl interrupt a gathering at the teahouse, apologizing abjectly. I knew the kanji for various apologetic words because I used them so often.

"Is it too much trouble?" I'd asked the girl in the comic book store. "Sorry, could you tell me where this address is?" I'd asked the woman in the coffee shop. And "I'm sorry, but I can't guarantee that I'll give you publicity," I'd told Chiyo.

In Show a Boy, apologies between women weren't routine. Chiyo didn't apologize to the young woman because the Cowboy wasn't available to lasso her friend, just as the young woman didn't apologize for interrupting our conversation with her complaint. In the strip club, women didn't have to answer to the language police.

The train had reached Zushi, the stop closest to Hayama. I readied myself to get out, almost wishing that I hadn't departed Tokyo. If I'd stayed put, I could have zipped over to Nezu to see if the address Kunio had listed for the school was real, and ask around about whether the artist haunted that neighborhood.

A bus ride and ten minutes' walk later, I did wish that I'd stayed in Tokyo. The lights were out in Takeo's family house, and when I rapped on the locked door, nobody answered. I needed a toilet. All the sherry I'd drunk at Show a Boy was making me hop up and down.

If Takeo didn't arrive home within the next five minutes, I resolved to visit the beach latrine, the fount of the thin, filthy river that ran into the sea. I would have to overlook the warning Takeo had given me not to walk by myself on the beach at night. "Why?" I had asked. With all the emperor's police guards nearby, Isshiki Beach seemed a stupid place to commit crimes. Takeo had mumbled something about the beach drawing rowdies.

I walked around the property, looking for a way into the house. The walled garden was a place in which I'd hoped to spend more time over the weekend. In the twilight, I strolled the overgrown lawn studded with plum and mulberry trees trained into graceful shapes. In the very back was a small Zen garden with a couple of large rocks, a small stone lantern, and a small wisteria. The focal point was a raked bed of purest white sand, a very distant cousin to the dirty blend on the beach. Takeo raked the garden's sand every morning into perfect waves, removing any leaves that might have marred its surface.

A pair of golden eyes glowed at me from the center of the sand, and I thought first of a demon before realizing that it was a cat. I looked at the cat but didn't make any friendly sounds. Cats make me uneasy. I heard a rushing sound and realized that the cat was urinating on the carefully raked Zen garden. As the cat kicked sand to cover its doings, I felt my own need growing more urgent.

The kitchen window was open. I could imagine that all I'd need to do was slide the light screen aside and I could be inside. The only problem was that the window was ten feet above where I was standing. I looked around for the ladder that Takeo and the roofers had used. Could they really have bothered to lock it up in the shed?

Apparently so. I gave up. I left the small bag containing the casual clothes that I'd worn earlier in the day next to the front door, with a brief note mentioning that I'd gone for a short walk and would return.

Then I set off for the beach, slipping out of my sandals once they filled with sand, hoping the damp feeling under my feet was caused solely by seawater.

The beach at night was a very different place than during the day. The families and Ping-Pong players were gone, but the open-air lean-tos I'd noticed before were filled with a mishmash of young people. Rowdy American sailors were ordering drinks with lewd names like Sex on the Beach for packs of single Japanese girls, Japanese couples were sipping huge mai-tais, and small pockets of Japanese men wearing sunglasses, tank tops, and tattoos were swigging Budweiser, a high-status imported beer. Some Australian men called out to me as I walked by, obviously mistaking me for a non-English-speaking Japanese. Usually I'd shoot something back at them in English, because nothing made a *gaijin* lose interest faster than a woman who could speak his language. Tonight I ignored them because I was intent on reaching the cement cesspool fifty feet away. I made it in, survived the stench, and was out within a few minutes. As I approached the bar again, looking for a place to wash my hands, I saw a slender girl wearing a bikini top and shorts, with her hair neatly pulled into two childish ponytails. Something about her reminded me of Rika, the intern from the *Gaijin Times*. When the girl's smile stretched wider and she startled babbling about the coincidence, I realized that the teenager *was* Rika.

"How nice to see you," I said, trying to figure out how I felt. Seeing her smiling face reminded me of how I'd instinctively liked her. But why was she here, an hour from the magazine office, at a fairly obscure beach after dark?

"Rei-san! This is great! I heard about your weekend plan, so I decided to come here, too. Will you join me and my friends for a drink at the bar?" Rika seemed so excited that I realized that she was at least halfway drunk.

"Sure. I need a place to wash my hands first."

"You can do that at the bar," Rika said. "They've got water there."

I followed Rika's slim hips back to the bar, feeling somewhat overdressed in my sand-sweeping dress. The handwashing facility she'd mentioned was the bar sink, a large standing tub with a hose running into it. Everything else in the bar was similarly crude. Lightbulbs hung crazily askew from the straw roof. There were a couple of large picnic tables and also some smaller tables that looked like the large spools for rope taken from a ship's deck. Hayama was a few kilometers from Yokosuka, where the U.S. Navy had a shipyard. I wondered if the spools were recycled.

Rika was not with anyone from the magazine; rather, she was surrounded by a bunch of fellow Showa College students she introduced so swiftly that I forgot their names. There was a boy with a scrawny build, who tapped long fingers decorated with blue nail polish against the table; a girl with hair that was frizzy and green, the probable result of having tried to go blond with a cheap dye; and another boy, who seemed unremarkable except for the fact that he was very drunk, sloshing beer across the table and carrying on giddily about how he had surfed a ten-foot wave that day and almost been killed.

I looked out at the placid bay and shook my head. Some people jokingly called the water Lake Hayama because it had so few waves. The fact that Takeo and his friends had surfed there wasn't very impressive to someone like me, who'd grown up in California. They'd wipe out the first time they attempted to surf at a real beach.

Rika poured me a glass of beer from the frosty pitcher of Asahi on the table. "Why are you here alone?" she asked.

"My friend had something else going on. What about you?"

"It's fun to come here at night. There's a very good *manga* shop that's open late."

"You went to Animagine, I bet," I said.

"Yes. How did you know?" Rika exclaimed.

I could have told them that Takeo had clued me in to the place, but I thought it would seem rather miserable to talk about a beau who had ditched me for the night. I said, "It's near a French café that I like."

"We could look together for ideas at Animagine, couldn't we?"

Rika was stressing the idea of Japanese teamwork, when all I could think of was protecting my image. Trying to get into the share-and-share-alike spirit, I admitted, "I went inside looking for . . . ideas." I turned my gaze to her companions, inspired by something that would bring them into the conversation and divert attention away from my project. "I was surprised by how many young men like to read comic books about schoolgirls."

The fellow with blue nails shrugged. "Only lonely guys read them. Losers. There was one guy who became so obsessed with the idea of raping young girls that he studied the technique in comics, and then raped and killed some girls himself."

I shivered. "So you don't believe those comics are a safe outlet for fantasies?"

"No," he said. "Why do you think so many girls get groped on the subway? It's because there are books and *manga* celebrating that act."

"Please remember, Rei-san, that sexual comics are only twenty percent of the comics market." Rika appeared embarrassed by her friend's lurid talk. "There are so many other kinds of *manga* that we should be writing about. There are series that tell fun stories about outer space, or cooking, or music. I'm sure that is what Mr. Sanno has in mind for the *Gaijin Times*."

"He is giving you a nice chance to oversee that project," I said.

"Oh, no, I am a very small part. But whatever I can do to help, I will."

"Rika doesn't know much about *manga*," the girl with the harshly dyed hair snapped. "It is a good thing the magazine is published in English, not Japanese."

"That's true." Rika looked glum. "I don't know nearly as much as the others in the *manga* club. I'm going to have to count on them for help."

I felt sorry for Rika, so I said, "Actually, the staff opinion is that Rika knows quite a bit. She came up with a very good direction for the piece I'll be doing on the artistic significance of *manga*."

"Have you found some good artists to write about?" Rika asked.

"I'm thinking about writing up a *doujinshi* called *Showa Story*. It's a version of *Mars Girl* that is more interesting than the original."

"I know it!" Rika said with excitement in her voice. "The artist graduated from Showa College this year. He's called Kunio Takahashi."

"Really?" Things were clicking together. Chiyo hadn't mentioned the name of the institution from which Kunio had graduated. Now, the comic's title had an additional meaning—homage to the place where the artist had studied.

"There was another boy from school in the group," Rika's blond friend said. "He's American, and he is heavily into *cospray*."

"What kind of spraying is that?" I was taking notes in my address book. I'd thought I was comfortable with the Japanese language, but ever since I'd started researching *manga*, I'd come smack up against a challenging new vocabulary.

"*Cos-play*," Rika said in an exaggerated American accent, dividing the syllables and enunciating the *l* so that the word was understandable to me. "It means dressing up like favorite characters from animation series. *Costume* plus *play*. Do you understand?"

"Now I do. It sounds wild!" I raised my eyebrows. "Do you know the students' names?"

Rika shook her head. "Since college is finished for the summer, it will be hard to find them. If the American is in the foreign-exchange program, he may have gone home for the summer."

"There is a Japanese girl in the group," Rika's friend said. "I think her family name was Hattori."

"Seiko Hattori?" Rika asked.

"Yes, that's it. Seiko Hattori," Rika's friend said.

"Great," I said, writing down the name. "I wonder if Kunio also engages in cosplay," I said. "I heard that he dresses in vintage clothing."

"He was older than me, so I didn't know him at all," Rika said with a little sigh. "But I have seen him dressed that way. He does look very sexy."

How many times had women commented on Kunio's looks? He really had to be something. *Six years your junior*, I reminded myself. Boy, did I feel old.

9

The moths flew into the lights and were zapped, the bartender ran out of bananas for daiquiris, and the clock's hands were edging toward eleven. Perhaps seeing the time, Rika reminded her friends that in less than half an hour, the last train to Tokyo would be leaving Zushi Station. After the blue-nailed boy whipped out a small cellular phone to call a taxi to get to the station, I borrowed the same phone to check if Takeo had returned to his house.

Still no answer. I felt a mixture of uneasiness and something close to anger about Takeo's absence and the locked door. I could walk back over the rocks to his house and wait on the doorstep, but I knew that if I was stuck there all night, I'd be very uncomfortable. As the taxi picking up Rika and her friends stopped on the beach road, I decided to do the sensible thing. I joined the group to take the taxi back to the train station.

What if something bad has happened to Takeo? I wondered, feeling guilty as we ran for the last train at Zushi Station, Rika's ankle almost getting sheared as the door closed behind her. But once I was on the train, there was no turning back. We made it to Tokyo Station just before midnight, making sprints in various directions to get on the last subway trains heading home. For a culture so dependent on trains, it seemed unfair that most of them stopped running at midnight.

Life in Japan was challenging, and I knew that I had it easier than most people. Rika and her friends lived with their parents in far-flung suburbs, but I lived autonomously near Sendagi Station in the northeast inner quarter of Tokyo. It was only a ten-minute walk from the station to my one-bedroom apartment on the first floor of a prewar house. The flat had the stale warmth of a place that had been closed up for the weekend, so I opened the windows to let in the night air. I had bars on the exterior of the windows, a protection that was probably unnecessary, given the extremely low crime rate in my old-fashioned neighborhood, which abutted Yanaka Cemetery. An unchained bicycle had been leaning against the back of house for the longest time, because nobody knew who had left it there, and to throw it away seemed unkind.

I hadn't found the beach to be very tranquil, and my time with Takeo had certainly been limited. It was good to be home. I looked around the familiar persimmon-colored room filled with Japanese antiques that I had rescued from the flea market and refinished. An antique child's kimono hung on one wall, and antique wood-block prints decorated the other. My futon took just a few minutes to roll out of the bedroom closet. I sank into its softness and wondered one last time about why Takeo had not been waiting for me.

I found out the very next morning at eight o'clock. The telephone by my bed shrilled, and when I picked up the receiver, Takeo's voice was almost as loud.

"So you're alive! I was wondering, given the bag of clothes you left on the doorstep. The note said you'd come back, but you did not, so I thought you might have gone for a suicidal night swim."

"No. I left the bag there at eight o'clock because I didn't want to carry it to the beach."

"The beach?"

"Your house was locked, so I went to the beach to use the latrine, and then I waited"—I decided to use that verb, instead of "passed the time drinking"—"at the bar. I called you twice. Because you still weren't back by eleven, I took the last train home."

"We weren't supposed to meet at the house."

"Oh?" I asked.

"I wasn't at the house because I was expecting you to get off at the bus stop near the *manga* shop. Isn't that what we agreed?"

"I didn't know that!" I could just picture what had happened. I must have sailed right past him, not looking out the window because I was so consumed with *Showa Story*.

"After the last bus passed the bus stop at eleven-thirty, I walked home."

I was positive that neither of us had said anything about meeting there. But now I remembered that as I'd waved at Takeo and run across the street to catch the bus, his mouth had been moving. I hadn't heard what he'd said. I'd made an awful mistake.

"Did you call out that you'd meet me at the bus stop when I was running to catch the bus?" I asked.

"Yes. Did you forget?"

"I never heard you. I'm so sorry. I did leave a message on your answering machine when I was coming in from Tokyo, but I guess you don't check your answering machine when you're out of the house."

"There's probably a code or something that would let me do it away from the house, but I don't know it."

"Actually, I thought of breaking into your house," I confessed. "I decided not to because I didn't want to be the source of any more repairs to that place. You have enough to do."

Takeo still sounded grumpy. "Yes, I'll be up on the roof today, and I'll probably start repainting the interior the day after tomorrow."

"So I guess you won't be spending much time in Tokyo this week?" I asked.

"No. I'm just too busy," he said, and hung up.

All that morning I thought about what had happened. People fell out over misunderstandings all the time. I was beginning to realize that I'd had a lot of such experiences in my life, which could mean only one thing: The misunderstandings were my fault.

There didn't seem much that I could do to mend this particular broken fence, so I crawled out of bed, had my usual prebreakfast run, and got on with the day. I was planning to take a walk to 1-2-8 Nezu, the location in Kunio's comic book, to see whether the old school really existed.

The area in question was on the other side of Shinobazu-dori, the main artery running through the neighborhood, along which two Chiyoda Line subway stations, Sendagi and Nezu, were located. I walked in the direction of Nezu, feeling consumed by curiosity. If Kunio lived so close to me, why had he wanted to receive mail all the way over in southwest Tokyo? It could be an issue of status. Having one's address in Taito Ward was a lot less glamorous than having it in Minato Ward, where Shibuya was.

I stopped at a police box for information about the exact block mentioned in the comic book.

The policeman was eager to talk. "Sure, there once was a school there. They closed it when I was in high school. What you'll find at that place is a small apartment building."

I looked at the policeman. He was in his early thirties, I guessed, a little bit older than me, and perhaps eight years older than Kunio Takahashi.

"Do you know someone living in the area called Kunio Takahashi?"

"Not personally . . . but if he lives here, he should be registered. Shall I check for you?"

"If it's not too much trouble. I'd guess he lives in the area around the school, if that's any help. Here's the spelling of his name." I held out the comic book, because I didn't want to attempt to write the complicated kanji that made up his name.

"*Chome* number eight, right?" The policeman opened a thick book filled with pages and pages of addresses and names, all in very tiny kanji pictographic writing.

"I'm not positive." He was referring to a numbered neighborhood subsection that was part of the school's address. "Are the Takahashis all listed together?"

"Not at all. Each family entry is organized by the street address. There are probably more than one thousand families in the *chome*. Maybe it will take some time to check for you."

I suddenly felt guilty. "You have so much to do. I don't want to trouble you like this . . . not when I'm unsure that this man is based in Nezu."

"It is your decision," the police officer said, slapping his book shut.

"Well, I mean, if you do come across it, I would be grateful," I said. I hated myself for indulging in such doublespeak, but the minute the policeman closed the book, I felt sorry that I was losing my chance for information.

He sighed. "I'll look. Come back in two hours."

In the interim, I decided to walk to the apartment on the site of the old school, following the directions the policeman gave me. Looking for Kunio was like following a Hansel and Gretel trail of crumbs. Or, in this particular neighborhood, it meant following torn-up bits of newspaper, snippets of rotting scallion, and the occasional wayward soft-drink can.

1-2-8 Nezu was really an alley off a street that ran west of the Nezu Shrine. Most of the houses here were old tin-roofed shacks. Cats lounged boldly on the roofs. I wondered what was up there that was so enticing. Perhaps it was just the Japanese custom. I'd never seen an American cat behave the same way. There was no evidence of any school, and I was thinking that the policeman had gotten his facts wrong, because there was only a parking garage.

A small tofu shop stood on the left of the parking garage—in old-fashioned neighborhoods, you could buy fresh tofu made by a specialist—and to the left of that there was an apartment building. Futons hung over the balcony railings on most of the windows, presenting a spectacle of colorful textiles in red, blue, and pink against the grimy stucco building. The top floor's balcony revealed a futon decorated with a Mars Girl cover. The futon was a good omen, I thought, just the nudge I needed to go investigate the building's interior.

Fortunately, the vestibule did not lock. Attached with rusty screws to a wall that needed paint badly was a battered gray letter box with twenty or so compartments. Each letter compartment was labeled with a surname. The labels had been slapped on by the various tenants, so the names were shown in styles varying from neat typing to almost illegible scrawls. I had the *Showa Story* comic with me to double-check the kanji for the name that I was interested in. I didn't need to open the magazine, though, because I recognized the clear, hand-lettering on the label for apartment 4A.

Takahashi, Kunio. I could guess without a doubt that his was the apartment with the futon hanging outside it. And because the balcony door behind the futon had been wide open, I could deduce that the artist was in.

10

I rang the buzzer at apartment 4A, and the door pitched open a little. It seemed to be unlocked. I rang the buzzer again and called out.

"Mr. Takahashi?"

There was no response. Not even after five minutes.

What to do, what to do. I supposed that Kunio Takahashi went out and had left his apartment completely unlocked. It was safe enough to do that in a neighborhood like Nezu. On the other hand, he could be lying inside, alone and injured in some way.

I moved away from his door and rang the buzzer of the one beside it. The peephole darkened, and a voice croaked, "What is it?"

"Ah, I'm trying to locate Mr. Kunio Takahashi." I straightened my posture, aware of the scrutiny that was going on through the peephole. "Do you know if he lives in apartment 4-A?"

"The one who's soooo good-looking?" The speaker had a strange accent that I couldn't quite place.

I rolled my eyes. "Yes, that one."

"He certainly does. Just go ahead, ring his bell. Lots of girls do." There was a hint of world-weariness in the person's voice. I was curious what she looked like. Probably she had no sense of the same about me, if Kunio was getting visitors day and night.

"I did ring, and he's not answering. But I don't think he's out, because the door is ajar. Do you think he might be injured or something?"

"You are persistent." The door swung slowly open, and I saw, to my surprise, a very odd-looking person. I was staring at somebody about my age who seemed to possess the sexual characteristics of both a man and a woman. The hair was a blatantly false tangle of lavender acrylic; the face, Kabuki-pale and with sparkling blue eyes; the body, voluptuous, and stuffed into a high-necked blue nylon leotard. A silver lamé skirt swept the ground, so I couldn't examine the person's feet. This had to be a transvestite, I thought. I could understand seeing such a fellow in Roppongi, but not in Nezu.

In my time in Tokyo, I had met many eccentric men, but this one crowned them all. I opened and closed my mouth, aware that I should make some kind of formal greeting, but completely overwhelmed by the fact that the old lady I'd thought I would be talking to was in reality a young man.

"My name is Rei Shimura," I said. "I'm here because I want to write about Kunio Takahashi."

"You don't recognize me." The man smiled, and it was his large, white, perfectly even teeth that helped me make the recognition.

"You're the host from Show a Boy . . . is your name Nicky?" I remembered the man whose voice had been as warming as the sherry I'd drunk.

"I don't look like Mars Girl all the time, but I'm going to a very important meeting today."

I was putting things together. "You must be part of Kunio's *manga* circle. You're the American! Do you study at Showa College?"

"I used to," Nicky said. "But the money from the bar's so good, I decided to take a little vacation from school. I flew over to Korea, and Chiyo-san got the paperwork done so I could have a legitimate work visa. I love Japan. I could live here forever."

"What about the girl in your group?" I asked.

"Seiko Hattori?" His made-up eyes widened. "Have you talked to her, too?"

"Not yet," I said. "Does she also dress as Mars Girl?"

Nicky chuckled. "No, she's an animal lover, so she dresses as Mars Girl's dog, a.k.a. the bitch. Get it?"

"Yes." I didn't smile at his antiwoman joke. It was jarring after his supreme courtesy toward women at the bar the night before. "So, can I ask you something? Since you work at Show a Boy, are you the one who came up with the clever idea of using that location as a mailing address?"

"Yep, the name of the comic and the mailing address were my brainchildren." He laughed as if he thought he was a great wit. "I told Kunio to ask about using the address because I didn't want her to realize that I had an interest in *manga*. She doesn't like us having outside work or hobbies."

"That seems unfair," I said. "Anyway, I'd like to talk to Kunio. When can you introduce us?"

"Are you sure you're up to it?" Nicky taunted. "The price of Kunio's artwork has gone up. Tell your bosses they're going to have to be serious about wanting him."

"Of course we're serious," I sputtered. "But journalists don't pay cash for interviews! The payoff will be in the expo-sure. After this story, your comic is bound to pick up some new readers. What is its print run?"

"About two thousand. We sell at *manga* shops and by sub-scription."

"That's kind of small, isn't it?"

"Not for a *doujinshi!* We're one of the most successful ama-teur groups."

"My article could increase your press run and do so much for you," I said rashly. "Introduce me to Kunio, okay?"

Nicky sucked air between his teeth, a Japanese tic that meant "no can do."

"I haven't seen him in a while. He went on a trip to see his parents."

"He came back from that trip. He brought sweets to Chiyo."

"Really? Well, I haven't seen him. I went in to water his orchids yesterday. Come to think of it, the place seemed to be rearranged."

Nicky had a key to the apartment and permission to go inside. I'd struck gold.

"Why don't we go in to look around?" I suggested. "I won't be able to rest unless I'm sure that he is all right."

Nicky rocked back and forth on his heels. "It would be disloyal to my friend to let you inside. On the other hand, if he's come home, maybe the money is there."

"What do you mean?"

"Well, I make a lot more money than he does because of working at the club, and I guess that I'm a sucker. I lent him fifty thousand yen to cover the cost of his trip home. He said he was going to bring me the money from his parents. He owed me more from before, too."

If Kunio was in financial difficulty, that surely was the reason that the phone number he'd given out was dead. I raised my eyebrows. "We both have an important reason to go in, don't we?"

Nicky reached onto a crowded table and picked up a key on a Mars Girl key chain. "Just for a minute. I'll come with you to make sure you don't try anything funny."

He shuffled into a pair of Teva sandals to walk the four steps to Takeo's door. He pushed open the door, exposing a room with all the windows open, so it was drenched with light. The building had been so dreary from the outside that I had not thought about the possibility of it's containing an artist's studio, but that was exactly what Kunio's apartment was like. The white walls were covered by taped-up sketches of scenes featuring Mars Girl. Each page of sketches was the same size as a comic book page. He probably had three books' worth of illustrations taped to his walls, all in sequence. It was all done to scale, so I could not make out the individual designs from where I was standing. The overall impression was a cheerful checkerboard in rich colors similar to those of the mural in Show a Boy. The colorful walls stopped only at the room's small kitchenette—and a half-opened door to a small bathroom.

"Just as I thought. He's not here," Nicky said. He slipped off his sandals to walk into the center of the room. Despite his rude language, he had some grace.

"The futon's hanging on the balcony," I said, remembering what I'd seen from the street. "That's got to mean that he slept here last night." I walked out to the balcony and straightened the futon; even though it had a big clip securing it to the railing, it looked as if the wind had whipped it. Touching it, I was surprised to find the cover was slightly damp.

I returned to the inside of the apartment and noticed that a cordless telephone was lying on the floor. Its base sat on a small table near the door. The telephone number written on a Mars Girl sticker on the base matched the one I'd been given at Animagine. I replaced the receiver and immediately picked it up to check for a dial tone. As I'd expected, there wasn't one.

A desk was covered with more sketches, and a *tansu* chest had a few drawers open, exposing papers and art supplies. The low tea table had some newspapers, a Mars Girl *doujinshi* that I hadn't seen before, and a half-full can of Asahi Super Dry Beer.

Nicky picked up the beer and took a sip. "It's only slightly flat. He probably opened it last night. So he's come back to the city and obviously has enough to keep himself in beer, but not pay me back. I haven't come across more than seven-hundred yen."

"This newspaper has yesterday's date on it as well," I said. I picked up the *doujinshi* and began paging through it. Mars Girl was there in all her violet-haired splendor, wearing an outfit just like Nicky's. I skimmed the boxed illustrations and realized that these were the exact illustrations that were papering the walls of Kunio's apartment. He must have photocopied his originals to form this sample, which was bound in a simple plastic cover instead of the usual glossy paperback cover.

I traced the story. Mars Girl was living in 1930s Japan, and she was staying with a family who seemed to believe she was a strange cousin from the country. She was asked to prepare rice on an old-fashioned stove, and there the conflict arose, because in outer space, as in modern Japan, electric rice cookers were the norm. After trying a variety of measures of rice and water, Mars Girl slipped off to a restaurant to buy rice. But in the restaurant, she encountered gangsters who were trying to extort protection money from the owner. She used a few swift karate moves to dispense of two thugs; however, the most sinister of them turned out to be a karate master who overpowered her and kidnaped her, taking her away in a cycle rickshaw. The gangster paid off the rickshaw driver in exchange for abandoning the two in the vehicle in an isolated spot under a bridge over the Sumida River. Then, over the course of five pages, Mars Girl's kimono was unwrapped, and the next illustration was of a steam-powered train traveling through a tunnel. So Mars Girl was getting raped—a typical cartoon fantasy. However, my spirits rose when Mars Girl wrapped her legs around the gangster's head in a surprise hold and broke his neck. With a bit of soy sauce, she dribbled an outline of the planet Mars on his face as the final humiliation before dragging him down to the river, where she discarded the body. The gory tale was wrapped up by Mars Girl returning to the rickshaw to discover a fresh boxed lunch, which she of course took home and managed to pass off as her own cooking.

"Country girls can take a long time to prepare a meal, but the taste is superb," the father of the household praised, while Mars Girl insisted—like a typical Japanese deflecting a compliment—that she was a terrible cook.

I was surprised that I could understand as much of the story as I did. I looked up after what felt like just a few minutes and saw that I was in the apartment alone. Where had Nicky gone?

I called out his name, and got up and traced a path back to his apartment. He answered the knock on his door after a minute.

"So you're done reading," he said, looking at the material in my hand. "What do you think?"

"Well—artistically speaking, the mural is superior to the comic. I'm planning to write about the comics, though. In fact, I could start by interviewing you about how much influence the circle has over the *doujinshi*'s content."

"I'd be happy to, but like I said, I have a matinee."

"You're going to a movie?"

He chuckled. "No. I'm running off to meet my hot Japanese girlfriend."

"Thanks for sharing so much information," I said in my most sarcastic manner.

"I'm kind of sorry for Japanese-American women." Nicky looked at me thoughtfully. "Let's face it, you can almost pass for Japanese, but your personality's all wrong. You can't possibly attract anyone here. You have boundaries, and they don't. Japanese girls are kinky. They do things you couldn't imagine."

I could have said a million things. Nicky, like so many of the foreign men I'd met in Tokyo, believed Japanese women had a

peculiar combination of emotional purity and sexual willingness that made them the ultimate mates. I could tell that Nicky
wanted to make me upset. He understood the kind of woman
I was. Well, understanding women was his job.

"It sounds as if you're better off as a stripper than a student," I told him.

"Yeah. I dance for them, and they slip money in my pants.
When they take me out before work—we call dates like that
dohan—they always pay for the hotel rooms, the alcohol, the
gifts. Everything!"

"These are career women?" I was incredulous.

"Hell, no! There are no career women here, that's what's so
great! My girls are the babes you saw in the bar: students,
office ladies, housewives. They can be twenty years apart, age-
wise, but once you're inside, they all feel the same."

I couldn't hide my disgust any longer. My grimace made
him laugh.

"Well, I'm going to see the others in the circle soon. I'll tell
them about your interest, and we'll see if something works
out."

"Kunio's the one I really want to talk with," I said.

A loud banging noise came from the hall, startling me.

"Sounds as if Kunio might have come home," Nicky said.

We went into the dingy hall, and indeed Kunio's door was
resolutely closed. Nicky tried to turn the doorknob.

"Open up!" he bellowed, hitting the door.

There was no answer.

"It doesn't make sense. The door was unlocked before, and
now it's locked," I said.

"Did you take my key ring with you on the way out?"

I winced. "Your key ring?"

"Yeah, I carried my key ring in with me, out of habit. It must
be in there now. How irritating."

"I'm so sorry," I said. "Maybe I could call a locksmith—"

"Don't bother. I don't really care to water his plants any-more, especially since I know that he's back. And I do have to leave. If I'm late for the matinee, my girlfriend won't like it. She's liable to whip me."

As Nicky spoke, he moved around the room, scooping up a child's Mars Girl lunchbox and putting in it some subway and telephone cards, money, and a lipstick. He shooed me out of his apartment. From the doorway, he said, "I should be seeing another circle member this afternoon. I'll ask if that person wants to speak with you. But I'll ask only if you promise to let me call you. Don't come creeping around the club again, or this building, okay?"

"Sure." I handed him my business card.

"I'll see if I can get you an interview. But if our comic runs in your magazine, we want to be paid."

"I'll have to ask the magazine staff about that first," I said.

"See you." Nicky brushed past me in a blur of taffeta and sweet perfume, a perfect she-boy on his way to the unknown meeting spot. It was only when he was halfway down the stairs that I realized I was still holding the Mars Girl prototype comic. The gap under Kunio's apartment door was too slim for me to slide it back.

In the end, I took the prototype, knowing that I could tell Nicky, when he called, that I had it. The whole business about the door locking was strange. I wondered if Nicky had pushed the button on the doorknob of Kunio's apartment door, caus-ing the door to lock after we'd left. He could have done that to force me to leave.

It was risky visiting strange men in their homes; my aunt and mother and about a hundred other people had told me that during the course of my twenty-eight years. Now I had to agree.

11

The message light was blinking on my answering machine when I got home, so I played back the tape, hoping for a message from Kunio Takahashi.

Instead the caller was Takeo, apologizing for being snappish over the phone earlier in the day.

"I was upset because I thought that something had happened to you. You've gotten in trouble before, and I guess I was expecting the worst. Call me when you have a chance."

My heart softened, and since I didn't know Takeo's cellular phone number by heart, I hunted around for my address book to find the number. Funny. The address book wasn't in my backpack, nor was it on my telephone stand. I tried to remember when I'd last used it and finally remembered that it had been at the beach bar in Hayama. I'd taken it out to check the phone number of Takeo's country house before I called using Rika's friend's cellular.

Could I have left the book at the bar? If so, chances were that it was either lost in the sand or had been turned in to the Hayama police department's lost and found. I couldn't remember the name of the bar, but I bet Rika would. However, it was Sunday, so I couldn't reach her until the next morning, when the *Gaijin Times* opened at 9 A.M.

"Rei-san! Why aren't you here?" Rika whispered into the receiver after I'd identified myself.

"I have no reason to be," I said, caught off guard. "I just called to ask if you know the name of the bar where we were Saturday night. I think I dropped my address book."

"It's called Bojo. But listen, Mr. Sanno is here today. He wants a full status report of all the stories in progress."

"Really? But it's just Monday!"

"This is what happens when a Japanese authority takes over, Rei-san. We have to *gambaru*—give it our all."

"If he had told me to come to the office, I would have. But he didn't say—"

"Yes, you are at a disadvantage because you are a free-lancer. Since we are all regular staff members, we came in on Monday as usual. And I really must go now, because Alec-san is waving for me to come back into the conference room. Just tell me one thing—may I give the progress report on your work? I would like to tell him what we discussed at the beach the other night."

I pointed out that it was dangerous for her to promise a story to Mr. Sanno that I possibly might not be able to deliver. "Can you just say I am in the process of tracking down a promising *doujinshi* artist?"

"I'll try," Rika said. "Yes, that is a good idea. I will say that is why you are not here. You telephoned to apologize and say that you are in the midst of a very important interview with Kunio."

"Please don't say his name, since it might not—" *Work out*, I would have said, but Rika had already chirped a cheerful good-bye.

I was no closer to getting my hands on my address book, so I tried to do something meaningful with my afternoon while waiting for either Takeo or Kunio to telephone me. I decided to straighten the apartment, collecting in the process any phone numbers and addresses that I'd jotted down on slips of paper. It was amazing how sloppy I was. There were phone numbers scrawled on the backs of torn envelopes and restaurant menus. Many of the numbers had been written down without an identifying person's name.

Kunio's apartment had been far tidier than mine. I thought about how there had been a few things on the table, but no real clutter of notes and magazines and dishes, as was the style in my place. It looked as if he had just stepped out—though that couldn't be, I realized.

A naturally tidy person would not leave a half-full beer on the table a full day after he'd started to drink it. He would have thrown it away. And the futon was damp. It obviously had hung out overnight and soaked up the previous night's rain. Nobody, if he was sleeping at home, would leave a futon outside.

So what had happened?

I imagined one scenario. Nicky had come home late at night, and Kunio, relaxing in his own apartment, had heard him. He might have left fast to avoid a confrontation over the borrowed money.

No, I decided, Kunio must have left at an earlier time the day before. Otherwise he would have brought in his futon. Nobody would leave a futon hanging out overnight, unless he hadn't come back home because of an emergency.

I was worried, although there was no good reason. I had been anxious about Takeo because he had not been at his home Saturday night, and he'd turned out to be angry but unscathed. Kunio was a grown man who could take care of himself. The fact that he'd not spent the night in his apartment was probably because he was spending time with one of the admiring girls Nicky had spoken about.

Wherever he'd been last night, there was still a chance that he had dropped by Show a Boy to pick up his mail. I called information to get the telephone number for the club, and dialed, hoping that someone other than Chiyo would answer.

"*Hai*," breathed a man with a scratchy accent.

"Hello, is Marcellus there?" I asked.

"Nobody's here right now. Who's calling?"

Nobody except you, I thought. I hesitated before saying, "I have a question about the artist who painted the walls."

There was a pause. "Why?"

Could this be Kunio on the other end? I chose my words carefully. "If he stops in for his mail, I would like to talk to him. It's about an excellent publicity opportunity. One that goes beyond a magazine article."

"Maybe he doesn't want publicity. That's what I've heard."

"You mean a young man straight out of college doesn't want to make money doing the work he loves?" I laughed softly, trying to make it sound like a joke. I had to get on the right side of this edgy guy, whoever he was.

"There's more to life than money. If you don't know that, I'm sorry for you."

I struggled for an answer, but he hung up on me.

The person on the other end of the phone had to have been Kunio. No matter how fast I made subway connections to Shibuya, he would be gone from Show a Boy by the time I arrived. Another idea was to stake out his apartment, but if he caught me doing that, it might alienate him further. I sighed. If Kunio ultimately refused to be interviewed, I could write a story without his participation. But Rika had probably already told Mr. Sanno that I was profiling Kunio. It would be a major embarrassment if I couldn't come up with the subject.

I made myself a cup of Darjeeling and sat down in my tidied apartment to think about the pros and cons. In the end, I decided that the messages I'd left with Nicky and Chiyo were enough for Kunio to decide whether to get into contact with me. In the meantime, I would locate another interview possibility—a talented artist who would welcome the chance to be written up in a glossy magazine.

Instead of trekking out to Animagine, I'd look for the new artist's work at a *manga* shop in Tokyo. A likely location for one would be Harajuku, a booming retail neighborhood that drew teenagers like cats to an open can of tuna. It was only about a half hour's subway ride to the west, but it had a completely different age demographic from the rest of Tokyo. There was no way to amble leisurely through the street. Instead, I was swept up in a dark blue wave of school-uniformed adolescents. I almost felt as if I were entering one of the schoolgirl comics that older men enjoyed reading, but no man would have liked being stuck in this moving mass of pigtailed soldiers who brayed with delight at a Ronald McDonald clown statue posed on a bench in front of the hamburger shop. Two security guards were stationed around Ronald to keep him safe from the crowd.

The statue was a hazard to foot traffic, I thought sourly as I got swept into the tide of girls once more, the momentum stopping from time to time as friends decamped to get their pictures taken in booths or ran into record shops.

"Excuse me, do you know where...," I tried to ask a teenager carrying a bag emblazoned with Doraemon, the robot cat from a famous television series, but there were too many shrieks for him to hear my question.

Fortunately, I was a few inches taller than most of the teens, so I was able to see a gaudy clothing boutique that had mannequins in the window dressed as animation heroes and heroines. I broke out of the pack, apologizing to the dozen girls I bumped into during the process, and tried to creep backward against the tide to reach the shop.

"Do . . . you . . . know . . . where I can find a *manga* shop?" I was slightly breathless when I approached the store's salesgirl who was dressed in the tigerskin costume worn by Urusei Yatsura, a female demon from an *anime* program that used to be on television.

"There isn't a retailer in this neighborhood anymore. But there is a coffee shop called Anime Kissa," she said.

"Does it have any connection to *manga*?" I asked because the word *anime* was associated with TV and video, not printed matter.

"Yes. If you go in and pay four hundred yen for a coffee or tea, you are allowed two hours' time to read the magazines in stock. It's a good way to catch up on series."

"So I can't actually take any comics out of there?" I asked.

"That's correct! But who wants to buy what you can get for free?" She laughed gaily. "Actually, that's the kind of saying that my mother tells me, but she doesn't mean it in reference to *manga*."

Two blocks later I turned left at a vintage jeans shop, looking for Anime Kissa. A narrow doorway led into a room that was filled with so much smoke that I had a coughing fit. The room looked almost like a library, because the walls were lined with bookcases filled with paperback comic magazines. None of the teenagers or office workers looked up to notice the intruder.

I went to the shelves, preparing to make a systematic sweep. According to the rules posted near the entry in Japanese and English, I wouldn't have to buy a drink until I'd brought my desired *manga* to a table. Then, as soon as a waitress met me to take the refreshment order, the two-hour clock would start ticking. If I ordered more drinks or something to eat, I could stay even longer.

I quickly passed the rows and rows of commercial comic books in favor of a few shelves of *doujinshi* in the back. There was one *Showa Story* comic with an appealing cover of Mars Girl landing on the deck of a classic Imperial Navy ship.

I took that along with an armload of about a dozen other amateur artworks, found an empty table for one, and began reading. In my case, reading meant skipping over kanji that I didn't know, so I was actually plowing through books at the same speed as the people around me. I read my way through two iced coffees and a piece of pumpkin cheesecake. I was looking for the spark of something interesting. Instead, what I found were monotonous copies of popular series, with the added excitement of sexual situations. Very boring—although I supposed that to some, these comics might be titillating. The only comic book I liked was *Showa Story*.

I noticed more of the customers in Anime Kissa were reading commercial comics than *doujinshi*. The bookcase where I'd gone to pull out some *doujinshi* was receiving no traffic at all. The only person who had picked up an amateur-designed comic was a young man in sunglasses who was chain-smoking with a newspaper in front of him and an iced coffee at his side. I considered approaching him for an interview—*Have you heard of* Showa Story? *Why do you like* doujinshi?—but I noticed with scorn that his head was not even tilted toward the page. It was aimed instead in the general direction of where I was sitting.

Maybe there was someone fascinating behind me. I pretended I had an itch on my upper back so that I could turn around and see, but the table behind me held a salaryman who was buried in a copy of *Jump*.

Perhaps Sunglass Man was gay and trying to encourage eye contact with the salaryman. I got up and took a few of the *doujinshi* I'd finished back to the bookshelf. When I sat down, I bent my head to study the next comic book, but kept an eye on Sunglass Man. He strolled over to the main comic section, then, as I'd suspected he would, went straight for the *doujin-shi*. He was interested in seeing what I'd read.

The magazines I'd returned to the shelf were salacious rip-offs spoofing *Sailor Moon* and *Neon Genesis Evangelion: doujin-shi* I had no interest in writing about because the artwork was not special, and what I could make out of the stories seemed very clichéd albeit rife with sexual positions. I didn't want the Sunglass Man to focus on me and what I had looked at. It was time to leave.

Trying not to be obvious, since he'd sat down once more in his seat, where he could keep an eye on me, I moved my handbag onto my lap and began counting out change to leave the wait-ress to pay for my coffee and cheesecake. I slid the change onto the table next to me and continued to pretend to read for the next five minutes. I remembered the salesgirl at Animagine telling me that the average Japanese took ten minutes to read a comic, so I didn't want to rush things and raise suspicion.

At last I closed the comic and rose to go to the bookshelf to swap it for another. I felt the man watching me, but I pretended not to notice. I returned to my seat and opened the new maga-zine. The instant the man had gone up to investigate which *dou-jinshi* I'd returned to the bookcase, I zipped out of the coffee shop.

I ran a few doors down the alley and dived into an electron-ics store, where I could hang out behind some stereo speakers and see through the window whether he passed. I didn't see Sunglass Man, but I knew he might be camouflaged in the huge wave of teenagers who were now heading largely toward Harajuku Station. It was five-thirty, time to head home to eat dinner and do homework. I wondered how many of the children's parents knew they were wasting their time shop-ping in Harajuku instead of attending after-school tutoring. I also doubted the parents would be pleased about the kind of men who lurked beside the teenage patrons of *anime* coffee shops. It could have been Kunio Takahashi, of course, which would mean there was no danger, but I'd blown a chance at an interview. The fact that Sunglass Man had black hair, and not red-brown as Chiyo had described, might simply mean that Kunio had gone back to his natural color.

The evening news was blaring from a television turned on in the back of the store, so I could listen to the latest developments as I awaited my stalker. Maybe it was just an idle fascination he'd had, and he didn't intend to follow me from the coffee shop. I was famous for my overreactions. I listened to the news, thinking about how a lot of people in Japan had serious problems. The Japanese Nikkei stock index had dropped another two points . . . thirty children had fallen ill from *E. coli* contamination of boxed lunches . . . a man had been found dead in the Sumida River.

A man had been found dead in the Sumida River. All of a sudden I lost interest in watching the street. I went to the back of the store and stood in front of the screen to take in the dirty green-brown river. I'd been there before, I realized, because I recognized it. Or had I? The neighborhood mentioned was one that was a little closer to Kunio's neighborhood than mine. I didn't think I knew it.

A local fisherman who had found the body was speaking to the reporter. In a quavering voice, he said, "There was a strange marking on the face. At first I thought it was blood, but now I think it was ink."

"A marking could be the sign of a gang," the newsman said, clearly attempting to coax the man into agreement.

"I don't know about that. Anyway, this person was not a regular man. You could tell from the clothes. Plus he was foreign, with blond hair."

"Please explain about the clothing!" the newsman encouraged.

"He was wearing a blue bodysuit. It was a strange foreigner—a young man dressed like a lady, with a silver skirt and high-heeled shoes."

"Was the body fully clothed or partially naked?" the newsman asked.

"Turn the camera off," another voice shouted from the television. A police officer had realized belatedly that the interview was going on. He began haranguing the reporter for interfering with police business.

I swapped the first fear that I'd had for a new one.

Kunio had not been murdered.

Nicky, his friend from next door, had.

12

I made my way out of the electronics shop and into the bustle of Harajuku, feeling both sad and stunned by the news. Nicky, misogynistic creep that he was, hadn't deserved to die. If I had trailed him to his matinee and later meeting with his comic book cohorts, he might have lived.

Outside Harajuku Station, there was a short pedestrian bridge leading to Yoyogi Park. Crouched along the bridge, young people dressed in costumes as shiny as the one Nicky had been wearing were chatting, playing boom boxes, and watching a tiny battery-operated television. So these were the *cos-play*, or costumed player, types that Rika and her friends had mentioned. They looked like Halloween celebrants trying to look like transvestites; they were too cute to be the real thing.

I approached a young man dressed as Sailor Moon, a well-known girl character wearing a sailor suit uniform. "Sorry to bother you, but I wonder if you heard the news . . . the news about someone dressed like Mars Girl who died?"

Through a pair of thick false eyelashes, the boy's eyes bugged out at me. "I don't play Mars Girl. I play Sailor Moon."

"I see that." I stopped, amazed that he wasn't at all interested in the prospect of a fellow animation enthusiast's death. "Actually, I've been trying to locate members of a *doujinshi* circle that puts out its own version of the Mars Girl comic."

"Ah, you mean *Showa Story*," Sailor Moon said, his voice a touch warmer. "The girl in the circle is the only one who we know. She dresses like a dog."

"That's exactly whom I'm interested in finding," I said, realizing he couldn't help me find Kunio.

"Seiko is always busy, even though she doesn't actually draw the comic. She's responsible for getting it printed."

"Can you give me a physical description of her?" I asked.

"Hey, are you weird or something?" He looked at me dubiously, as if I, in my jeans and T-shirt, were a much more eccentric character than he in his schoolgirl uniform. Well, around his stomping grounds it was true.

"I need to know what she looks like if I'm going to find her," I said between gritted teeth.

"Oh. Well, she has long yellow fur and whiskers. She wears a black leather dog collar. She's very distinctive."

"You don't know what she looks like outside of the costume?"

"Oh, you won't be able to identify her that way. I've seen her once without her costume, and she just looks like a typical Japanese girl!"

"Did you . . . did you happen to hear of any men who dressed as Mars Girl?" I asked Sailor Moon, not hoping for much.

"Seiko-san said that the *amerikajin* in the circle played Mars Girl. I think his name was something like Nikko."

Nicky. I thought of telling Sailor Moon that I thought Nicky was the dead one. However, I didn't know for sure, and I didn't want to start false rumors. I thanked Sailor Moon and spent a few minutes looking for Seiko in her yellow dog costume, just in case she was around. After twenty minutes, I gave up and continued on my mission. Next stop: Show a Boy. When I reached the club, Marcellus was standing outside, offering leaflets to female pedestrians.

"Miss Rei, say hey, walk this way," he warbled as I approached. The happy rumble of his voice made it clear that he didn't know what had happened.

"I have bad news," I began.

"You're not going to be able to promote the club in your magazine? Well, that's fine, *chérie*. I can smooth things over with the *mama-san*."

"It's about one of the men who works here," I said.

"Are you still looking for Kunio? I tried to tell you before, he's a painter, not a host—"

"I'm talking about Nicky." I'd decided that since Marcellus was a close coworker of Nicky's, he needed to know my worry.

"He's not here yet. Chiyo might fire him, she's so angry that he's late." Marcellus raised his eyebrows theatrically.

"Well, actually, she should go to the police. According to a news broadcast I just watched, the body of a foreign man was found in the Sumida River."

"There are plenty of foreign men in Tokyo," Marcellus said, but his voice quavered. "It cannot be Nicky. He will be arriving any minute."

"I pray that I'm wrong. It's just that he was dressed in a special costume when I saw him this morning, and the dead man they were talking about on television was wearing the same thing. A Mars Girl costume."

While Marcellus had been listening, he had kept his arm idly outstretched. Now, as a teenage pedestrian tried to take the offered flyer, Marcellus was caught off guard. He staggered, then caught himself. He apologized to the teenager, and when she was out of earshot, he asked me, "Did you see his face?"

"No. The body was covered. Anyway, you or somebody who knows Nicky well should go to the police."

"But I can't! There is too much danger."

Danger. He must have been paranoid about the police. "Of course I understand," I said. "I know it's hard to deal with the Japanese police. I'll try to think of someone else . . . actually, I heard the name of another member of the *doujinshi* circle: a girl called Seiko Hattori."

"Oh! The one . . . like a dog?" Marcellus asked.

He did know a lot about *Showa Story*, I was realizing. "It sounds as if you know her. Maybe you could suggest to her that she go to the police?"

"I don't know her well. Seiko-san used to come inside for the show sometimes. But the *mama-san* didn't like her there. She was banned."

"Wow. Is there any way that you can put us in touch?"

Marcellus looked uncomfortable. "All I know is that she was Nicky's classmate at Showa College."

"Well, maybe she can help me make the identification."

"You are so concerned, Rei-san," Marcellus said softly. "Why? Did you love him, too?"

"No, of course not." I felt my cheeks getting hot. "It's just that I saw him earlier today, and I wonder if there was anything I could have done to stop him from meeting his end."

"There is no reason to believe he has met his end," Marcellus said soothingly. "Why, he will probably walk in soon and we will all laugh about your worries."

"I wouldn't laugh," I said. "Not when somebody's died."

Marcellus scrawled something on a leaflet and gave it to me. "Call me at home tomorrow morning. I'll tell you that he came in, all right?"

"Thanks." As I walked off, I wished that Marcellus was right about my fears being ungrounded.

◆◆◆

I have lived long enough in the city to have a number of good friends to turn to in times of emergency. Interestingly, most of them are men. First is Richard Randall, my best friend and ex-roommate, who was away for the summer leading Japanese tourists through London and Paris. The others are Ishida-san, an antiques dealer who can detect fraud at fifty paces, and my cousin Tsutomu "Tom" Shimura, a doctor at St. Luke's Hospital, who keeps peace between me and my Japanese family. And finally, I know Lieutenant Hata, who works for the Tokyo Metropolitan Police in the Roppongi District. Lieutenant Hata is still so formal with me that I don't know his first name. However, the fact that I'd given him assistance a couple of times made him likely to take my call. I thought it would be better to make contact with him before I pressed on with Kunio or Seiko.

I arrived home and flipped through my business card collection until I found the dog-eared card that the lieutenant had given me one year earlier. There was a first name on it, but I was too illiterate to read it. I called the station and found out Lieutenant Hata's shift had ended in midafternoon. I gave the precinct's secretary a message asking him to telephone me first thing in the morning.

So I was left with myself for the night. I drained a can of Asahi Super Dry Beer and went restlessly from room to room—which didn't take much time, since my apartment was six hundred square feet—thinking about the state of things. I kept the television on and flipped from channel to channel, watching irritating game shows until the news came on at eleven.

The Sumida River corpse led the news on every channel. There was still no identification of the foreigner, who was now described as a European man between twenty and thirty.

After the news segment had ended, I opened the comic book that I'd taken from Kunio's apartment. How uncanny that the scene of Mars Girl's struggle had taken place at a river and involved drowning a man. I studied the five pages containing scenes of Mars Girl getting the better of her attacker. Red bridge, green-black water. The location looked very different from the modern but run-down area where the corpse had been discovered.

I looked back at the television screen, where a reporter was describing the alleged disfigurement of the corpse's face. A strange circle had been drawn on the forehead in dark red ink. The fisherman who had found the body had re-created the marking on a piece of paper to show the reporter.

The mark was a rough approximation of the symbol Mars Girl had drawn on the forehead of the slain gangster in the comic book. Whoever had killed the foreigner was making a reference to the killing in Kunio's comic book. Either he'd been in Kunio's apartment and looked at the walls, or he had paged through the prototype comic book that I held in my hands.

"Shimura-san, you have described many unusual theories in the time that we have known each other. This is the strangest yet."

On Tuesday morning, Lieutenant Hata stood next to me on a loading dock overlooking the sandy strip next to the Sumida River where the foreigner's body had been found. Hata's eyes were on a barricaded area still being searched for clues by police using metal detectors, sieves, and all manner of implements. I followed his gaze, thinking how ironic it was to be observing these beachcombers fully clad in dark blue uniforms after having lain so recently among the nearly naked on the beach in Hayama.

"My strange theories are sometimes wrong," I said. "But when I know something that might be helpful, I don't know of a better person to tell about it than you."

"Thanks," the lieutenant said. "You mentioned that you wanted to show me the comic book?"

I handed it to him, open to the page with the scene of the gangster's death.

"It is similar," Lieutenant Hata said, turning the page. "It's uncanny. All the close-up illustrations of the face have the planet marked on the forehead."

"You've seen the victim's forehead, then?" I asked, being careful to use the word *victim* instead of Nicky's name. It was almost as if by not saying the name, I might guard against a bad outcome.

"Just in photographs. And the planet on the real man's head is not as beautifully stylized as in the *manga*."

"You're saying that the real-life marking doesn't look like the work of an *anime* artist?"

The lieutenant shrugged. "It's hard for me to judge. I'm not the art expert."

I seized on that. "I'll let you know what I think of the murderer's artistic abilities when you show me the body."

This was the second time I had voiced my interest in going to the morgue. When Lieutenant Hata had called me first thing in the morning, I'd said that I wanted to try to make an ID. To my shock, he had said that he didn't think it was a good idea. I hadn't known Nicky long enough to be a good judge of his identity, according to standard police thinking. It seemed that once again, I found myself stymied in Japan because I wasn't part of an in-group.

"Shimura-san, you know that I cannot take someone who is not a close associate of the deceased into that room for a viewing. I understand your curiosity, given the coincidences in this comic book."

"It's not that I'm eager to see the corpse," I said, feeling a mixture of anger, incredulity, and hurt. "But since nobody's coming forward, I'm the best bet that you have."

Lieutenant Hata shook his head. "Why is it that you feel every murder in Tokyo is connected to you?"

"I am connected, given that I have this in my possession—supposedly the only one of its kind." I flapped the Mars Girl *doujinshi* at him. "I was watched in a *manga* coffee shop by a shady-looking man who knows I'm interested in *Showa Story*. I'd feel better if you caught up with him and asked why he was so interested."

"Are you saying you think that the artist who drew the scene is the murderer?" Lieutenant Hata asked.

I shook my head. "No. I don't know, but I wonder whether the culprit knew the members of Nicky's circle. Nicky didn't want me to come along and meet them yesterday. Maybe it was because he sensed danger."

"I can't follow up on that until we have a firm identification of the body. When that comes, I think the line of inquiry you propose is very good. But until that time—"

"Nothing can happen," I said bitterly.

There seemed only one thing to do—find somebody who cared about Nicky enough to bother showing up at the morgue. I had an idea about who could pull it off, but with my luck, she'd probably say no.

13

Rika had seemed pleased that I wanted to take her to lunch.

"Is it about the *manga* story?" she asked when I arrived at the *Gaijin Times* office to pick her up after my meeting with Lieutenant Hata. Alec Tampole was out of the office trying to interview Harry Connick Jr. This meant that I could steal away with Rika without her having to ask his permission. Rika was still officially Alec's editorial assistant.

"Yes," I said. "It's getting complicated, and I need your help. But we should sit down at the noodle bar before I tell you."

We walked through Jimbocho, the area in Kanda that was lined with wonderful small bookshops. I'd spent many happy hours looking for the antique illustrated books that were the precursors of *manga* and *doujinshi*. The sun was shining and the Virginia Slims models—pretty young women wearing smart green-and-white suits—tried to slip free cigarette samples into our hands.

"What a shame you have to work like this," I told one of the girls, remembering the smoky hell of the *manga* coffee shop. "People will die because of what you're doing."

"A free gift! Please enjoy!" the woman kept reciting, not even looking at me.

Rika took the cigarettes and said, when we were a few steps away, "I'm not going to smoke these, but I had to take them to save face. Rei-san, you embarrassed her!"

"I'm in a very touchy mood," I said. "That's part of the reason that I need your help."

The restaurant that I had in mind served *somen* noodles in a cold-water bath. The serving method was particularly ingenious: A metal-sided "river" was set into a long counter, with whirlpool-like jets. The noodles raced downstream past all the diners, and the goal was to reach with the noneating ends of one's chopsticks into the stream and catch a bundle. Small bowls of dipping sauces at each place insured the cold noodles could be seasoned according to personal taste. At less than $7 for a serving, this was definitely a lunch that I could afford.

"Should we do this in English?" I asked Rika in my mother tongue.

She smiled. "Of course! Although you must not laugh at my poor English."

"Don't worry. Rika, you told everyone at the magazine that I was going to interview Kunio Takahashi about his work for *Showa Story*, didn't you?"

"I had to tell, so I made it sound very good. I described how this was a particularly artistic comic book, and Mr. Sanno loved the idea. They are going to make it the cover story." Rika dug into her bag, pulling out a small silver steel rectangle. She pushed a button, and the screen lighted.

"What's that?" I asked.

"You've never seen one? It's a Palm Pilot. I can take notes on it, so it's very good for reporting," Rika said.

"All right. Here's the big problem. Kunio's disappeared, and his next-door neighbor—a guy called Nicky who was part of

Showa Story's creative circle—is dead. Or at least I think he's dead."

"Could it be Nicky Larsen?" Rika asked. "He is the foreigner who hung around with Kunio at college. Why do you think he's dead?"

I told Rika the story about how I'd visited Kunio's apartment and had the encounter with Nicky. I filled in with the description of Nicky's bizarre costume, and how I'd recognized his Mars Girl clothing on the dead man on the evening news.

Rika typed nonstop as I went through the story. At the end she asked, "Why don't the police want to let you view the body to check that it's really Nicky?"

"I'm not supposed to know him well enough to make a judgment."

"I've met him only a few more times than you. I never saw him in the Mars Girl costume. I only know him to look manly." She paused. "That is the correct word? *Manly?*"

"That's right. I think your college connection is really helpful. If you called the police hotline, I bet they'll let you to take a look. But you'd better not mention that you've seen him only a few times."

Rika was silent for a long moment, and I wondered if she was thinking that seeing a dead body would be more than she could bear. I'd seen three corpses in my lifetime, and they were stamped indelibly into my senses. The unexpected sound of a cat's meow made me remember a woman with beautiful pale skin. The sight of a certain model of Toyota summoned up a middle-aged man slumped over in the passenger seat. I did not wish for someone as young and naive as Rika to have the kind of memories that I did.

At last Rika spoke. "I am surprised that you asked me, Rei-san. First to come to lunch, and now to help you identify the body. I wonder how many more things you will ask me to do."

"I'm sorry," I said. "You don't have to do it."

"Actually, I am happy and surprised that you asked. I had a feeling that you . . . well, that you wanted to write the story alone. You did not want my help, even though I had an interest in the topic."

I looked straight at Rika. "That's not what counts anymore. We're not going to be able to write any kind of article about *Showa Story* if all three circle members are dead or missing in action."

"But that's exactly why we must write it! It is a really exciting article now. If it turns out that Nicky died and Kunio cannot be found, we have information to write a story that is much better than anything that could appear in *Asahi Shinbun* or the *Japan Times*."

I had brought her in because I needed her help to answer a question. But now I saw that she had a separate agenda. "Actually, Rika, I hate to think of profiting from somebody's misery."

"That is because you did not train as a journalist, Rei-san! I did!" She hit a key on her Palm Pilot that made a loud beeping sound, as if to emphasize her point.

I threw up my hands. "Well, I'm happy to share credit with you if there's a story to write. But first we need to get that body identified."

"Yes, that's the first thing. We must establish that we have a victim. Oh, I hope so!"

"Rika!" I couldn't hide my horror. "I thought you liked Nicky!"

"Do you realize that this story could get me a job on MTV Asia? Or CNN?"

Her ambition was so raw. I felt revolted, then remembered what I'd been like a few years ago. When I first immigrated to Japan, I was desperate to get a job at a museum. I'd have done almost anything to make my application noteworthy. I was only doing my current mishmash of jobs because I'd never achieved my dream employment.

Thinking about that made me realize that the *Showa Story* article under consideration certainly wouldn't boost my arts career the way past articles had. Still, going ahead with the article would at least answer the question about whether it was Nicky lying dead in the morgue.

"When you call the police, don't mention my name," I instructed her carefully. "I bet that if you identify yourself as a student who met Nicky several times, that should be enough. Of course, they might want to probe your background a little bit. Police are naturally suspicious."

Rika toyed with her pigtail. "That should be easy. I'll mention that we know each other through Showa College's animation club. I don't have to tell them that I'm working on a story for *Gaijin Times* if they don't ask about it."

"I just have one more suggestion." I paused, searching for the right words. "You must be completely honest about whether you recognize the corpse. If you aren't positive that it's Nicky, you must say that. I won't be disappointed."

"Yes, we could still do the *Showa Story* article even without a dead man," Rika said cheerfully. "The focus would change to our search for the missing circle members."

The only gap in Rika's equation was that we'd have to find a source to say something by the article's end.

I wasn't used to having someone else take over. It made me nervous. I stayed with Rika while she telephoned the police from the noodle restaurant's vestibule.

"I'd like to come in and identify the corpse." Rika spoke loudly over the restaurant din, and I saw a few diners glance at her in curiosity. Yes, it was good that we'd had the bulk of our conversation at the noodle counter in English.

"They want me to try!" she said gleefully after hanging up. "I'm going over to the morgue after work. I'll be there at five-thirty, and I can probably call you with the answer shortly after that. Will you be home?"

"Yes," I said, knowing that I'd be pacing my apartment the same way I had the night before. This would be best. I could keep an eye on the evening news to see whether the police would break the news of the body's identification to the press.

"I'll talk to you then. Rei-san, I cannot thank you enough for helping my career with this story. You are an incredibly kind person."

We parted outside the noodle shop and I headed toward Kanda's JapanRail station, stopping in at a few of the used-book stores to see if anything good was for sale. I found myself paging through a water-damaged paperback book illustrated with black-and-white wood-cut drawings that told a story with written commentary in blocks alongside each picture. I read onward and saw a man and woman tumble across the pages, the woman's kimono opening just enough to show the curve of her breast. The illustration, however tasteful, was similar in theme to the modern *manga* that I'd seen at Animagine—yet the type of paper and printing technique told me the book had been printed in the late nineteenth century.

As I paid for the book, the dealer noticed a copy of *Showa Story* peeking out of my book bag.

"That looks like nice paper. May I see it?" he asked.

"Sure." I handed it over, and to my surprise he did a curious thing: sniffed the paper.

"Ah," he sighed. "The best."

"It's like art-book paper, isn't it?" I asked.

"That's right. This paper, which is called Contessa, is made in Singapore. It's acid free, and one would expect to see it in art books, not in comic books! But this is Tokyo. Everything's available if you've got the money for it."

"How do you think some college students in their twenties could get hold of such a paper?" I asked.

"Hmmm." He paged through the comic book. "It's photocopied—one can tell by the slight loss of resolution. The work was done on a color photocopy machine. They had to go to a photocopy shop, and the shop probably carried a variety of high-quality papers."

I thanked the dealer for his intelligence, but decided privately that going from photocopy shop to photocopy shop across Tokyo would be a logistical nightmare—even if I screened out ones that did not carry Contessa paper. Besides, I wasn't so sure that the dealer's theory that the paper came from a shop was right. Seiko, Nicky, and Kunio had a connection to Showa College. They could have raided the college's art department for the paper.

I went home to rest my aching body in a bath foaming with blue salts from Hakone, a gift from my aunt. I was just drying off when the telephone rang.

"Rika-san?" I said quickly when I picked up the phone. I had decided to show her some respect by addressing her with the formal honorific suffix -san rather than the affectionate but slightly belittling -chan that others at the Gaijin Times used for her.

"Sorry, Rei," came the answer in Japanese. At first I leaped at the thought that the caller was the mysterious Kunio. But as the masculine voice continued a litany of my crimes—why hadn't I returned his telephone calls, where had I gone?—I realized the caller was my distraught boyfriend, Takeo.

"I really have been trying to talk to you, but I lost my address book at the beach," I said.

"Why didn't you call the School? They'd give you my cell phone number." Takeo sounded exasperated.

I had no excuse to give him, so I said, "Sorry, I'm glad you called."

"May I come over?"

"Okay, but we're going to have to stay in until I've heard from someone on the phone. It's about the article."

"See you soon," he said, and the warmth was back in his voice.

14

Takeo showed up at my doorstep in half an hour. For a change, he'd left his Range Rover at home and taken the subway.

"I didn't realize that you knew how to take the Chiyoda Line," I said, kissing him once I'd closed the door. I didn't want my neighbors to think that I was wild.

When we broke apart, Takeo said, "I should take the subway more often. It's great being pressed up amidst all those bodies, thinking all the time of yours. Thanks for not dressing." He stroked the light cotton fabric of my robe.

"Um, I actually just took a bath. I meant to get dressed again. . . ."

"What's the point? Here, this is for afterward. I brought your favorite tarts—the ones with butter cream and mandarin oranges." He handed me a pale green box that bore the seal of Mitsukoshi department store.

He looked cheerful and relaxed as he kicked off his Birkenstock sandals in my apartment's entryway and then began unbuttoning his shirt.

"Takeo, let's enjoy those tarts right now. I'll put on the kettle for tea, or would you prefer sake?" I moved out of his grasp.

"Since when do we practice tea ceremony with each other?" Takeo laughed delightedly. "What do you want to do, go backward in time?"

Yes, I thought. *I want to go backward one day to the time when Nicky told me that he had to go to an important lunch meeting, and that I couldn't follow him. I should have said, "I'm coming with you," no matter what, and my presence might have saved his life.*

I must have let out a sound, because Takeo said, "What is it?"

"I—I'm just sitting around waiting for bad news." I watched him amble into the LDK—the Japanese acronym for a combined living, dining, and kitchen space. Even though I had tidied up that morning, my kitchen counter was packed with drying dishes, ripening fruit, and assorted tea-making equipment. The low tea table where I ate and conducted most of my business was covered by paper—daily newspapers, the *Showa Story* prototype I'd picked up at Kunio's place, and my most recent find, the nineteenth-century book of woodblock prints.

"May I?" he asked, setting the box squarely atop the antique comic.

"Actually, it's rather precious." I crouched down beside him and slipped the comic out from underneath. The pages were open to a rather gratuitous sexy scene. The woman had a slim, realistic figure, save for the fact that she was completely hairless—ah, that Japanese aesthetic!—but her male partner had an organ the size of a late-August zucchini.

Takeo blinked. "Wow, have you changed the plan? Are you going to write an article on historic erotic comics? What a great idea!"

"No, it's just for me. What I mean is, it's not part of the article I'm writing for the *Gaijin Times,* but perhaps I can learn from it." Realizing how damning that sounded, I corrected myself. "That is, I hope to learn more about the popular culture of the Meiji period."

Takeo smiled at me. "I can teach you. There's a wonderful old text called *The Pillow Book* that I got out of my father's library. I know some of the moves by heart."

"You're depraved!" I said, smiling, although I was not in the mood. "Let me do something with the sweets. I don't anything to contaminate the antique paper."

I moved around my kitchenette, swiftly putting the tarts on a blue-and-white Imari plate and warming a little bit of sake on the stove to pour into an earthenware flask. Sake tasted good with sweets. Asahi Super Dry Beer did not.

I placed everything on an antique red-and-black lacquer tray that sat on two short legs, a table unto itself, and took it to Takeo's side. A courtesan's behavior, when my nerves were jumping up and down inside. When taking a forkful of tart, I accidentally dropped a mandarin orange segment down the front of my robe. Takeo snaked a hand between my breasts to find it.

"Here's my opening," he murmured, maneuvering me backward on the *tatami* mats.

"Not just yet," I said, rolling away.

Takeo sighed heavily. "I'm sorry, Rei. I've been oblivious. You must be hoping for the telephone call."

"Yes. Crucial information is about to come. Forgive me, but I feel as if I'm jumping in about a thousand different directions."

"You're hoping that artist guy will call. Kunio Takahashi." There was an edge to his voice.

I shook my head. "He's not interested in cooperating. This call I'm waiting for is from Rika, the intern I told you about. We're working a new angle together. I guess I should tell you about it."

Takeo poured a glass of sake for me, neatly taking over my role as host. "Well, first let me congratulate you for moving past your original competitive feelings toward Rika. You never needed to worry, *neh?*"

"If only it were so easy," I said, taking a sip of sake. I'd bought the liquor at a very old brewery in the Japanese Alps town of Takayama. It had the subtle taste of pine needles, and I wanted to serve it quickly, before its taste deteriorated. It seemed fitting that I would sip ceremonial liquor while waiting for news of death or life.

"You're saying that you're still angry at Rika?"

"No." I showed him the *Asahi Evening News* article about the dead foreigner. "Did you hear about this?"

"Yes." Takeo wrinkled his nose. "Gay-bashing. I thought that was only a problem in countries like the United States. It's highly unusual here."

"I don't think it was gay-bashing. The man who died was dressed up to look like Mars Girl. Men who dress as female characters usually do it just because they like a character, not because they want to be a woman."

"*Mars Girl*? Was that one of the ones we translated together?" Takeo asked.

"That's right. The commercial strip served as the inspiration for the *doujinshi* that I became interested in later."

"Oh, you're talking about that *doujinshi* you bought at Animagine? I didn't get a chance to translate that, since you took it with you."

"I have another one of their comics, too, a prototype that I picked up yesterday. The problem right now is that the death scene for the young man I mentioned is identical to the story told in the prototype."

"Wow. What are you doing about that?"

"I sent Rika to the morgue to try to identify the body."

"Why didn't you go yourself?"

"Lieutenant Hata didn't think I had seen Nicky enough times to be able to make a firm identification, but I suspect it's just as much because I'm a foreigner," I said, feeling defensive. "Rika has seen Nicky about the same number of times that I have, but because she's Japanese, the police will take her more seriously."

"Don't be so paranoid about being a foreigner," Takeo said, smiling. "Not everyone is suspicious of you."

"Then why can't I rent an apartment without a Japanese guarantor? And why must I always carry an alien card?" I fumed. "One of the things the reporter said about the dead foreigner was that he wasn't carrying his alien card. That detail made him sound extra deviant!"

"The alien card–carrying obligation is going to change soon," Takeo said. "That man was probably entitled to work here, as you are. When I was studying in the United States, my visa didn't allow me to work. So what's fair?"

"But you don't need to work," I protested.

"Come on! I wanted to work then, and I want to work now." Takeo put his cup of sake down with a click. "I feel terrible having to scrape by doing home renovation because my father doesn't think I'm good enough to take over the school."

"Of course you're good enough," I said. "It's just that your ideals are too strong for him." The telephone rang, and I sprang for it.

"I have news, Rei." It was Rika, sounding very excited.

"Did they let you see him?"

"It was—it was really horrible when I was in there, Rei-san. The only way I could keep from fainting was to concentrate on making notes for the article."

"Mental notes?"

"No, I brought in my Palm Pilot. The policeman at first didn't want to let me use it, but I told him that I needed to type a mantra in order to keep from getting sick, so he allowed me."

Smart move. I felt the strangest twinge of jealousy that she had been the one taking the notes.

"The notes helped, because I could write down things about his appearance and check them against my yearbook later. I even asked the coroner to move his lip so that I could examine the teeth, but rigor mortis had set in."

"Yuck," I said.

"I remember clearly that Nicky's teeth were beautiful, and so were this man's. I explained that, and the police were impressed. In fact, they offered to pull aside the sheet so that I could see more of his body. I think they thought we had been, you know, boyfriend and girlfriend, and that I could check his private parts to make certain of the match."

"Rika! You didn't!"

"Yes, they were very excited to have me there—but suspicious, too! They asked where I had been during that afternoon, but of course I had an excellent alibi—answering telephones at my internship. I didn't bring up *Gaijin Times*, because they might be suspicious of me as a member of the press. I said Sanno Advertising instead. It's all the same organization, really."

A slight deception. I guess it didn't matter much to Rika, but it worried me a little. I hoped her fib about her place of employment wouldn't come back to haunt either of us.

"Could we return to the main topic? Did you recognize the corpse?"

Rika sighed. "Yes, it's him. And I'm not saying it because it would make a good article, either. I'm certain that this is the foreign student I knew from our campus."

"What happened when you told the police what you thought?"

"They believed me. They told me that there had been a tip that the victim might be Nicky Larsen, and they were waiting for a witness to come forward and make the identification."

"Did they ask you a lot of questions?"

"Well, after I told them Nicky was not a boyfriend of mine, they asked if I knew the names of any students who knew him better. I said that I didn't know."

"What about Kunio Takahashi and Seiko, the girl who dresses like a dog?"

"If the police put those two in prison, we won't get to interview them," Rika said. "Let's interview them first."

"I'm no great fan of the Tokyo Metropolitan Police, but I think they should know some things," I sputtered, noticing Takeo had stopped drinking sake and was concentrating on listening to the conversation. Rika and I were speaking English; Rika had initiated the language choice, and I guessed it was because she didn't want to be understood by people around the phone booth. Takeo had an excellent command of English. I imagined the bits of conversation I'd uttered, especially about the police, were making him curious. I reminded Rika, "This Kunio Takahashi interview might never take place, anyway. He had someone give me the message that he doesn't want to be interviewed."

Takeo was sitting bolt upright now. He made a motion with his hand that looked as if he were picking up a telephone receiver. I got it: He wanted to listen to what Rika was saying. I shook my head and mouthed, "Later."

He looked puzzled, and it hit me that his English ability did not extend to lip-reading.

"We have a commitment to Mr. Sanno," Rika whined into the receiver. "He is expecting an article about *Showa Story*. We must deliver what he has asked for."

"Let's meet tomorrow to talk things over," I said in the same soothing tone I'd heard my psychiatrist father use over the telephone to the occasional distraught patient who called him at our home. "And again, thank you for being brave enough to go to the morgue. You are the one who came through with the identification."

The silence stretched between us.

"I'll be there at one," Rika snapped, hanging up without saying good-bye.

15

The instant I put down the receiver, Takeo was all over me.

"Was it he?"

"Couldn't you tell from my side of the conversation?" I asked, remembering how intently he had listened.

"I only heard half of it."

"Rika says the body was Nicky. She based her identification not only on the face, but on some details she noticed before, like his teeth. There are plenty of foreigners running around with pierced ears, but not all of them have good teeth."

Takeo raised his eyebrows. "So your theory was right on the mark. You're turning into a crime reporter."

"I don't want to write about murder," I confessed. "I could hand everything over to Rika, but then . . ."

"You might not be asked to do another story for the *Gaijin Times*," Takeo finished.

"I really need the money. Even though, at this point, I'm coauthoring this article with Rika. But two hundred and fifty thousand yen split in two is still good money." At the current dollar-yen exchange rate, my share would be almost $1,200.

"Isn't Rika ineligible for salary because she's an intern?" Takeo asked. "She should be pleased enough to be credited as a researcher. I'd describe her visit to the morgue as assisting with research. You're writing the article."

"I just don't know if I should muddle into an area in which I have no expertise. This isn't about antiques anymore."

"The story still ties into art," Takeo pointed out. "Why not write an article about the *Showa Story* series, mentioning in passing that the gifted artist for the series could not be found for an interview, and that his colleague was mysteriously murdered? Do it your way."

Boyfriends weren't supposed to be like this, I thought sourly. They were supposed to want you to stay out of trouble, safe at home under the covers and in their arms. Hugh had been like that.

Takeo splashed more sake into my half-filled cup. "Let's see. Where shall we start?"

"I think I've figured out the storyline of the *manga* I bought at Animagine, but would you help me with a full, careful translation of the prototype I found?"

"I thought you'd never ask."

An hour and a half later, I had a word-for-word translation typed into my laptop computer. The central plot—Mars Girl's attempt to buy cooked food to trick the family she was staying with into believing she could cook—was the same as I'd guessed from the illustration. Takeo translated the long passages of back story that I didn't understand. Mars Girl had been sent from the year 2000 into the early 1930s to try to prevent a terrible historical event from happening. She had been told by her outer-space bosses to show up at the home of a middle-class family who lived in the city. Making up a story about being a long-lost country cousin, she was welcomed in. While Mars Girl struggled to gain intelligence on what she needed to do to save Japan, her host family tried to figure out who she really was. The mother had hopes that the new cousin would be a wonderful housecleaner and was stunned by the young woman's woeful inability. The father decided Mars Girl might be a nice plaything for him, but his awkward passes were humorously defeated. The young son of the household feared that Mars Girl was competing for his inheritance, so he started a subtle campaign of dropping insects into her food and bed at every opportunity.

"Poor Mars Girl!" I said, utterly caught up in the situation. "She should just check out and get her own apartment."

"In 1930s Japan? Impossible," Takeo said. "Besides, the story tells us that she is needed to protect that family, as well as society, from a great evil. On the day that Mars Girl ventured out to buy some cooked rice to pass off as her own home cooking, she stumbled across a gangster threatening the owner."

I'd assumed on my brief pass through the comic earlier that the gangster wanted money. But in Takeo's translation, it became clear that the gangster was trying to pressure the owner into paying a tax to a new political party.

"The party in this comic is even more extreme than the conservative imperialists who led Japan into war," Takeo murmured. "In this next frame, the gangster is explaining the party belief that Emperor Hirohito was an illegitimate claimant of the throne. The party members were asking businessmen to contribute money so that the gangster at the top of their organization could raise an army to overthrow the crown."

"That is so hokey!" I said.

"Oh, but it could have happened. A lot of businesses before the war—and even today, a half century later—must make regular payments to gangsters to protect their shops from theft and their families from violence. What if all those payments no longer were distributed among various petty criminals, but went to a central source?"

"You'd have one very rich man," I said.

"A powerful man with the wrong kind of ambition and ties to the military could accomplish a lot. Think of Yukio Mishima."

He was talking about the famous writer who, with a cadre of right-wing army officers, seized the headquarters of the Japan Self-Defense Forces in the early 1960s. The takeover ended when Mishima, with the assistance of one of his aides, killed himself.

"So Mars Girl was sent to stop this gangster political party," I said.

"That's right." Takeo continued with the rest of the story—how the gangster kidnapped Mars Girl with the intention of rape, and Mars Girl then killed him by means of strangulation, dumping his body in the river. She then picked up the rice that the gangster had taken from the restaurant, and brought it home to her family, who was very pleased with her cooking for a change.

"The problem is that Mars Girl realizes that the gangster she has defeated is just one of many underlings trying to secure funding for the new party. They've infiltrated the military. In this final scene, where she's washing up the rice bowls, she is wondering if she can find a way to truly save Japan. The story will continue in the next issue."

"With the artist missing and the author dead, how can the series continue?" I said. "Well, I guess that most of the readers will return to the regular, commercial *Mars Girl* comic series."

"I like this amateur series better than the commercial one. I don't know how you selected this particular story, Rei, but it's excellent. I don't read comics, but I'd buy this one."

"I chose it for the art," I said, remembering how I'd felt when I'd first seen the magazine wrapped in plastic at Animagine. "But now the whole alien theme is really appealing to me. In a way, it's like my own story."

I was nowhere near as strong as Mars Girl, but I did have powers that were different from others'. Being a foreigner in the midst of Japanese, I could look around and see insecurity and tensions that nobody else did. And by Japanese standards, I'd learned my etiquette on a different planet.

"I'm glad you're not destined to go back to outer space." Takeo leaned over to kiss me and added, "I'm heading out to the house in Hayama tomorrow. Do you want to come with me?"

With genuine regret, I said, "How I'd love to go—but I'm already scheduled to meet Rika. However, if you're going to Hayama, perhaps you could do a small favor for me." I told him that I was pretty sure I'd lost track of my address book at the beach bar.

"What's the bar called?" Takeo asked.

"Bojo. It's an open-air place with a straw roof and funny tables—they look as if they were rolled off a ship's deck. "

"Bojo!" Takeo exclaimed. "I can't believe you went there by yourself."

"What's the problem?"

"Didn't you notice a number of men wearing dark sunglasses? Even though it was nighttime? And did you notice the tattoos?"

"You're saying it's a gangster hangout?" I was unable to resist an incredulous smile.

"That's right. You thought the gangster subplot in the comic book was unrealistic, but I can tell you it's only too real an occurrence. They lurk at the beach. Everyone pretends they don't notice them, but they're at that bar. Ever notice there are no decent Japanese patrons? Just foreigners, who don't know how dangerous the situation is."

"Well, you don't have to go there," I reassured him. "I can just telephone them to find out if they've got the book. What's the area code for Hayama?"

"Zero-four-six-eight. But would they have a telephone in an outdoor bar?"

"I don't know. I'll see what the operator tells me," I said, already dialing information. "Hello? I'm trying to get the number for Bojo, a commercial establishment on Isshiki Beach."

But there was no listing. I gritted my teeth, thinking how ironic it was that every other schoolgirl seemed to have her own cell phone, but a business such as Bojo could flourish without a regular telephone or flush toilet.

"I'll go there for you," Takeo said.

"No. You said that men in sunglasses made you uncomfortable." I stopped, struck by a memory of Sunglass Man, who had been watching me in the *anime* coffee shop.

"What is it, Rei?" Takeo seemed to sense my change in thought.

I said, "I hate to admit that you're right. I ought to be more wary."

"I'll get the book for you," Takeo said.

"Really, I can do it myself—"

Takeo interrupted me with a surprising, hard kiss. It ended as abruptly as it had begun, and the next thing I knew, he was out the door.

16

I woke up a bit later than usual on Wednesday morning and turned on the television right away. A tabloid news program was already in full swing. Topic: Nicky Larsen. Police had finally identified the gaudily dressed body washed up on the banks of the Sumida River. The newscaster gave more details: Mr. Larsen had been a Japanese-language major at the University of Minnesota who had come to Japan in 1998 to study at Showa College. He enjoyed Japanese animation, and the bizarre costume he'd been wearing when he died was that of his beloved Mars Girl.

So the cops had gotten out the news, and other journalists had acted quickly and broken the story. Well, they didn't know he was part of *Showa Story*—just that he was an animation fan. I had something interesting that they didn't. Still, I was a little envious of how fast, and smoothly, the news team had picked up on the story. The picture on the screen changed to the head-quarters of Dayo, the comics publisher that produced the gen-uine *Mars Girl* comic that *Showa Story* had imitated.

Mr. Mori, a spokesman for the company, looked like a typi-cal forty-five-year-old salaryman in his dark gray suit. He fairly droned a statement from a sheet he held between his hands.

"It is sad news that an admirer of *Mars Girl* has died. The situation is especially poignant, since Mr. Nicky Larsen was a foreigner who had traveled many miles from his home in America to enjoy Dayo's best-selling series. Our goal at Dayo is to produce comics that entertain and enlighten." Mr. Mori's face twitched; it made him look as if he didn't believe what he was saying, or was about to sneeze. "Unfortunately, those young people who create their own comic books using our characters are infringing on copyrights. The artists at Dayo who produce the real *Mars Girl* work very hard. Our efforts are compromised when imitators charge money for unauthorized depictions of our series."

Mr. Mori bowed, revealing a balding semicircle, and the screen changed to a commercial.

As a woman crooned about toilet bowl cleaner, I tried to filter her out and understand the subtext of Mr. Mori's message. It seemed as if Dayo was using Nicky's death to make a jab about *Showa Story*'s copyright infringement. This struck me as cold-blooded and also rather surprising. I'd been told by Rika in the staff meeting that comics publishers didn't care about copyright infringement. Did she really know . . . or was this another example of one of her quick, casual untruths?

Could the Dayo company be somehow involved in Nicky's death? Kunio had suddenly vanished, ostensibly to collect money to repay debts. Could he have been collecting to make a settlement with Dayo? If so, why would he have taken on all the financial load himself and not shared it with Seiko and Nicky?

I went out for my morning run. I was starting later than usual, so instead of cool air, there was a warm, humid fog, and heat rising up even from the cement pavement, toasting my feet. I saw a neighbor walking her golden retriever and was reminded of Seiko Hattori, the *manga* circle member who allegedly dressed as Mars Girl's dog. I ended my run early, and instead of drinking my usual Aquarius or Pocari Sweat, I chose a cold Georgia Coffee from the vending machine outside Sendagi Station. I had enough change in my shorts pocket to jump on the Chiyoda Line to make a visit to Showa College.

I'd been to the college once for a film festival; it had been a dark winter evening, and I'd gotten the impression of a modern office complex rather than a place devoted to scholarship. It was the architect's fault; many buildings had gone up in the boom-boom 1980s, and they were the standard white Tokyo boxes that become gray fast and do nothing to improve the landscape. It was a shame, because I was willing to bet that the campus had once been nice. The college was founded in 1928, shortly after Emperor Hirohito had come to power. Reflecting the emperor's personal taste, marine science was an important department; his original museum of marine biology was still one of the leading draws on the campus. It was a round building built of stones with windows shaped like portholes. Because it was old and quirky, of course I considered it the most attractive building.

A campus map mounted outside the museum showed tiny photographs of the various buildings corresponding to the various academic departments. I couldn't see the word *art* anywhere. I wondered if the department was housed in another building, such as communications. I would check with the administration. Scanning the building names printed in kanji characters, I triumphantly recognized the symbol for "admissions office" and set off on a smooth cement path toward it.

As Rika's friend had mentioned, the regular school year was over, so things were quiet. There were no bicycles leaning in the bike racks, and no students sitting on the steps. Still wearing my shorts and tank top, I was the only person walking around who looked remotely collegiate. A few grown-ups in business suits walked by with briefcases; professors, I imagined, doing summer research. It was past 9 A.M., so I figured the offices had to be open.

I entered the mauve-and-white room that was the admissions office, and before I could speak, I was handed a form written in Japanese. It appeared to be some sort of preliminary application. The receptionist, a kind-looking middle-aged woman who wore glasses on a necklace chain, waved to me, indicating that I should sit down on one of the plush chairs.

I remained standing, and told her, "I'm trying to get some basic information about students . . . and the art department."

"There is no art department here," the receptionist told me. "Some of the students enjoy art as a hobby, and there are clubs for it, of course. You may indicate your interest in the application."

"Where are the art hobby clubs located?" I asked.

"The second floor of the student union. But I'm very sorry that it's closed for the summer. Can you come back in late August?"

"Um, actually, I'm visiting from America," I said semitruthfully. I was sure the Japanese government would like to think of me as a visitor and not a permanent resident.

"*Ah so desu ka!* We have programs for foreign students. Your Japanese was so good that I did not realize—I gave you the wrong application—"

She began frantically rummaging through a series of folders.

"Please don't go to any trouble," I apologized. "It would be a great help to me, though, if I could meet a particular student I heard about who is interested in the same things as I am."

"Well, it is a bit irregular for me to do this, but seeing as you've traveled so far, I will ask the registrar if he can help." The woman seemed relieved to be able to pass the buck. "What is this student's name?"

"Seiko Hattori."

"All you know is her name? Not her major?"

"Well, I have heard that she is in the *manga* club."

The receptionist frowned. "The Japanese immersion program here is very rigorous. Those who come to Japan seeking only to play at *manga* can be disappointed in the college experience. We had an American like that, and the dean does not want the experience repeated."

"Oh, I agree. Are you talking about that boy who was in the news—Nicky Larsen?"

"He was so consumed with *manga* that he dropped out. And then look at what happened!" She shook her head. "I'm going to telephone the registrar right now. While you wait, you can look at our student publications in the reception area."

I located the Showa College yearbook on a rack, and since I wasn't sweaty anymore, I sat down on a small mauve-and-cream print chair. The chair reminded me of the kind of customer seats one encountered in banks, sized at an elementary-school-student scale—seats that made one feel small in the face of the authority behind the counter. The receptionist obviously had thought I was young enough to be in the undergraduate program, which I suppose was a compliment of sorts, but I don't think she was very happy about my interest in comics.

I paged through the yearbook; fortunately the *manga* group was called Comic Club, so I was able to easily identify the picture. Two rows of students were mugging for the camera, some wearing costumes, some holding their fingers like rabbit ears over the head of the person in front of them. Before looking at the faces too closely, I checked the text for names: Nicky Larsen, Kunio Takahashi, Seiko Hattori.

Nicky was easy to spot: his blond head was higher than everyone else's. He was wearing a long leather coat and looked pretty glamorous. I could see why Chiyo had hired him for the host bar. Kunio Takahashi, standing to his right, was dressed in what looked like a vintage tuxedo complete with wing-tip shoes and gloves. He was wearing sunglasses, so I didn't get much of an impression of his face, except that he had a pointed chin, giving a rather pixielike character to his face. He looked almost like an animation character. I considered whether he could be Sunglass Man, who had watched me in the *anime* coffee shop a few days earlier. The picture was too small for me to decide, and the sunglasses were a different style, but I did think that Kunio was probably close in height to Sunglass Man.

Why did Kunio have to wear sunglasses in the picture? I groused to myself. It was so unfair. Seiko Hattori was on the other side of Kunio. I'd been thinking to myself that since Kunio was supposedly so hot, she might have been a girlfriend—especially since Nicky had called her a bitch. It sounded like they had some past bad history.

In this picture, Seiko was standing with her hands flat against her thighs, smiling into the camera as if she owned it. I had an impression of long straight black hair and a round, softly pretty face. In other words, she looked like half the Japanese college students or office ladies that I saw on the street. I couldn't pick her out of the crowd.

I went through the back of the book, looking for an index to see if there were more photos of Seiko and Kunio. There was no index. Instead, there was page after page of advertisements, in English or Japanese, congratulating graduates and the various extracurricular organizations. There were a number of pages showing support for the volleyball team, and one especially showy page congratulating members of the journalism club, which included Rika Fuchida. Reading the fine print at the bottom of the page, I saw that her parents had paid for the advertisement. Well, that was normal for American high-school and college yearbooks, too.

An ad with a smiling Mars Girl holding a diploma conveyed congratulations to the whole animation club, courtesy of Hattori Copy Shop. The advertisement listed the participating students' names. Kunio, Nicky, and Seiko were listed along with twenty others. There was one name I'd expected to see there but didn't: Rika's.

Looking at the ad, two questions cropped up. First, I wondered if the people running Hattori Copy Shop had any connection to Seiko Hattori. Second, I was curious why Rika hadn't been featured in the *manga* club photo. Rika had told Mr. Sanno she was active in the Showa College *manga* club, but she was turning out to have been less of a player than I thought. Maybe, like her friends had suggested, she was a nonplayer.

"Not available," the receptionist said suddenly.

"Hmmm?" I'd been so lost in Rika's absence from the animation club that I hadn't heard the full sentence the receptionist uttered. With Japanese, I always had to listen very carefully to a whole sentence to understand it.

"It seems that Seiko Hattori used to study here as an English major. She is no longer enrolled."

"Did she graduate?" I asked.

"No, the last year she completed was her third. We have a four-year program." She sighed. "This is a private college, and scholarships are few, I must tell you. Perhaps, with the economic crisis, her parents couldn't afford it any longer."

Three members of a *doujinshi* circle, all missing from college. Somehow I doubted it had anything to do with the current economic crisis.

"Nicky left after his third year as well, didn't he?"

"Technically he was enrolled as a senior this year," the receptionist said. "It's just that he didn't come to class."

"You know a lot about Nicky Larsen without having to call the registrar."

"Oh, as you can imagine, the staff was very concerned after he died. We heard just a few days ago. He's on people's minds."

"Did you know him personally?"

She shook her head. "He completed the application process while he was a student in the United States. Therefore he didn't have any reason to enter the admissions office. The foreign-students office dealt with him, but because it is summer, it's closed."

"I hear that he had a Japanese friend called Kunio Takahashi who recently graduated."

"You are so interested in particular students who are not enrolled here any longer, *neh?*"

Oops. I'd crossed a line, and I was in danger of being found out.

"Um, well, these were the names I was told," I said. "I'd like to take this application and be on my way, but I really am impressed with this yearbook—is there any way that I can buy my own copy?"

"The student union sells copies, but since that is closed, you could try to find a copy at the shop that printed it. Hattori Copy Shop is very close by, just outside Takadanobaba Station."

Hattori Copy Shop was the same company that had placed the advertisement congratulating the animation club. Excellent. I smiled my thanks and was on my way to the station. The copy shop was easy to locate; it was a typical mom-and-pop store with a big sign in the window reading COPY NOW! ONLY 5 YEN. I thought of dashing in, but I realized it was only twenty minutes till my lunch date with Rika. The perils of rising late, I thought sourly. Rika was on a tight schedule at the magazine, so I owed it to her to be punctual. I checked the hours of the copy shop, which were posted on the door, and hurried off to my meeting.

◆◆◆

Rika got to the restaurant at nearly the same moment as I did, and we found seats together just before the noon rush hour. As always, the service was like lightning. The goal of the place seemed to be feeding people, and releasing them, as quickly as possible. Some restaurants had no conversation allowed, in an attempt to speed things up even more. The fact that we were talking was arousing a few evil stares from people standing in the doorway waiting for tables.

"I went to your school today," I said between bites of tofu. I didn't want to eat the same thing I'd had the day before, so I was picking at a cold plate of the delicious soybean curd generously slathered with soy sauce.

"How did you have time to visit my college? I thought you were concentrating on writing our story," Rika said.

"Nicky and Kunio went to Showa College. Don't you think that makes the campus a good place to do research?"

Rika waved her hand airily. "School's not in session."

"The admissions office is open. I saw a yearbook."

Rika's eyes flickered. "Were you able to get a photo of Kunio and Nicky?"

"I couldn't remove the book, but I saw that the *manga* club photo included them as well as Seiko Hattori. But you weren't in the picture."

"I was more active in the journalism club. Didn't you see my photo there?" Rika sounded casual.

How was I going to get her to confess? I eyed her warily and said, "Did you even belong to the *manga* club?"

Rika coughed. "Not exactly, but I am a fan. I went to their parties."

Now I understood. When Rika's friends at the beach said that she didn't know much about *manga*, they'd been telling the truth.

I didn't reply, waiting to see what would come. After thirty seconds, the words came out of Rika in a rush.

"At our staff meeting, I mentioned being part of the club because I certainly know people in it. I'm practically a member."

"I see." I was learning a lot about the little intern who could. I looked at her for a moment, knowing that she was feeling uncomfortable, and I realized that we wouldn't get very far if I turned into an accusing force.

"Let's talk about another thing I'm interested in—the gang connection. My friend Takeo thinks the beach bar where I met you has many gangsters drinking there. Is that true?"

"Don't say that word!" Rika whispered.

I always forgot that one wasn't supposed to utter the word *yakuza* in public, lest one of the gangsters themselves overhear and become angry. But I was speaking English. The term had probably floated by most people.

Rika took a deep swallow of water and then said, "I'm not one of them. I'm just a normal Japanese girl!"

So Rika had thought, when I mentioned that Bojo was a *yakuza* hangout, that I believed she was in the crime world. Her fear was ludicrous enough to make me laugh, but I knew she was in a delicate emotional state, so I didn't.

"I know you're not involved in that," I said. "Most people drinking in those places aren't involved. But there were a few male customers with tattoos and sunglasses. I didn't get close enough to look at their hands."

Hands could be a giveaway for a gangster who'd slipped up once or twice. The traditional penalty for misdeeds within the Japanese underworld was said to be a severed finger.

"I'm giving my best to this article," Rika said. "I have already examined a naked murdered man. I made many notes in my Palm Pilot for you. However, I will not walk up to one of these men to do an interview. There is no connection between the Bojo

Bar and this article, other than the fact that you and I talked about our plans there!"

I sat back in my chair, thinking that it would be a lot easier to skip interviewing a gang member. Why did I feel that we had to?

"Rika, you know I can barely read Japanese," I began. "Nevertheless, when I buy wood-block prints, I look for the artist's seal in the lower right corner," I said. "Because I've studied for so long, I know the seals better than a lot of people, but not as well as a veteran. On the TV news, the reporter suggested that the sign on Nicky's forehead was a gang marking. I would never have thought of that before, but you know, it really makes sense. Nicky worked at Show a Boy, a strip club run by a very tough *mama-san*. There is a possibility that she hired gangsters to kill him—or that gangsters with an interest in the business killed him to send her a message."

"So why is the answer to interview strange men at the beach?" Rika's words came out in a passionate rush. "Why not go back and speak to that *mama-san?*"

"I might do it," I said. "There are actually a lot of things we both could do. Since you have the connections, you could find Seiko Hattori while I pursue the gang aspect."

"Before we begin making such interviews, we must check with the magazine. Mr. Sanno might not like the angle. The *Gaijin Times* is all about selling things, not digging up knives hidden in the beach sand!"

"Mmm, that's a nice metaphor," I said. "May I use it for the article?"

"Not until we speak to Mr. Sanno!"

"But that's jumping the chain of command over Alec," I pointed out.

"I'll talk to Alec first, then I'll wait until Mr. Sanno is in a good mood."

I lost my temper then. "Rika-san, it sounds like you don't want to report this story with me."

"Please give me time, Rei-san. I would like to present Mr. Sanno with my impressions of the corpse, including my diagram of the design on the forehead. Only then can he understand your desire to interview criminals."

I shivered, thinking about how grisly the article was going to be. And also, without doubt, how people would enjoy it. In Japan, there were so few murders per capita that they all received plenty of attention. I'd seen the excitement on television about the strangely dressed foreign body that had washed up on the riverbank.

"Very well. While I wait for you to get me an answer, I'll do some more background work. One last thing. Are you really sure that the body you saw was Nicky's?" I asked. I still had a flicker of uncertainty about launching into a series of potentially dangerous interviews based on an identification made by Rika. I wished I could check out Rika's story about Nicky's body characteristics with Lieutenant Hata, but I couldn't reveal to him that I'd sent her there, could I?

"I'm sure that it was Nicky," Rika said, giving my hand a reassuring pat. "Don't you trust me?"

17

After Rika and I parted, I still had two items on my agenda: visiting the Hattori Copy Shop, which was probably open through early evening, and talking to Marcellus. He was due to go to the club by midafternoon, so I made him my top priority. I ducked into an NTT phone booth and pulled out from my bag the leaflet on which Marcellus had written his home number.

"Have you had your coffee yet?" I asked when Marcellus answered the phone with a sleepy *hai*. Or *hi*. It was hard to tell which language he used for his telephone greeting, because the English and Japanese words sounded the same.

"Who is this?" Marcellus demanded.

"Rei. Remember, the one you told to walk your way? We've got to talk about Nicky. Are you alone?"

"*Oui*. I'm glad that you called. I could not talk the other day because of the *mama-san*. She has been jumping out the door to spy on me. She's nervous."

Now I knew I had to see Chiyo again. "Do you think she might have had something to do with Nicky's death? And what about Kunio?"

"I thought that you did not know whether Nicky died. Is there some news?"

I told him about Rika's evaluation. "Of course, there are other men with that physical description in Tokyo, but the clothing, the good teeth, and the blond hair made it sound like Nicky," I said, finishing up my description.

"I believe you," Marcellus whispered. "Oh, the sorrow of it. He was like my brother. My American brother. He taught me about rap music and break dancing. I owe my act to him."

"I'm so sorry for your loss," I said.

"I do not want to hear what Chiyo thinks when she learns the truth," Marcellus said. "She has no heart. In the time that Nicky has been missing, she has cursed him. She believed he moved to a bar in Roppongi that's copied our dance show. Chiyo said that Nicky has no loyalty to the group, that he was an example of the worst possible *gaijin* character."

"Well, she'll hear his name on television or in the papers. Then she'll probably feel guilty for all that she said."

"Or guilty for other reasons!" Marcellus sounded ominous.

"What do you mean? Does this relate to the danger that you hinted about earlier?"

There was a long silence. "I have to think about what I can tell you," Marcellus said at last.

"Do you think that Nicky's death could be related to the *yakuza*?"

"Don't say that word!" Marcellus cried.

He had become so Japanese. "All right, I'll say *g-a-n-g*. Are you aware of such groups' involvement at the club?"

"No! Our customers are women of normal background. They would like to rape me, but they are not technically criminals. Just women being *naturelle*."

"What about visitors during off-hours?"

"I cannot discuss that."

"All I'm trying to do is figure out whether someone who

stopped by your bar killed Nicky. If you won't tell me, just think about keeping yourself safe."

Marcellus snorted and said, "*Ma chérie*, when I came to this land, I believed it was the safest place on earth. In a tourist guide I saw a photograph of a Japanese village by the sea, with kind elderly ladies walking the road carrying baskets of vegetables. Consider where I must work, and the young ladies who try to tear off my clothing every night! The real Japan is a great shock."

"I understand," I said. "Can you get out of the city for a while?"

"I met a lovely lady who would like me to do that." He sighed heavily. "The difficult part is that it pays more to be a rape artist than to catch fish from the sea. I wear handcuffs of gold. *Comprends-tu?*"

I comprehended. I thought about what it would be like for Takeo if he couldn't be a gentleman do-it-yourselfer in Hayama. He was a bit too lean to make the stage at Show a Boy—not that Chiyo would allow him onstage. So what could a man without options do? Might he turn to a life of crime?

I left the phone booth, which had become a hothouse, given the sun beaming down from outside and the general July humidity. My cotton knit dress that had looked so fresh and neat going off to lunch was now plastered to my body. I looked as if I'd gone swimming. To try to restore my appearance, I stood close to the air-conditioning vent in the subway car—that was the only cool spot I could find on my short ride to the Hattori Copy Shop. I checked my reflection in a small mirror above a water fountain on the subway platform when I was getting out, and I was satisfied that I looked more or less decent. I stopped at the station's news kiosk, mindful that I needed to buy something to photocopy. I had in my backpack several copies of *Showa Story*, but I didn't want to tip my hand by using them. In the end, I settled on buying the Asian edition of *Newsweek*.

I approached the small shop, which was fronted by glass, looking to see who was inside. There were no customers on the small row of chairs lined up against the window; I could see a counter, behind which was copying equipment and two employees. As I got closer, I saw one was a middle-aged man, and the other a young woman. The two were in conversation; as I drew close to the door, I could tell it was an argument. The man was shaking his finger at the woman, and she was backing away. I wanted to hear for myself what they were talking about, so I quickly pushed open the door.

A bell jingled, announcing my presence, startling the woman, who, without even glancing in my direction, went through a door into the back of the shop. All I could see was that she had shoulder-length hair and a slightly chubby figure clad in Pepe Jeans. I thought she was probably under thirty, but I couldn't tell for sure. I wondered if it was Seiko.

The man, who had remained standing in the customer service area, nodded at me and uttered the regular *irasshaimase* welcome that was given to customers entering a shop. He looked at me expectantly.

I opened my mouth and said, "Hattori-san?"

"Yes. What can I do for you?"

"I need some articles photocopied," I said. "The thing is, I would like to use a very good paper for it."

"We have many high-quality papers. I can show you a selection." He went to a shelf and began collecting samples of sheets. "What kind of quality do you want, exactly?"

"Ideally, a paper called Contessa."

"Ah, that's better for artwork, and it's oversized, by the way. Didn't you say that you are just photocopying articles?"

"The articles have color photographs," I said swiftly. "It's got to look good."

"I'm afraid that I'm out of stock of Contessa right now, but I can get it within a month's time. That probably is too long a wait." He looked at me shrewdly, and I wondered if he'd seen through my feeble excuse.

"That is a long time," I agreed. "What else can you offer me? Oh, and I was wondering, are you Seiko's uncle?"

"I'm her father," Mr. Hattori answered. "Do you know her?"

"A little bit," I said after a second. I'd been listening to some rustling sounds in the back of the store that had suddenly stopped. "Does Seiko-san work here?"

"Yes. I'll tell her that you said hello."

"Oh, how convenient that she's in the shop. May I say hello to her?"

"She's actually gone out to lunch. I'll tell her you stopped in, if you give me your name."

It was two-thirty, not exactly a typical Japanese lunch hour. But maybe they had to work through the normal lunch hour, because that was when customers had enough free time to come in for service.

"You wanted to leave your name?" Mr. Hattori was staring at me rather quizzically.

"Rei Shimura," I answered him, handing over my Rei Shimura Antiques card. Who knows, Seiko might be interested enough in my visit to telephone me later.

"Ah, you work with antiques. I can understand your interest in high-quality photo reproduction. Do you want me to create an advertising flyer for you?" His voice was a bit warmer.

"No," I said, feeling silly that I hadn't just brought in some photos of my wares. "It's a news article for a, um, language class that I teach on the side."

"Well, how about selecting the paper? Here is a choice that is comparable to Contessa. I'm sure you'll understand that prices are higher than five yen for this type of paper."

"Do you have anything in the twenty-yen range?" I didn't want to blow a lot of money on this copying project, since I'd have to explain it to the accountant at the *Gaijin Times*.

"Here's something that's suitable for photo-quality repro-duction that costs thirty yen per page. I assume you want a color copy made?"

"Yes." I was flipping through *Newsweek*, looking for an arti-cle worth copying. I stopped at one about police efforts to crack down on Japanese gangs. I figured that it made sense for me to be photocopying an article on a Japanese topic.

"How many copies?"

Since I'd said that I was teaching a language class, I should have more than one made. However, I knew color copies were going to be expensive.

"Two." Seeing his disappointed expression, I added, "It's a very small class."

"Teaching English isn't big business anymore, is it?" Mr. Hattori asked rhetorically. "Ten years ago, it was a good career choice. But now it's not so good."

Seiko was an English major, I recalled from the conversation at the admissions office. I wondered if another reason that Seiko's father had made her leave school was the fact she was studying English.

I handed Mr. Hattori the magazine flipped open to the arti-cle about Japanese gangsters. I saw his eyes widen slightly at the topic, and he looked at my face again. I smiled benignly.

Mr. Hattori went a few feet behind the counter and began the process of making a color copy. It took a minute or so, but he kept his back turned, as if to discourage further queries about Seiko.

I used this time to glance around the shop. The walls were decorated with framed examples of photocopied and printing jobs. I didn't see anything as obvious as a *Showa Story* cover on the wall, but I didn't need to see one to be fairly certain it had been printed here. Seiko could have done it on the sly, when her father wasn't watching. She could have been the one who used up all the Contessa stock.

"All right, then. Each color photocopy is two hundred fifty yen, plus sixty yen for the special paper, plus tax—your total is five hundred eighty-eight yen."

I paid it, getting a receipt so that the *Gaijin Times* would reimburse me.

"Thank you for your business, Miss Shimura." Mr. Hattori lined up the sheets and slid them into a perfectly sized red-and-white-striped bag. The bag's pattern looked familiar. I'd seen another one like it somewhere.

"You're welcome," I answered, taking the bag. "Oh, when would be a good time for me to catch Seiko in person?"

"She's so busy. It's quite hard to tell."

I had a feeling that she'd be busy whenever I came in. I exited the store, no closer to finding Seiko than when I'd gone in.

I walked around to the back of the shop and saw a Toyota Town Ace van parked in a narrow space adjacent to the shop. I crouched down to take my notebook out of my backpack. I was going to record the license plate specifics and see if I could use that information to get a home address for the Hattori family.

I heard the sound of footsteps and looked up. If this was Mr. Hattori, I'd have to make some kind of excuse.

It was a young woman with shoulder-length hair and a stocky frame whom I'd seen earlier. She wore a red-striped cotton tunic over her jeans that matched the pattern on the shopping bag Mr. Hattori had put my photocopies in. She looked a lot like the yearbook picture of Seiko Hattori, only minus the confident, happy expression—and plus a black eye.

I saw the young woman look back over her shoulder into the copy shop, and her pace quicken as she walked away from it. She was crossing the parking lot where I was crouched behind the van. She didn't notice me because she was busy fumbling in a large backpack for something. I caught a flash of what looked like yellow fur—could it be her dog costume? She stuffed the fur back in, pulled out sunglasses, and put them on.

As I began to trail her, Seiko turned around, glanced at me, and then walked casually toward the street. Maybe it was a normal occurrence, in this area of few sidewalks, for pedestrians to cut through the copy shop's parking area. Seiko stood poised on the edge of a crosswalk. When there was a break in traffic, she cut across. She was jaywalking, something not ordinarily done in Japan. Citizens were not supposed to cross streets until the corny musical melody told them that it was safe.

I hurried to catch up with her; by the time I reached the crosswalk, the electronic "walk" jingle had started and I smoothly crossed the street. I saw Seiko's striped tunic bobbing ahead of me, almost but not quite lost in a crowd of other young people. But then, to my surprise, her swift walk turned into a run.

Perhaps she was scared of someone she'd seen in the crowd—or else her father had warned her about me. If I'd been wearing my trusty Asics instead of sling-back Bally pumps, I would have taken off after her. She wasn't a fast runner—I could have caught up within half a minute. But because I was feeling so impaired by my shoes, I struggled through the crowd in a race-walk. My head was starting to ache. It had been a long day, and this chase was not something I'd expected would end it.

Seiko's run ended at a bus stop, just as a large bus pulled to a noisy halt. I wanted to laugh at myself. She wasn't a fugitive, just a person trying to catch a bus. Time, and the long queue at the bus stop, were on my side; by the time I reached it, the stoplight at the intersection had gone red, so the bus was still waiting. I climbed on, so intent on locating Seiko that I forgot to take a paper ticket marking my embarkation point. I was reminded by a schoolchild.

"Sorry," I murmured, and made my way to the back. Seiko Hattori was snuggled in a seat along the window, her face half hidden by a comic book. She was still wearing the dark glasses, most likely to shield her bruised eye area from the public gaze.

I hung out, holding on to a rail while standing in the aisle, staying near Seiko. A large grandmother type who'd been standing ahead of me in the queue for the bus had gotten the seat next to Seiko. The two were politely ignoring each other, standard bus etiquette.

Before I'd jumped on the bus, I'd thought I could slip off when Seiko disembarked, follow her to where she lived, and approach her later for an interview. Now I realized that could be very, very far away. The bus's destination, lit up in lights over the driver's head, was Shinjuku Station.

I cleared my throat and said, "Excuse me."

Instead of Seiko, the old lady sitting next to her looked up at me. "Even if you are pregnant," she said loudly, "I have as much right to this seat as you."

There was a rustling sound as the other passengers craned their heads to get a look at us.

"I'm not hoping to sit in your seat, I just want to say hello to her—"

"When I was pregnant, I kept myself clean," the lady said. "No dirty kimono. Also, I kept clean when I had the babies."

This must be a direct reference to my now very wrinkled knit dress. I was more angry than embarrassed.

"I'm not pregnant!" I whispered as loudly as I could. I wanted to call the old lady an *obatarian,* a nickname that combined the Japanese words for *grandmother* and *battalion* and meant a relentless, annoying type of senior citizen, but I didn't dare.

Seiko glanced up at last, then reburied her nose in her magazine. The volume in her hands was a comic book with extremely graphic sex. It might have been *Showa Story*, but I wasn't going to lean over and stare. "Hattori-san?" I whispered.

Seiko didn't look up.

"I'm a friend of one of your friends."

Still no response.

"Can't she hear?" The *obatarian* clapped her hands loudly, causing everyone around us on the bus to glance over. We were becoming an odd situation, the kind of story passengers would recollect later at the dinner table for family amusement.

The sharp clap was just a few inches from Seiko's ear. She finally broke her scrutiny of the magazine and looked at both of us with clear annoyance.

"Aren't you Seiko Hattori?" I asked.

She nodded cautiously.

"I'm a great admirer of *Showa Story*," I said. "I wonder if I can ask you something about it."

"Who are you?" Her voice was husky, not the standard chirp that most girls her generation had. To talk in a high-pitched voice was a symbol of friendliness, efficiency, and femininity. But Seiko's voice was as sexy as a torch singer's. Not what I'd expect from a round-faced girl wearing a striped pinafore over jeans.

"My name is Rei. I looked for you in the copy shop, but your father said you were out." I reached into my backpack and handed her my business card.

"It's rude to reach in front of others," chided the *obatarian*, who was blocking my access to Seiko.

"Would you like me to help you move to a silver seat?" Seiko said to the old lady in her low, smoky-sounding voice. The bus had several special seats for seniors that were colored silver to match the color of their hair. Rules posted above the seats said they had to be given to senior citizens or handicapped persons. The seats were placed not in twos, but facing

into the aisle so that no senior would have to crawl over anyone's legs to get in or out.

"*Ara!* So rude!" the obatarian exclaimed, staying firmly in
her place.

Seiko mouthed at me, "*Chotto matte.*" Wait.

I moved back slightly in the aisle so that neither the old lady
nor Seiko felt hemmed in. Seiko shut her magazine and tucked
it away. After a couple of minutes, she rang the bell indicating
that she planned to get off the bus. She nodded at me.
Gratefully I realized she was allowing me to follow her off.

Seiko made a little pardon-me bow to the *obatarian* and got
to her feet. I held my breath, waiting for abuse.

Instead of standing, the *obatarian* moved her knees to one
side so that Seiko had to crawl over her to get off.

"Girls these days!" she grumbled.

Seiko paid her bus fare with a ticket she tore off from a little
strip she was carrying in her wallet. Based on that information, I guessed that this bus stop was close to her family home.

We got out on a wide street that bordered the university
where Takeo had gone. Like Showa College, it was on summer
recess. The area was quiet, and more upscale than where I
lived.

Seiko looked at me uncertainly. I imagined what was going
through her head: *I've invited a stranger to get off. Now what do I do?*

I spoke first. "Could I invite you for a cup of coffee?"

"I'd rather have a real drink," she said.

"Sure." Suddenly I was feeling that I was dealing not with a
copy shop clerk anymore, but a femme fatale. Seiko led me
into a side street that had a small plaza containing the kind of
slick restaurants that were threatening to swallow traditional
Tokyo. There was a Royal Host coffee shop, as well as
Kentucky Fried Chicken. Seiko pointed toward Henry Africa,
a mock Asian colonial tavern.

"They have a happy hour right now."

I was glad I'd brought my backpack with a wallet. I'd need to use a credit card to handle Henry Africa. The last time I'd been inside one, I'd been stunned by the English-language menu and the high prices. I supposed Henry Africa was a thrilling international experience to someone who'd grown up in Japan. After all, I spent many hours in Japanese restaurants, dreaming of my future life, when I was growing up in San Francisco.

The bar was aggressively air-conditioned and held just a few salarymen and foreign corporate types. An unsmiling young foreign man—a blue-eyed blond, just like Nicky—motioned to the bar. He probably expected we were there trying to meet men. I shook my head and said to him in English, "A quiet table in the back would be better."

Upon hearing my English, he raised his eyebrows and said nothing, just showed us to a table. I thought of Show a Boy and its male foreign dancers who were there only to please the Japanese women. This fellow could have used a few tips.

I went to the bathroom to freshen up, and when I came back I saw that Seiko had ordered us both glasses of sherry. When it turned out that my sherry couldn't be sent back, I handed it to her and asked the waiter for an iced coffee.

"You don't drink?" Seiko asked when the waiter was gone.

"I'm, um, not feeling that well right now." I wanted to keep my wits about me.

"Which American place is your homeland?" Seiko asked in a proper conversational tone.

"California." Everyone in Japan knew it. Usually they would repeat the state's name and then sigh in wistful appreciation. *Beverly Hills 90210* and *Baywatch* had done a lot to color impressions. Seiko didn't make the sighing sound, I noticed. She stayed blank.

"Thank you for agreeing to talk to me." I figured that I'd better get things going. "I'm hoping to interview you for an article that will run in the *Gaijin Times*. Have you heard of it?"

She nodded. "Yes. My American friend, who was at Showa College with me, read that magazine sometimes. It reviews restaurants, right? Are you planning an article about photocopy shops?"

"No. Our management is planning a shift to a *manga* format. That's the reason I want to speak to you about *Showa Story*."

"How did you find me?" Seiko began fiddling with a silver hoop in her ear. I noticed that she had about five piercings in her left earlobe, and three on the right.

"I was given some information at Showa College. You're not studying there anymore?"

"My father made me quit." She said it without emotion.

She'd had to quit, just as Nicky had quit. Kunio had had to leave his apartment. They were running scared from something. I asked, "Was he upset because you insisted on studying English?"

"No. When I started two years ago, my father had enough money, but now . . ."

"Sure. The economy is tough," I said. "But it's really tough on you to have to leave. I understand you were part of a circle of students who created *Showa Story*."

"*Showa Story*'s dead," Seiko said. "I didn't want to explain to you on the bus in front of all those people. I guess you don't have a story anymore."

"Can you tell me about the history of the group?" I asked.

"Kunio-san, who does the art, started drawing the comic book two and a half years ago. I met him in the *manga* club about a year and a half ago. I helped with the printing. Nicky, who was our American member, had ideas for stories and wanted to make translations."

"Where is Nicky these days?"

"He's dead," Seiko answered sharply. "Don't you know that?"

"Um, I wasn't sure if you knew the facts—"

"How could I not know? It's all over the news." She buried her face in her hands, and her shoulders rocked for a moment.

She looked up and straight into my eyes. "A couple of days ago, Nicky said something about a girl reporter wanting to interview us. I suppose that was you."

I sighed. "I really am an antiques dealer, but I sometimes write about antiques and art for the *Gaijin Times*. You can look in last month's issue and see something by me if you don't believe it."

"So many comics to choose from! Why ours?" Seiko continued to sound defiant.

"I want to write about *Showa Story* because I am interested in Kunio Takahashi's artwork. It's really quite extraordinary. Then came Nicky's death." I paused, thinking about how she might interpret my role in the death. "If the attention I paid to the group somehow caused the tragedy, I'm very sorry. But if I go through with the story now, outlining the death, someone may read it and come forward with evidence to catch Nicky's killer. We can't bring him back, but we can make sure the killer is punished."

"You're right. I should be thinking of what's best for him." Seiko reached a finger under her glasses, and I guessed that she was wiping away a tear, or wanted me to think that.

"Let's not talk about Nicky for a moment. I never met Kunio Takahashi. What is he like?" I asked.

"Well, everyone says he's good-looking," Seiko mumbled. "He's not my type, so I can't tell you that I find him to be that. I do think he's a very smart, calculating boy."

"How so?"

"Well, he always wanted the best deals on everything. I know now that he allowed me in the circle because he wanted free photocopying. Good paper, too."

"Did you secretly photocopy the magazines at your dad's shop?"

Seiko shook her head. "No. My father wanted to help. He produced the magazines for us, and in exchange, we gave him the profits we made from magazine sales."

A cozy relationship—similar to Sanno Advertising's hold on the *Gaijin Times*, I thought.

"Could Kunio have killed Nicky? Was there rivalry, unhappiness, anything like that?"

Seiko shook her head. "No. We admired Kunio's talent so much. I described to you already how Nicky and I were doing technical things, working on translations, distribution, printing. We really were there to help him. We both love *manga*, but we can't draw them. We needed to work with someone who could draw. Plus he had this fantastic history background—he was a history major. That really helped with the illustrations."

"Do you think Kunio's dead?" It was an abrupt change of topic, but the way she was talking about Kunio in the past tense made me fear she thought the same thing that I did.

"I have not seen him in a while, but I'm sure he's safe. He has a way of coming out on top. Getting what he wants."

She had mentioned safety. It reminded me of the fears that Marcellus had expressed to me.

"Do you know a man named Marcellus?" I asked.

"From Africa?" She sounded startled.

I nodded.

"He's a dancer at the place where Nicky had a part-time job. They were friends, but I think that Marcellus was a bad influence. He was the one who told Nicky to leave college to work full time and make more money. It made me sick, because Nicky didn't have to leave college. I did."

"I've been to that club. The *mama-san* mentioned that she'd banned you from the premises."

"She was horrible." Seiko bit her lip. "She only likes girls coming in large groups. I came alone, and she was suspicious of me. So she made me leave."

Something was missing from Seiko's account, I sensed. I decided to get back to more pressing issues.

"What about Dayo, the company that publishes *Mars Girl*?" I asked. "Were they pressuring you to stop producing the comic?"

"Oh, you're thinking about that because of what they said on television," she said. "We never heard any complaint from them before. But I did hear of them. . . . Kunio mentioned getting some correspondence from them. When Nicky asked to see the letter, though, Kunio wouldn't show him. There were some things Kunio kept private from Nicky and me. Even though we worked well as a *manga* circle, we weren't really such a great group of friends."

"Well, I think you're great to be talking to me," I said, noting the way she'd said *Nicky and me*. I was starting to suspect that Nicky might have been the one she loved. "There's so much I want to ask you."

Seiko froze at that. "I should go back. I ran out of the shop because I'd had an argument with my father. I needed a drink. But I've got to go back."

"Do you live at home with him?" I asked.

Seiko nodded. "That's why I've got to apologize. There's nowhere else I can go."

I felt a premonition of something bad. "Are you really safe there, Seiko? How did your left eye get hurt?"

"It's not hurt. Why are you saying a crazy thing like that?"

"I saw you before you put on your sunglasses. I was hit in the eye like that once." I chose my words carefully. I wanted her to understand that I was sympathetic.

"Please, let's discuss something else," Seiko said.

"Did your father hit you?" I asked softly. "Maybe he thought you weren't doing your job right in the copy shop? Or because you were grieving for your *gaijin* boyfriend?"

"No! I don't know what kind of journalist you are, but that certainly isn't a question relating to art and *Showa Story*—"

"What about the *yakuza?*" I whispered the word, mindful of how paranoid it made people. "I brought in an article about Japanese gangs to be photocopied at your shop, and your father seemed shocked by it."

Seiko stood up.

"Where are you going?" I asked, realizing I'd tried to go too far with her, too fast.

"The toilet," she said, but from the way she grabbed her handbag, I knew she was not coming back.

"Please, I'm sorry. I just want to talk to you a little longer—"

But there was no chance. She flung open the bar's heavy wooden front door and was gone.

18

I'd done it. I'd finally landed an on-the-record interview with a member of the *Showa Story* circle, but I'd also scared her off. What kind of success was that?

I used my credit card to pay 3,000 yen—about $28—for the two glasses of sherry and my iced coffee. The only perk was that in her haste to leave, Seiko had forgotten the comic book she'd been carrying with her. I slid it into my shopping bag.

"You're leaving us so soon? What a shame," the waiter said, watching me take the magazine. I guessed he'd wanted to look at it himself. He took a sip of my untouched sherry as soon as I'd left the bar. Only a foreigner would taste someone else's drink; Japanese had a distaste for sharing food, just as they had a distaste for sharing trouble. Seiko had proved that to me.

On the street, I located a bright green NTT pay phone and dialed Takeo's cellular phone number. I'd decided to finally memorize it. Was this a sign of emotional commitment for me?

He picked up on the second ring. "Hi, Rei! You'll never guess where I am."

"On top of the roof?"

He laughed. "No. Driving back into the city for paint. My workmen are finishing the roof and I'm working on the interior. What are you doing?"

"Kicking myself."

"*Heh?*"

"Um, I mean I'm angry with myself. I had an interview with Seiko, one of the members in the animation circle, and in my questioning, I managed to scare her off." The telephone line beeped, reminding me that I had only a few units left on my telephone card before I'd get disconnected. "I'm about to get disconnected," I told Takeo.

"Will you be at your apartment in an hour?"

"Yes."

"I'll see you after I've—" The phone went dead.

I made my way home on the subway, thinking all the while of how I could have handled Seiko better. When I got home, I went straight to the answering machine and saw a message light blinking. Hoping to hear Seiko's voice, I instead got Rika's, telling me that Mr. Sanno was excited about the direction the article was taking and wanted to speak to me the next morning at ten.

Great. The *Gaijin Times* had taken over my life completely. I hadn't seen a client on antiques business in days. There was a backlog of new people I needed to shop at the flea markets for, and some old clients who wanted me to go to an auction in Kyoto for them. All I could do, really, was promise to come through with the things they needed after the article was done.

I made a few client calls and was just trying to get the apartment into a semblance of decency when there was a knock on the door. I opened it and Takeo walked in, wearing a paint-smeared T-shirt and jeans. He thrust a nicely wrapped box from the sushi shop down the street into my hands.

"I didn't know if you'd had dinner."

"I forgot to eat," I said ruefully. "No wonder I've been feeling so frazzled."

"So, what happened?" Takeo went into the kitchenette and, after washing his hands, proceeded to lay the sushi in a pleasing arrangement in a rectangular dish.

"I met Seiko. She works at her father's photocopy shop. She has a black eye and won't say who hit her. When I asked, she ran out on me."

"You're thinking the killer hit her, and she just barely escaped?"

"No. Actually I was thinking it was her father—they were having an argument when I walked into the shop. Of course, I don't know. My invasive question scared her off. About the only thing I got out of the interview was the knowledge that she didn't like Kunio very much, and that he'd had some direct contact with Dayo, the publisher of the commercial *Mars Girl* series."

"That's good information." Takeo poured cold barley tea from the pitcher in my fridge. I helped him carry everything to the tea table. It was going to be a nice, light, high-energy meal.

"*Itadakimasu.*" Takeo said the customary word of grace and reached for a piece of salmon-topped rice.

"Do you say *itadakimasu* when you're alone?" I asked.

"Of course. I'm casual in so many ways, but when it comes to food, I want things to be right. Somehow, saying it makes me feel connected to other people. Do you say it?"

I shook my head. "I always say it when dining with someone here, but not when I'm alone."

"Eating alone is depressing."

"Exactly!" I said. "Now, Seiko did something that I found really hard to do—she went to the Show a Boy club alone. That atmosphere is all geared to wild packs of women. Chiyo didn't like Seiko's being there, and in fact banned her. I want to find out what Seiko did that was so awful. Also, I have a new

Showa Story comic book to read," I said. "Seiko left it behind in the bar. How's that for luck?"

"I don't know about luck. Maybe she left it for you on purpose." Takeo still sounded morose. "I don't suppose you need help with a translation of this one. Your reading skills are improving."

"I'd really like to have your help with the translation," I said. "But I've got to warn you—from my first glance through, this one looks raunchier than the others."

"I'll suffer through it," Takeo said, winking at me. His expression changed after he'd started paging through it. "I'm not sure how much of this you're going to want me to translate. The words are just awful."

"I'm going to transcribe everything you say. It's just too hard otherwise." I got out the notebook I'd been using for the article.

"Okay. Well, you take a look at it by yourself first."

Takeo left the magazine sitting on my tea table, so I had to pick it up. Almost as if it were contaminated by something, I thought, opening the worn cover with care.

The story started during the war, about five years later than the period in which the previous *Showa Story* comic took place. Mars Girl was looking for a job in a factory so that she could help the family she was staying with. Within the first few pages, she headed off to search for employment wearing a fitted midcalf dress her host mother had made from an old futon cover. Kunio had perfectly captured the period clothing style and the economic hardships of the time.

"This plot seems like the best one yet," I said.

"Just wait," Takeo said.

I wondered whether Takeo meant that the story was going to be even more fantastic. I happily turned the page and followed Mars Girl into an auto plant.

"Mars Girl is asking, 'Are there any jobs available?'" Takeo translated. "The foreman says, 'You're too delicate to work the machines. Go away.' Mars Girl is thinking, 'I'm tougher than most soldiers. If only he knew.'"

Dejected, Mars Girl walked with her head down from factory to factory. Either there were no places for her to work or she was not qualified. As I looked over the comic, I remembered my own first miserable job hunt in Japan. I was turned down from many places for a good reason, though; I couldn't read. It was a problem that haunted me even now, making me dependent on Takeo for help with the article.

I read more. Mars Girl was standing before a military recruitment center with a banner across the door.

"Work . . . women . . . does it say 'jobs for women'?" I asked. I was reading aloud as much of each line as I could, and asking Takeo to translate the rest.

"That's right. And the next thing that happens is she goes into the place, is served a cup of tea, and is interviewed by this man . . . he is a major in the army. 'There's something foreign about you . . . are you from another land?' the officer asks Mars Girl. 'No, I'm Japanese,' she replies. The thought bubble over her head showed her musing, 'What else can I say? That I was born in outer space?'"

I smiled at that. I'd felt the same way so often during my time in Japan.

"'Do you live with your mother and father?' the officer continues. Mars Girl replies, 'No, they're dead. Right now I'm boarding with my aunt and uncle. I need to earn money for the household,'" Takeo read. "The officer says, 'Very well. I have a good job I can offer you, but it involves traveling. Room and board are included, so you can send all your earnings home.' Now Mars Girl is in a quandary. She's afraid to leave Tokyo, because she believes she has been sent from outer space specifically to protect the way of life in her family's neighborhood. She asks, 'Do you mean I'd become a soldier?' The officer laughs at her. 'No, no. You'll be a maid to the officers. We have some rest houses spread throughout Asia. The job would not be a long-term one, but it pays well, and you would have the pleasure of serving your country.'"

"What are Mars Girl's political beliefs?" I asked Takeo.

"They're never stated. Mars Girl's thought bubble has the message, 'It is my duty to help the host family eat. I must take this job.'"

The next several pages showed Mars Girl meeting other women placed on transport to the military job. All were young and malnourished. Some were Korean, I could tell from the traditional long-skirted costumes.

I turned the page and saw the rest house, a shabby villa overlooking the sea. It was perhaps the island of Okinawa, I guessed, from the palm trees. In the guest house, there were women working who wore the traditional batik dress of Okinawans.

"Why so many maids for one building?" I asked Takeo. "This has got to be one detail Kunio's gotten wrong."

The maids were taking in the new girls for orientation. They were told to disrobe, and here Kunio showed the women's nudity. But instead of being lascivious, he showed how bone-thin and sickly the young women looked.

"The drawing here reminds me of the German expressionists who painted people showing the ravages of war. Like Käthe Kollwitz," I said admiringly.

"I don't know all the artists that you do," he said.

"You grew up with a real Miró on your wall," I said, remembering a painting I'd seen a while back in his family's Tokyo penthouse.

"Yes, but the only reason the painting's there is because it has flowers. We're limited to floral themes, haven't you noticed?" Takeo sounded weary as he returned to translating the story.

"The girls are given thin robes to wear, and assigned to bedrooms. Each room has several dirty futons on the floor. When

Mars Girl asks about the next day's hours, an officer slams the door shut, locking it from the outside. 'You shouldn't be so bold,' Mars Girl's roommate cautions her. 'We need to know when the workday starts, and we cannot work in such thin clothing as this. I want my underwear back!' the feisty Mars Girl replies."

"I think I know what's coming," I said.

"Yes, it's about slave prostitution. It's pretty hard to take."

I turned the page, and I didn't need Takeo's translations anymore, because the action was so clear. Two soldiers arrived and spent a few moments deciding which of the female workers they'd like to rape first. Mars Girls stepped in to defend her colleagues, but belatedly discovered that her special amulet, usually worn on a chain around her neck, was missing. Without the amulet, her superpowers were gone. She had just the strength of a woman, nothing more.

The crimes against the women unfolded in excruciating detail. It was typical for Japanese artists to show genitalia in exaggerated forms, so I shouldn't have been surprised by the graphic details of these illustrations. I felt physically ill, though. The girls were so helpless against the soldiers, who were both violent and humiliating.

I pushed the magazine away and shut my eyes, wishing I could erase the picture of Mars Girl's mouth opened in a scream, and then being stuffed with a soldier's penis.

"It does turn out to have a happy ending. Mars Girl gets hold of some of the soldiers' sadomasochistic tools and turns an erotic encounter into a bloodbath," Takeo said.

I shook my head. "Didn't this happen in the earlier comic that we looked at together? Mars Girl was raped then, too. You know, that's the flaw in this series that I absolutely hate. If Mars Girl is a superheroine who can beat up all these men, why does she manage to get raped?"

"I wonder what Seiko thought of it," Takeo said.

"That's an interesting point. What if the inspiration for this story is somehow connected to her personal history? Maybe she had a great-aunt or someone like that who told her this story." I shook my head. "This stuff about comfort women isn't in history texts that college students would read."

"Remember, it's fiction," Takeo said.

"What do you mean by that? Are you saying that you don't believe the Japanese military kidnapped and violated women in the worst ways possible?"

"No, I believe those things happened. But this comic strip must be fiction. I mean, students wrote it. Not historians. And there's something creepy about it. . . . It's not just supposed to make you feel horrified. It's supposed to excite the reader."

I shut my eyes to concentrate. He was making me think of something that had been said to me a while before. I opened my eyes again. "Nicky, when I met him, mentioned the sexually risky things Japanese women would do with him. I didn't press him for details because I was so offended. I wonder now if he was talking about S and M, which really is what this rape story is all about."

Takeo leaned over and ran a hand down my face. "Looking at this material probably makes you want to swear off sex forever. Or at least men."

I smiled back. "You're not like that. I couldn't do without you."

The last time, I hadn't been in the mood to be touched because images of dead Nicky had been burned into my brain. But this night, I was ready for consolation. I kissed Takeo thoroughly, tasting the wasabi in his mouth, feeling the heat run through me. I was surprised when he backed off.

"I'm, um, going to have to go back to Hayama tonight," he said. "The house is just so much work."

"You can't go yet!"

"Well, I'd feel terrible driving off. I came to get the paint, check in on how you were doing, and go back. Really, Rei, that was the plan." His eyes were widening, because I'd already pulled off my dress and was starting to unsnap my bra.

"I'm taking a shower," I said, standing up and stepping out of my panties. "I think you need a shower as well. It will refresh you for your drive home."

When I was bending down to adjust the water temperature to a pleasant warmth, I felt his hands on my hips. He was naked, as I'd hoped. I sprayed him with the handheld shower, and once he was clean, he turned it on me.

There was a different feeling to the sex; I didn't know whether it was a subconscious reaction to the comic book we'd just looked at, but I found that I didn't want to speak to Takeo, and I didn't want soft caresses. I wasn't technically rough with him, and neither was he with me, but we coupled with a force and speed that were new and wildly exciting. While we were toweling off, I remembered the bathroom window was wide open to all the neighborhood. Our pleasure had probably been broadcast all the way to the tofu shop. I whispered my embarrassment into Takeo's ear, and he laughed softly.

"Everyone in Japan makes love in the bathroom occasionally. Now you're not such an alien, my darling."

"I don't know," I said, leading him into my small bedroom, where the windows were closed and the air conditioner was blasting. I threw a towel at him. "Did we really make love? It seemed—wilder, somehow. Is there a different Japanese word for that kind of thing? Just like there are so many different words for rain."

"There is a word, but it's not something I want you to learn. It doesn't reflect you."

"How so?"

"As you said the other day, you're more the type who likes air-conditioning and fresh sheets. And gentle kisses, I think."

"Do you really have to go now?" I had a prickling sense of unease at being alone.

"I have to get up at the break of dawn to work with the painters," he said. "Hey, why don't you come with me?"

"Can't. I've got a *Gaijin Times* meeting in the morning. So we're both tied up."

"You know, plenty of people live in Hayama and commute to Tokyo for work. It's an ideal situation," Takeo said, buttoning up his jeans.

"Don't tempt me," I said, trying to decide whether Takeo was just talking about the fact I could get in quickly the next morning or was suggesting a more permanent arrangement.

"I wish I could." He smiled tenderly, not making the decision any easier for me. "Rei, I'll be thinking about you during my drive. And though I know people say this all the time, I really mean it. Be careful."

"I promise," I said, closing the door after him and using all three bolts.

19

I walked into the conference room at the *Gaijin Times* the next morning and saw immediately that the power had shifted. Mr. Sanno was still at the head of the table, but Rika was on his right. There was an empty place for me on the other side of Rika, near enough that I had to inhale the Egoïste cologne Mr. Sanno had spread liberally over himself. I wondered if the scent was overpowering Rika, because she looked ill. All the bluster and aggressive behavior of the past two days were gone, and she was slumped low in her chair like a little girl. A wacky Pebbles-style topknot and a shrunken pink T-shirt decorated with Belldandy from the *Ah! My Goddess* cartoon series added to her childlike aura.

That morning, I had chosen a dress that I thought would steel me for conflict. I was wearing a black, slim-fitting sheath from my mother's late-1960s collection that I knew made me look as slim as Rika, for once. The dress had a genius design: very stripped-down and elegant, almost Michael Kors. That's what Karen, my friend who was the fashion editor, had told me when I arrived a few minutes early.

"You look like an office lady," she teased. "Shouldn't you

have worn something more rough-and-ready? The expectation now is that you're leading a murder investigation."

"So what's the right outfit? Dark glasses and one of those windbreakers that say POLICE across the back?" I didn't hide my irritation, especially since my dress was so tight that I could barely sit down. Unfortunately Mr. Sanno caught me in midscowl.

"Hello, Miss Shimura," Mr. Sanno said. "Your art story has turned into a murder mystery! You have an aptitude for making news."

"Oh, no. I'm afraid it was a matter of unlucky events taking place," I answered. It wasn't polite to take credit for anything.

"Congratulations—I hear you talked to Nicky Larsen. That will be a real coup, the story from the victim a few hours before his murder."

"I didn't write down anything that he said," I admitted. "When we spoke at length, I believed he was an unimportant neighbor to the artist Kunio."

"Still sounds like an interview to me." Alec Tampole, who was sitting close to the end of the table toying with an unlit Mild Seven, put down his cigarette and looked at me with an expression that I didn't like.

"I cannot accurately report what he said if I don't have a record of it."

"Don't you have a memory?" Alec asked patronizingly.

"I could summarize things, sure, but that doesn't seem very honest. Not without notes."

"The subject is not alive to contradict what you write," Mr. Sanno said rather callously. "You don't have much of a problem."

"Write it up dialog-style," Alec said. "Summary doesn't read very well."

I nudged Rika. She was a journalism student; she surely could quote some manual to tell them that they were suggesting unethical behavior. But then again, Rika was a lowly intern. I shouldn't have been surprised that she kept quiet.

"Rika took notes at the morgue," I said, trying to nudge her into taking part. "She did a fine job of getting some evidence of her own on her Palm Pilot."

"It is Rika-chan's duty to answer the telephone," Mr. Sanno said, surprising me with his coolness. He had fairly twinkled at Rika when he admired her animation knowledge the week before.

"There's, um, a bit of interviewing to do in areas that I don't have much expertise with," I said. "Somebody needs to interview management at Dayo about *Showa Story*. After all, *Showa Story* was ripping off their mainstream publication." I looked directly at Norton, who was the business reporter.

Norton shook his head. "Ordinarily I could help, but I'm on deadline to finish a story on the economics of *manga*. I don't think that I could help you girls. Sorry."

Before I could bristle at his use of the word *girls* for Rika and me, Mr. Sanno spoke.

"Since you're busy, Norton-san, Rei-chan will follow up on that angle." He glanced around the table, picking out Karen. "How about the costume aspect of the death? Could there be a fashion feature?"

I could see Karen flinch. "I worry that people think it might be . . . tasteless," she said at last.

"Nonsense. And call up a few of our advertisers, tell them you'll try to mention their shops in the story. It will be good for revenue."

"I'll try my best," said Karen. "I think there are some boutiques in Harajuku that specialize in that kind of fashion."

"I'll take photographs of live Mars Girl wannabes," Toshi, the photographer, added.

"You could also take pictures at Comiko, the animation convention this weekend. There are bound to be a lot of amateur artists or comic book enthusiasts there," I explained to the group, all of whom were staring at me with flat expressions. "Maybe some of them knew Nicky and might have pictures of him from past conventions."

"Why haven't you interviewed Kunio Takahashi? Isn't he a big part of the story?" Mr. Sanno asked.

"Maybe he'll be there," I said, not wanting to admit I hadn't had the interview with Kunio that Rika had mentioned on Monday. "And I'll interview an editor at Dayo about their attitude toward *Showa Story*."

"Very good. That makes work for everyone except Alec," Mr. Sanno said.

"There is the chance Nicky's death might have a gang connection," I said rather wickedly. "I suppose that Alec, with his vast experience at this magazine, could interview one of his sources in the *yakuza*."

All heads turned toward the entertainment editor who would be king. He smiled an awful phony smile. "You mean because you're too scared to do it?"

"No, because we're supposed to be a team!"

"Well, I actually think of myself as operating on a higher level. Maybe I can spearhead the whole project. You know, keep an eye on everyone."

"Fine," Mr. Sanno said, barely looking at him. "For those of you who don't know, the stories are due in one week's time. By next Thursday, at the latest."

"But what about the gangsters?" I said.

"We should include them, by all means. But please take care, Miss Shimura," Mr. Sanno said.

Now I was doing half a dozen things, plus one. It was amazing to me that the men on the staff—save for Toshi, the photographer—didn't want to help put together what was potentially the most sensational feature ever to run in the *Gaijin Times*.

"Why?" I asked Rika during a hurried consultation in the ladies' room afterward.

"Those foreign journalists can't read Japanese," Rika answered with a hint of amusement in her voice. "When you started handing around photocopies of the *Showa Story* comic book, they looked terrified. They don't want Mr. Sanno to know how useless they are at doing more than reviews of pizza parlors and compact discs."

"I don't read much Japanese, either," I said.

Rika looked at me pensively. "Still, you know more than anyone about this story. It belongs to you. I think you know more than you're saying. I wonder if you kept something back at the meeting."

"If I'd mentioned Seiko, nobody would have wanted to interview her."

"Yes, we still need to get that interview. I will try to do it, Rei-san. To help you."

"You?" It was on the tip of my tongue to tell Rika that I'd already met Seiko and had a disastrous outcome, but I didn't. As Rika had said before, I was holding back.

"You do that," I said, wondering if she would put together the clues and make her way to the Hattori Copy Shop.

I left the bathroom and got into the elevator to go down to the first floor. When the doors finally opened, Alec Tampole was inside.

"Hi," I said, squeezing into the narrow space next to him.

He moved so that his hand brushed against my hip. "Nice frock. Hey, no stockings underneath?"

"I wasn't aware of a *Gaijin Times* dress code."

"There is none," he said, breathing heavily. "But there is a code of conduct."

"Oh, really? I haven't seen it posted." I looked at my watch, wondering how long this elevator ride was going to take.

"It's unwritten. But anyone who's taken a single journalism

course should know the basic rule that you pay your dues before telling experienced people what to do."

"Oh, you sound like a Japanese manager. How funny. Especially when you can't even speak much Japanese."

I'd scored a direct hit, because his face flushed and he thundered, "I know what you do when you're outside this office. Believe me, I have my sources. All I can say is you better watch your back."

He gave me a hard little shove when the elevator door opened. I shoved him back, and then I got out.

20

I tried to reach Mr. Mori, the public affairs officer, before I showed my face at Dayo Publishing. However, he was tied up in interviews, and the secretary who answered my call couldn't tell me when he'd be able to answer my phone call, let alone see me.

It reminded me of a time I wanted to buy a fantastic set of Edo-period lacquered trays. The owner hoped to sell to an internationally known museum rather than a vulgar, moneyed person. I showed up to finesse the deal with my hair combed the wrong way, wearing a borrowed pair of glasses—in short, looking as academic as possible. While there, I spoke only English and made a few vague references to a "Japanese living-arts tableau" in which the trays would be used. I was able to buy the trays for a client who, due to his extremely vulgar income, shall remain nameless. The "living-arts tableau" turned out to be a luncheon to which I was invited. I hadn't lied once.

The prop that I was carrying with me to Dayo that day was the prototype for the yet-unpublished *Showa Story* comic. I wasn't sure if I'd show it to anyone at Dayo, but I had it in my backpack because I'd come straight from the *Gaijin Times* art department. Just before I left, the art director had made color photocopies that might illustrate my story—the story that was due the following Thursday. Just thinking about that made me ill.

Dayo Publishing occupied the third and fourth floors of a spacious, shiny green office tower in central Tokyo. Stepping into the hushed offices decorated with blown-up covers of their best-selling comics, I felt suddenly insecure. This was not a place where combing one's hair the wrong way would help. The receptionist who took my name card was wearing a stylish polyester dress without a single wrinkle, making me notice that the linen sheath I'd been wearing for a few hours was now as wrinkled as a paper bag.

Mars Girl wasn't displayed on the wall, I noticed immediately. If she was such a treasured brand name, why wasn't she there?

I decided to speak English, on a whim. "May I speak with Mr. Mori, please? I'm here from the *Gaijin Times*—"

"*Gaijin Times*?" The receptionist's implausibly skinny eyebrows arched upward with some emotion.

"It is an English-language publication—"

"Oh, yes. I know it." She waved both hands at me, as if trying to subdue me. "Sit, please. I will call for tea."

I sat, mystified, on an uncomfortable red sofa shaped like a pair of lips as she got on the phone to someone. Less than a minute later, a sprite in a purple polyester pantsuit materialized with a steaming porcelain cup of Darjeeling. I overheard the receptionist whispering into the telephone.

"From one of the big foreign newspapers . . . Yes, the *Times* . . . I'm not sure if it's the *Times* of London or the *New York Times*. . . . Yes, I will do that."

I tried hard to look like I wasn't listening, but it was apparent that when I'd said "*Gaijin Times*," the receptionist had not understood it was a title unto itself. She had interpreted my words as the literal translation, which meant "the foreign English-speaking person's *Times*." Most likely she thought it was a *Times* published in Britain or the U.S.

Now she wanted my business card for clarification. The only way around it was to hand her my personal card, which simply said REI SHIMURA ANTIQUES and had Tokyo and San Francisco addresses. San Francisco was my parents' address—strictly for show. I explained to the receptionist, "I'm a stringer—that is, a local correspondent—who covers Tokyo arts for the *Times*. Is it possible for me to learn a little more about *Mars Girl*?"

She tapped her chin with a perfectly pink fingernail. "You would like to speak to the editor who supervises the series?"

"Sure." I hadn't known whom exactly to ask for, but she'd made it easy.

"Mori-san would ordinarily have made arrangements to take you, but at present he is dealing with the local press on another matter. I will therefore send you directly to the art department." She placed the card carefully on the center of her desk's blotter and got back on the phone. Then she made another call, said a few words, including what sounded like "Ros Angeres Time-zu." *Los Angeles Times*. The receptionist had made that decision about my employer's identity based on my California address.

"You are very kind," I said, sticking to exaggeratedly simple English. The more I kept the language distant, the fewer things she'd ask. Most Japanese people don't venture into complicated English conversations for fear of making mistakes. This girl, with her perfect brows and nails and wrinkle-free clothing, was probably more agitated about making mistakes than most. I noticed how she'd strategically not asked the actual name of the paper I worked for, but guessed about it from my address. Not that San Francisco was near Los Angeles, but if it was in the same state, that was enough.

The sprite in purple reappeared to escort me to the art department, which was one floor higher. I'd heard that the "creative" and "business" sides of advertising agencies and media publications often were separated like this. But the art department was no cheerful, creative jungle. Instead there were rows of neat drafting tables with workers bent over them, interspersed with computers. Dayo Publishing's art department could have been a bank office if you swapped the bank employees' navy for the funky casual look that the workers wore.

We were met by a woman in her twenties wearing a suit of sorts—hot pants with a jacket in the same pink polyester double knit. Her legs were covered by white tights. As she ushered us to the conversation area—a pair of purple leather love seats—I was surprised to learn that this hot-looking woman wasn't another office lady but Hiroko Shima, managing editor for *Mars Girl* and three other *manga* series. I was thrilled. I'd expected a managing editor to be a man.

"So, people are interested in *Mars Girl* in the United States?" Hiroko Shima spoke very good English with the slightest trace of a California "Valley" accent.

"Yes, she has a global—or should I say galaxy-wide—appeal," I answered with a little laugh. "I'm trying to learn why she's become so popular that other artists in Japan are knocking off the comic."

"Actually, I agree with you about the wide appeal of *manga*, especially the series that are animated for video. I spent my junior year at UC Riverside," she said with a bright smile. "There were so many *anime* clubs that I had trouble deciding which one to join. So I joined them all. I didn't get much studying done that year."

I joined in her trilling laughter. Hiroko was engaging in the kind of ostensibly carefree girl talk that was supposed to help us form an alliance.

"Do many women draw comics? I've heard many of the fans are women," I said, smiling. I was very glad that Mr. Mori had been too busy to see me. I had a feeling I could get exactly what I wanted from Hiroko.

"Slightly over half of the main artists for our comics are women. It takes a woman to write a comic that excites women."

I followed up the softball I'd thrown her with a harder pitch. "What about the schoolgirl comics? The ones where the girls get raped, and so on?"

Hiroko waved her manicured hand in a dismissive gesture. "That's an old, misunderstood story. Of course there's a little sex in certain series. Those series are as likely to be written by women as men. I think the ones by women have a little more, um, sensitivity and romance. . . . Hey, is this on the record?"

"Why not? I think you're fascinating. But if you can introduce me to the originator of *Mars Girl,* I can turn the focus onto her. Or him."

"I probably could do that," she said. "Manami Oida is here today. She originated the series six years ago; it first appeared as part of a compendium of many comics. We gave her the chance to create a monthly *Mars Girl* magazine a year later."

"She is absolutely the one I want to talk to! Thank you!" I gushed.

"She comes just two afternoons each week. Usually she spends her days working out of an office near her home. But you're lucky this is a Thursday. She's here Mondays and Thursdays."

"Is that typical? I'd think creating a monthly magazine is a full-time job. Are the others I see in the office also working part time?"

Hiroko shook her head. "No, they're here all day, every day. They do the rote things—lettering, setting up covers, doing general kinds of artwork. They're not involved in creating sto-

ries. As you can imagine, the story writers are the most important element in the comic. The art in our comic is relatively
simple and straightforward—it is the spellbinding adventures
of Mars Girl that cause our readers to buy and buy again."

"I must confess to you I haven't read every *Mars Girl* comic
published," I said.

"Don't feel bad. The series has been running for five years
with a monthly issue, so what does that make? Sixty issues to
read? You've got better things to do with your time."

"Do you read each issue?" I asked.

Hiroko nodded. "Actually, yes. That series is one of my personal favorites. I like the power she has. The way she lives
within a traditional Japanese structure, but lashes out from
time to time."

"Has Mars Girl ever done time travel? Has she solved
crimes in another era?"

"Oh, no. Our version—the original Mars Girl—lives in the
future! She is a twenty-second-century woman. She has the
heart of a typical Japanese girl but the strength of a super-
human. You cannot kill her. She's thrown down ten flights of
stairs and she jumps up, ready to fight. Wouldn't we all like to
do that?"

I changed tactics. "What do you think about what the amateur series *Showa Story* has done with its version of the character—taking Mars Girl back into pre–World War II Japan?"

Hiroko crossed her legs, making her shorts ride up a little
higher. I had the sense it was a movement she used frequently
in interview situations. Maybe it distracted any men who
were doing business with her, but it didn't affect me. She
asked. "Why do you ask me about *Showa Story*?"

"I'm sort of an art critic."

"Sort of?" Hiroko's friendliness was changing to frost.

"My area is Japanese art history. My article involves a discussion of how *manga* have evolved from wood-block prints.

That's why I asked what you think of Mars Girl in a pre–World War II background."

"You must keep this off the record." Hiroko looked at me intently.

I nodded, knowing that Rika would disapprove of my acquiescence. I told myself that it was more important to learn something than it was to print it.

"To answer what I think you're really asking—what do we think about *Showa Story*'s appropriation of our character— well, we have known about it for a while. Many *doujinshi* groups create comic books based on different Dayo products. Our general policy is to ignore them. They do not produce enough copies, and they aren't sold in enough places to steal market share. I would also argue, based on my experience in college *manga* clubs, that there can be positive results from *doujinshi*. If Mars Girl is cool enough to inspire an under-ground comic, she's pretty cool indeed. Until now, *Showa Story* provided us free advertising."

"Do you know if anyone at Dayo Comics was in contact with the *Showa Story* circle?"

She shook her head. "We have more pressing things to do with our time."

"But what about your spokesman's reaction? On television, he hinted that *Showa Story* had engaged in plagiarism."

"The circumstances around that death put the *Mars Girl* series in a bad light. We have to make it clear that our Mars Girl is not their Mars Girl. We can't have a controversy like the one that occurred over *Pokémon*. You heard about that, didn't you?"

"Of course!" A few years ago, all across Japan, several hun-dred children watching one episode of the animated show *Pokémon* had suffered seizures. Stories appeared worldwide about whether the culprit was really a blinking strobe effect or a more sinister side to Japanese animation.

"The only reason I'm talking to you is that I don't want stories appearing in Los Angeles talking about the evils of Japanese animation. I'm being direct so that you will better understand the situation, I hope." Hiroko looked straight at me, all the coyness gone.

"I can assure you no such stories written by me of such an ilk will ever appear in Los Angeles," I said emphatically. "One last question, strictly theoretical: Would a publisher be upset with a photocopy shop that was printing an unauthorized *doujinshi*? Could the publisher accuse the shop of trademark infringement?"

"No! I've been trying to tell you that *doujinshi* publishing does not disturb us. As Mr. Mori said, it's not really fair that they get tax-free income resulting from use of our characters, but that's just the way it is. I am very upset that a crime was committed that relates to our icon. But naturally, I feel bad for the American man who died. It's tragic, isn't it?"

She was so forthcoming, but was she for real? I tried to figure that out as something at her waistline beeped: a cell phone. She unsnapped it from her mod white patent leather belt and held it to her ear.

"Is Oida-san available? I've got a reporter to meet her," she said.

I watched her face as she said yes a few times, and finally clicked off.

"You can meet the *Mars Girl* artist. But please, no questions that might embarrass her. She's a very shy person."

I raised my eyebrows at that but didn't comment as I followed her through a warren of computer cubicles into an area where drafting tables were packed closely together in a similar way. At first I thought the slightly plump, middle-aged woman wearing bottle-thick glasses had to be a visitor to the department, because she looked so hopelessly square next to the mod Hiroko. But when she put down a pencil on the drafting table and I got a glimpse of an outline of Mars Girl on a piece of paper, I realized she had to be the head artist.

She smiled at me and spoke first. "This is the first time we meet, Miss Shimura. I am Manami Oida. I beg your consideration."

Her words were the standard Japanese greeting. They sounded right coming from her. It did make me reflect, though, on how Hiroko hadn't used the same words. She was young and modern, like a lot of the women drinking at Show a Boy. Manami Oida, in her white polyester blouse and black wool skirt, was the opposite.

I parroted my own rote greeting back and then got down to business.

"There are so many admirers of your series," I began.

"Oh, no! We are trying hard to make an amusement for the young readers, but these days, new comics are growing! I don't think we're so well known."

"You may have heard that some of your fans started their own amateur copy of the magazine."

"Yes, *Showa Story*. I've bought many copies. It's absolutely beautiful! Much better than our product, don't you think?" Manami Oida beamed, and her boss, Hiroko, smiled in a strained, artificial way. Hiroko probably didn't like hearing that the *Mars Girl* rip-off was better than the original.

"Oh, I don't know about that," I said. "Since they are students, they have leisure to work on the stories as they like."

"I sent a letter to *Showa Story* once, congratulating the three young people involved in its production. I suppose they weren't interested in correspondence with someone my age, for he never replied."

Was Manami being sincere? She was too nice. I shook my head, unable to fathom it. I said, "I heard that someone from Dayo sent Kunio Takahashi a letter. Perhaps it was you."

"So that's what this is about!" Hiroko said. "A man named Kunio Takahashi—not Nicky Larsen?"

"I didn't specifically address the letter to Takahashi-san," Manami Oida said. "However, if he is the main artist, I would like to meet him. Could you arrange that for me?"

"I wish I could," I said. "The only other living member of the group that I can find is Seiko Hattori. And I'm afraid that she doesn't draw."

"I'm always looking for gifted artists to render my series. That's what I wrote in my letter. If Takahashi-san contributed his talents, perhaps *Mars Girl* would be in the top five again."

"Until last year, *Mars Girl* had the fifth-largest circulation of all the monthly comic books," Hiroko explained. "Right now, we're number ten. Can you just put it that way in your article? That we are in the top ten?"

"Um, sure," I said, making a show of writing the phrase "top ten" on my notepad. "I was wondering how much such an artist might earn drawing for you."

Both women exchanged glances.

"Actually, I don't know," said Manami Oida.

"Mmm, let's just say about a fifth of what the series origina-tor earns. Drawing is an important job, but it is not as creative as what the series originator does."

Not very tempting for Kunio, I thought. I had probably come to a dead end in that direction. I needed to get back to Nicky. "Oida-san, for how many years have you been drawing comics?"

"Seventeen years," she said. "I used to illustrate children's books, but I moved into *manga* publishing because it was more regular employment. I enjoy it very much."

"Where do you create your drawings?" I asked.

"My hometown of Kurihama. It's quite pleasant there. Would you like to visit my studio?"

"Um, I only have time on Mondays."

She pressed her lips together. "Mondays I come here to Tokyo. There are staff meetings, that kind of thing."

"Does it take all day?"

"Well, let's see. I arrive here around nine-thirty in the morning, and I must stay until at least three."

"Are those the hours you worked this past Monday? The seventeenth?"

Hiroko interrupted. "I think she's had enough questions. She's got to get back to work."

"Yes, there really is a lot to do," Manami Oida apologized. "Last Monday, the Monday you're asking about, I was in the office from nine-thirty to six. We were so busy nobody even went out for lunch."

Ten minutes later, I was at Tokyo Station, waiting for the subway train to pull in and thinking about what had happened. Now I knew what had happened between Dayo Publishing and Kunio Takahashi. Kunio had opened the letter Manami Oida had sent and boasted a bit about it to the other members of the circle. There was no other connection.

A recorded jingle told me the train doors were about to close, so I jumped on and headed west toward home. The Marunouchi Line at this time of day was only lightly crowded with students and housewives. Because there was room, people were doing slightly inconsiderate things such as putting a shopping bag on the seat to them, or sprawling their legs out so it was impossible to sit in the neighboring seat. So in effect, the train had as few seats available as it would during rush hour.

I stayed standing, because the only space left was near a man wearing a gauze mask covering his mouth and nose. The last thing I needed was to come down with a cold. I had about a week until the article was due. The deadline frightened me, since even the easiest column on antiques took me five days to write and polish. The *Showa Story* investigation was ongoing, so there were days of research ahead before I could sit down to write.

As we pulled into Kasumigaseki Station, I could see a horde of suited government workers waiting on the platform. The mass seemed impenetrable, but I knew that once the doors slid open, the crowd would part in two neat wings to allow the disembarking people to leave the train, then fill the void efficiently. A lot of people were getting off with me; Kasumigaseki was the ground zero for Japan's government. I stepped off the train, my eyes scanning the wall for directions to the Chiyoda Line, the subway to which I needed to transfer to get home. I was so busy looking into the distance that when a passenger bumped against my back, I almost tripped into the gap between the train and the platform. In a rare example of hands-on concern, a blue-suited bureaucrat on the platform caught my arm, enabling me to step to safety. I thanked the man, but he had already boarded the train before I could press the issue. Japanese etiquette meant never acknowledging when you do something nice for someone. I moved on, the summer heat wrapped around me like a scratchy thermal blanket. Treading up the sticky staircase in my stacked heels toward the Chiyoda Line, I knew that it would be even more miserably hot outside. In Tokyo, the humidity was the killer. I wished I were at the beach with Takeo.

I moved a fraction more slowly than the crowd, due to the impractical styling of my dress. I promised myself that if I ever made it up the stairs, I was going to sell the dress at a consignment store. My mother would kill me, but her dress was really cramping my style. Most of the people who'd been on the train with me were a half flight ahead. How pitiful for me, a twenty-eight-year-old woman, to be outpaced by men my father's age. There was only one figure moving as slug-gishly as I: the man with the bad cold.

As I approached the top of the flight of steps, I thought I heard him say my name, though his words were muffled by the gauze mask.

He had stopped and was facing me. I nodded to affirm my identity but didn't move closer, for fear of his germs. He was walking up a step to be closer to me, I realized uneasily, and I took a step away from him just as his arm flashed out and punched me in the jaw. The punch sent me backward, sailing through the air, back down the staircase. My body glanced off the cement steps and then rolled over and over, down the length of stairs. My first thought was for my sensitive knees, so I pulled my thighs tightly to my chest. I was rolling, rolling, rolling. No time to think about my head or neck or back.

My ricochet down the staircase ended against something soft and giving.

A soft, fuzzy animal had caught me. A great big dog. *No, I have to be dreaming,* I thought as I stared into the eyeholes of my rescuer's costume. Japanese eyes, streaked with tears, peered back at me. I'd been caught by Seiko Hattori.

21

"Are you all right? Oh, it's my fault! I saw that you were having trouble walking—I should have helped you!" Seiko hadn't stopped talking all the while the paramedics were checking me out and placing me on a board. I was talking back, to reassure us both.

"The fall wasn't bad. But I told you, I didn't fall on my own, I was pushed!"

"But Rei-san, nobody was there. I told you." Seiko had lifted off the dog head that was part of her costume, so I could see her face in full.

"Were you on the same train?"

"Yes. I was in the compartment behind you. When you gave me that business card with your address yesterday, I became curious. This morning, I followed you from home to the *Gaijin Times* and then to Dayo Publishing."

"In the dog costume?" I was shocked that I hadn't noticed.

"No. I was dressed normally. I must resemble a typical Japanese, because you didn't notice." Seiko smiled weakly. "I carry my costume in my backpack. I changed into it in the rest room of the Dunkin' Donuts across the street from Dayo.

When I saw you went into Dayo, I got to thinking that I would like to visit there, too. I decided to wear the clothing of the *Mars Girl* dog so they'd think I was just a typical fan."

"I see. But you didn't go there?"

"No. By the time I'd made my plan, you had come out, and there was something about your expression that made me think you'd figured everything out. So I decided to follow you on the train, but I stayed in the next car because I thought you'd find it strange for someone dressed like a dog to speak to you."

"While you were on the train, did you see a young foreign man wearing a Porno for Pyros T-shirt anywhere?" I remembered Alec and the concert T-shirt he had worn to the *Gaijin Times* meeting that morning.

"Um, I wasn't looking closely, but I do think there were several foreigners on the train. Didn't you notice?"

"No. I'm about as unobservant about foreigners as I am about typical Japanese." I was joking, but my body was hurting terribly. All my instincts told me to reach around and rub my bruised upper vertebrae, but that was dangerous. I might have a spinal cord injury. Only after an X-ray would it be safe to move. Thinking about the possibility of paralysis was terrifying. I bit back a sob and asked, "Well, did you see a Japanese man wearing a gauze mask? You know, the kind of mask that keeps you from spreading germs?"

Seiko hesitated. "I didn't see anyone touch you, but there were several people on the steps. . . . I was too involved in catching you to notice!"

"So you saved me. Seiko-san, I don't know what to say." In truth, I was still a little confused about what had happened. Something that Hiroko had said about Mars Girl popped into my head—she falls down ten flights of stairs and gets up and fights. Had that allusion to the comic been a warning to me? Were the forces at Dayo more upset about my visit than she'd let on? Or was it Alec?

"The stationmaster is mortified that such an accident happened in his jurisdiction. He wants to know if you request a certain hospital, so that you are satisfied," Seiko rattled on.

The stationmaster's face swam over me. His brow was covered with sweat. He was worried that I might sue for damages, I bet.

"St. Luke's International Hospital. My cousin works there. It's funny. I was just thinking about trying to avoid catching a cold, and now I'm going to the hospital. Well, I'll be fine there. You can go back to, um, whatever you were doing."

"But Rei-san, you are in danger!"

"Not anymore." *She falls down a flight of stairs, and she gets up ready to fight.*

"Sei Roka Byouin," said Seiko to the paramedics, using the Japanese pronunciation of the international hospital's name. "Do you want me to telephone the *Gaijin Times* to say that you've been hurt?"

"No." I paused, thinking it over. "Well, maybe you'd better say something. If I'm indisposed, I'm not going to be able to finish the story."

"Really?" Seiko's eyes got big. "Isn't there someone who could help you there?"

"I suppose there is one person." I gave her Rika's name and telephone number. Now Rika would have a chance at interviewing Seiko, too.

"I know that girl," Seiko said. "She went to college with me. I didn't think she was old enough to graduate."

"She didn't graduate. She's doing a summer internship," I said.

"Oh." Seiko's expression remained grave.

"So you know Rika. What's she like?" I asked, but there was no time to get an answer, because just then the paramedics lifted me up and started carrying me out of the station. Seiko put my backpack next to me on the board. Being carried up endless flights of stairs was actually pretty embarrassing—I was aware of how people glanced at me quickly, then looked away, as if shocked at the sight of an injured person. I wondered if it was because I was young—maybe they thought I was a subway track jumper. Suicide was on the rise in Japan, and I supposed that a young woman like me, presumably unlucky in love or job, was a likely candidate.

The paramedics wouldn't let Seiko ride in the ambulance, but she made her way to St. Luke's via subway and was there to see me after I'd come out of various X-ray machines and was standing up, looking at the X-ray pictures on a light box with the radiologist, Dr. Natsuki, and my cousin.

"You're like a cat. Nine lives, *neh?*" Tom said. The X-rays showed that my spine had not been thrown out of whack, and my head had escaped injury. The aches I felt were a pulled muscle in my back, bruised bones, and the beginning of bruises that would show their ugly faces in the next forty-eight hours.

"I don't know whether I should credit my survival to your care or our shared genes," I said to my cousin. Tom was the emergency-room attending doctor at St. Luke's. It was a high-status job for a man as young as he was—just thirty-four—but Tom's life was far from perfect. He worked long, hard hours at the hospital, and after that, he went home to his parents, who were now pestering him to get married. Tom told them he was too busy to make any woman happy. He spent 90 percent of his waking hours in the emergency room, and in fact, my arrival was the first time we'd gotten together in months. Dr. Natsuki seemed to sense this, and after giving me a container of Valium to take as a muscle relaxant, he faded away, leaving me to talk with Tom and Seiko.

"Tell me about the man who hurt you. The officer who accompanied you here didn't seem to know anything."

"It's probably because he didn't want to record what I told him," I said bitterly. "The station manager told the policeman that I was confused by the accident. He said that although I claimed that I'd been punched, nobody had seen an attacker. Then he questioned Seiko."

"What about this mark?" Tom touched my tender jawline

Seiko piped up. "I think the mark didn't show right away. I'm really sorry, but I couldn't say that I saw the person. When your body was rolling down the stairs, all I could concentrate on was stopping it—you know, breaking the fall."

"Thank you for what you did," Tom said. "You saved my cousin from serious injury or even death."

"It has been a bad-luck day," I said. "You know, when I was getting out of the train, I almost fell onto the tracks. I thought it was because I was distracted, but I think there might have been some pressure on my back. I didn't suspect anything at the time. But now I think there's a good chance the push from behind came from the man with the mask."

"A mask? You mean the sort that criminals wear while committing robberies?" Tom asked.

"Well, my backpack wasn't taken or anything like that, but he was covered. He was wearing one of those gauze face masks that people wear when they have colds or allergies. It's similar to the kind you would wear when in surgery—"

"Yes, yes. Above the mask, what did you see? What about his eyes? The condition of his skin? Clothing, shoes? Any tattoos?"

I sat back in the chair, but no memory came. "I don't know. To tell the truth, I was trying to stay away from him because I didn't want to get any germs. The eyes are a big blank—I can't even honestly tell you if they were Western or East Asian. His clothing must have just been—normal. I would have remembered if it was a very nice business suit, or a construction worker's pantaloons and boots."

"Age?"

"His thick hair makes me think he was under fifty, although he could have been wearing a wig to create that impression.

He was walking slowly up the stairs, which you'd think meant he was older, except of course he was waiting for me."

Tom took away my empty cup of tea. "So what kind of people are you running around with now?"

I rolled my eyes. "Men who work as strippers by night and dress themselves as animation heroines by day. I'm writing a story for the *Gaijin Times*."

"That sounds different from your recent column on the Heiwajima Antiques Fair."

I shrugged. "The magazine is going through changes, so is my antiques business. I need to write the story to keep my bank account from going under."

"Forget about the money. Your life is worth more than a few thousand yen."

It was more than a few thousand yen that Mr. Sanno was offering to me. It was a chance for partial redemption. Nicky had died, perhaps because of me. I owed it to him to find out who had done it.

"I'll ask if your doctor will recommend that you stay a few days in the hospital. Your condition is excellent, but I don't think you should go home without company. I'm not going to bother asking you to come to our house, because you ran away the last time you stayed, and my mother was so upset."

That had been a year and a half before. I smiled at the memory. "This time, I know how to take care of myself. All I want is to go home now."

"I'm so sorry, Rei, but I'm on duty. I can't escort you. There must be someone else who can do it."

Seiko said in a quavering voice, "Actually, I have afternoon duty at the copy shop. I think that I am already half an hour late, and my father will be angry. I'm so sorry that I can't take you, Rei."

"It's all right. I just need to go off to the ladies' room for a second, and after that, I'll get back to thinking about whom I can ask to come for me. Richard would have been great, but he's in Canada right now."

"Do you need a glass? You should take the first dose of Valium."

I wrinkled my nose at him. "That stuff killed Marilyn Monroe! I'm not going to take it."

"You don't have to take anything." Tom raised an eyebrow. "If ibuprofen is a strong enough painkiller for you, just take that."

"The tablets I take for my runner's knee? Great. I don't even need to buy it. I've got plenty at home."

"If it's all right, Rei-san, I'll take my leave," Seiko said. "I will call you to check how you're feeling."

"Thank you so much, Seiko." I bowed toward her and Tom, and then hurried off to do my business.

When I came back, Tom was not where I'd left him. I walked around and went back into the emergency room, where I found him in consultation with a nurse. I'd taken a lot of his time, I realized, feeling guilty. The emergency room chief didn't need to personally oversee my treatment, but he was doing it because he was my relative.

When I found Tom, he snapped his fingers and said, "What about having Takeo Kayama pick you up? Do you still see him?"

"I do, but he probably can't come to get me. He's forty kilometers away, painting the interior of his family's country house."

"Good, that means he'll be able to receive this phone call. What's the number?"

"I don't know," I lied.

"Very well, then. I'm going to have to call my mother—"

"Please don't," I begged. "Oh, I've got an idea. Call this number." I opened my backpack, which I'd left in the hospital's lounge area, and fished out the Show a Boy leaflet I'd been carrying around for almost a week. "The handwritten number on the back belongs to a friend of mine named Marcellus. This time of day, he's definitely home."

I had closed my eyes for what seemed like just a few minutes, and then I heard Marcellus's voice.

"I'm very glad you called on me, Monsieur Dr. Tom-san," Marcellus murmured. He was using all manner of titles in an effort to be polite. From between my lashes, I could see that he was dressed in one of his flashy nylon athletic suits, the ones that had tear-away sides to the pants. They were done up neatly now; one would never dream that this was a sexy dance costume.

"It's so kind of you to make time in your schedule to help my cousin. She's so . . . well, accident-prone," Tom said, sounding a bit stilted. I guess he hadn't realized that the friend who spoke English with a French accent was actually African. "I just need someone to escort her to her apartment, and then, um, tell the neighbors to look out for her. I'm happy to provide the taxi fare, because I don't think she should take the subway right now."

"But are you sure she's ready to be released? She's unconscious!" Marcellus whispered.

I guess that I looked that way, lying back in one of the waiting room's lounge chairs with my face turned away from the crowd—I was tired of being looked at. I turned to face Marcellus, opened my eyes, and announced, "I'm fine, and it was very nice of you to come. I hope I am not interfering with your work schedule?"

"Three o'clock. Actually, I'm going to take you quickly to your place, speak to the neighbors, and then go to my place of employment. I'm scheduled to start there in an hour."

"Are you sure that's enough time? I hate to inconvenience you," Tom said.

"Not at all. Miss Shimura is a good friend indeed, and I take it as a compliment that she called on me for assistance." Marcellus was exuding all of the charm he could muster, and I could see Tom relaxing. He hailed a taxi for us and waved good-bye until we were out of sight, standard Japanese good manners. I settled back in the car and sighed. My nightmare was over.

Marcellus stroked my hand. "What misery you've been through! Do you think it's related to what happened to Nicky?"

"Yes. That's why I wanted to see you. And frankly, I think we should skip the stop at my apartment and go straight to Show a Boy. I want to show Chiyo that I'm not scared, given there's a chance she could be involved in things."

"You're still thinking she's behind Nicky's death?"

"All I can think about right now is who's after me. This creepy Australian editor from the *Gaijin Times*, Alec Tampole, threatened me just before I went out today, and Rika, the magazine intern who's helping with my story, doesn't seem to like me much, either. I also wonder about Seiko—what a coincidence that she happened to be on the scene when I got hurt, though I know that it must have been physically impossible for her to have hit me and then run down to catch me. Perhaps it was a two-person job."

"A gang, maybe. It sounds like the *ya-san*," Marcellus said.

"Now that's territory that I think belongs to Chiyo," I said.

"She's not one of them," Marcellus said. "I keep telling you."

The taxi stopped at the club; I reserved Tom's money to give back to him later, and paid for the cab myself. When we entered the club, I sensed a different feeling. It was early enough that the female clientele had not yet arrived, and some of the boys were sitting at the bar, drinking juice or soft drinks and talking in low voices. They stopped when I came in.

"Hey, it's not show time yet," said the boy who was wearing lederhosen, the same outfit he'd had on when I saw him last.

"I'm here to see Chiyo-san."

"Oh, I remember you now." Lederhosen Boy looked at me appraisingly. "The day before Nicky died, you came with your questions."

"They weren't about Nicky."

"Nevertheless—you ask questions, then he dies." The dancer had ice blue eyes, which he fixed on me until I looked away.

"Hans, it's okay," Marcellus cut in. "Where's *mama-san*?"

"She's having her sherry," Hans answered.

I gave a curt nod to Hans and walked on with Marcellus.

"Are you sure you want to do this?" Marcellus whispered to me. "I fear that after your accident, you are not so strong."

"I'm fine. Just a bit bruised."

He opened a door and there she was. Chiyo was stretched out on a chaise longue with a large glass of sherry on a small table beside her and a telephone clamped to her ear.

"Yes, yes," she was saying. "Your reservation for tomorrow evening is confirmed. Party of sixteen. Party theme of *Evangelion*. Come in costume, and we will provide everything else."

After some more conferring, during which she continued to speak with phony courtesy, she hung up and turned to me with a scowl. "Shimura, you look terrible. What are you doing coming in here wearing such a dirty dress? Marcellus, why aren't you working the door? What's wrong with you?"

"I look this way because somebody punched me so hard I fell down a flight of subway stairs. Perhaps because of you."

Marcellus had melted out of the room when I was speaking, so now Chiyo and I were alone.

Chiyo purred, "Why would I do something like that?"

"Because you don't want me looking for Nicky's killer. The killer might work in this club or be a friend of yours, or something like that."

She snorted, "I'm surprised that you don't think I killed him myself! The police detective visited, asking about my whereabouts that day. Ridiculous. Of course I had an alibi."

"You would never kill with your own two hands—you'd send *yakuza* thugs to do it."

Chiyo laughed—a long, nasty cackle. "Little girl, what an imagination you have! I'm just a hardworking entrepreneur. I'm not part of a criminal conspiracy."

"Gangsters have been spotted here."

She shrugged. "All my dancers have probably seen the men who come and demand payments from me, just as they take payments from almost all the other entertainment establishments in this neighborhood. Those men are extortionists. If they learn one of the dancers is illegal, they'll go after him, promising to fix his papers in exchange for a series of fees. They are like jellyfish, sticking their painful tentacles everywhere."

"Are you current with your payments?" At her blank look, I said, "Are they angry with you for any reason? I was thinking they might have killed Nicky to get a message to you."

"Absolutely not!" Chiyo cried. "I have a ledger, just like at the bank! Every time I pay, I put my personal stamp, and they put theirs next to it."

It *was* like the bank. I couldn't believe the highly organized nature of things. Changing tactics, I asked, "Has Kunio come back?"

She shook her head. "No. I have many pieces of mail for him. I telephoned his apartment, but it's disconnected."

"That's what I found when I called him last week. Why didn't you give the letters to the police?"

"Why should I? They are interested in Nicky, not Kunio. Would you like to take the mail? I have no use for it."

Chiyo stuck her feet in marabou-trimmed slippers and shuffled over to a desk. She opened a drawer and held up a box covered with brocade-patterned paper. "This is what you'd like, right?"

"Um, I wouldn't mind looking at it, but is that . . . is that legal in Japan?"

She laughed. "You are a very funny girl to worry about the law! Here, take it all. But let me remind you, I'm busy. I don't want you to come back with questions anymore. You never spoke to me, and you didn't get mail from me. Understand?"

"I'll keep it off the record, but I do have one last question, about a young woman called Seiko Hattori. You banned her from this place. Why?"

Chiyo sighed heavily. "She was Nicky's girlfriend."

"Really? You're sure she wasn't just a friend?" I had suspected that Seiko had strong feelings for Nicky, but because she wasn't a glamorous-looking young woman, I'd assumed they weren't reciprocated.

"He treated her miserably while she was here, though she kept looking at him with cow eyes. It was so awful that the rest of the clientele noticed. Being females, that kind of treatment made them angry. It was bad for business. With Seiko gone, Nicky was no longer distracted, and he could perform with his regular charm."

I picked up the box, which I could see included letters and some returned copies of *Showa Story*. "Thank you. I don't know why you're being so helpful all of a sudden."

"The police aren't doing much. I think it's because they think my boys are lower-class. A *gaijin* freak wearing a wig and a dress—why shouldn't he die? Our country is better off without foreign boys who play at *manga* during the day and corrupt Japanese women at night," Chiyo said in a low, intense voice. "I care about my business, and I care about my boys. Less than two years ago, as you mentioned, you interfered in my life, and that forced the closing of my business. But because of what you did, you saved one of my hostesses' lives. I won't forget that."

"Thank you again," I said, stunned by Chiyo's words and the tears she was wiping away with her pudgy fist. "Do you, um, see that particular hostess anymore?"

"Tonight," Chiyo said. "She's got a good job now, and she's bringing in some of her girlfriends from work to see the show. She says it's nice to have men catering to her after all those years of waiting on them."

"Tell her hello from me," I said.

"I will. Can you see yourself out? One of my boys can carry the box for you if you need help."

"It's not heavy," I said, and gave her a little wave as I left the office.

22

The phone was ringing when I made it to my apartment, via taxi, as I'd promised Tom. It turned out that he was on the line.

"Rei, you're finally answering. I was worried about you," Tom said.

"I just got in."

"What? It took two hours for you to get from the hospital to home?"

"I, um, asked the taxi to make a detour. I thought it best to pick up some supplies I needed so that I would be able to relax at home for the evening."

"Great. Actually, I'm being paged. Got to go." Tom rang off.

I took a bath and washed down an ibuprofen tablet with a glass of milk. I had no intention of taking the Valium that Dr. Natsuki and Tom had recommended. I wanted all my faculties intact.

I spread the letters into piles. First came three copies of *Showa Story* that the post office had been unable to deliver. I tried to scan the addresses of the places the magazine had gone, but there was a postman's stamp over the lettering, which was all in Japanese, so I felt pretty useless at doing anything outside of reading the city names—Kawasaki and Tokyo—and the postal codes. The back issues were all of the same issue, the first one I'd picked up at Animagine.

There was a letter from an art supply company, a letter from a cleaning company, a letter from an insurance company—all were standard junk mail. There was only one letter with a hand-addressed envelope. It was in a red-and-white striped envelope that looked familiar.

Hattori Copy Shop. *Oh, my goodness*, I thought. It looked as if Seiko had written Kunio a letter.

Tired as I was, I rifled through the bag that had carried my photocopies made at the shop and found my receipt. Sure enough, it had the shop's phone number printed on it.

I dialed and was relieved when a female voice answered.

"Seiko-san?" I asked.

"No, this is her mother. Who's calling, please?" The woman on the other end sounded tired but not unfriendly.

"I'm a casual acquaintance. I have something that belongs to her that I wish to return."

"Well, she'll be in the shop starting at ten tomorrow morning. You can speak to her then."

"I really need to speak to her tonight—"

"She'll be in tomorrow," Mrs. Hattori said, and hung up.

I stared at the letter. How I itched to open it. But I knew doing that was against the law in the United States, and probably in Japan as well. I wasn't going to use information I'd gathered illegally. On the other hand, if Seiko had sent the letter, wouldn't she have the right to open it?

She'd said that she didn't like Kunio very much. Was that the reason she had written to him? Because she couldn't stand to have personal contact?

I held the letter to the light and tried to sense what was inside the thin envelope. It seemed like a very light piece of paper. There was obviously no contraband inside—just a communication.

I didn't think I'd be able to sleep with such a worry on my mind, but eventually I did, though in the morning I felt terrible. The fall down the stairs was showing its effects on my skin—a line of bright bruises down my back, on my buttocks, one arm, and one leg. I also had a bruise on my jaw where the man had hit me. I thought for a minute about taking the Valium Tom had given me, then dismissed that thought. I needed to be sharp to handle what was coming.

I put on a pair of light cotton shorts and a T-shirt by habit, then realized I was probably too achy to jog. So I made myself a pot of tea, and once I was fortified, I placed a telephone call to the stationmaster's office at Kasumigaseki to ask whether any progress had been made on tracking down the man who'd hit me.

"Are you the lady who fell down the stairs?"

"It wasn't exactly a fall. An assailant pushed me."

"Nobody saw any such person of the type you are describing. We have on record that a lady called Rei Shimura wore unsafe shoes and slipped and fell."

"Well, then," I said, feeling bitter, "maybe I should report my shoes."

The stationmaster didn't rise to my bait. He said stiffly, "The Metropolitan Police were here yesterday, and they agreed that there was no evidence of a crime committed."

"It happened to me. I know."

The employee made another grunt and hung up on me.

I was in a cranky mood as I dialed Lieutenant Hata. It was just eight o'clock, and he was in the office but not available to come to the phone. I grumbled a little bit about important information that I had, and the secretary promised to have him return my call.

I cleared off my tea table only to cover it once more with piles of all the materials I had for the article. On one side was a stack of *Showa Story* issues and Takeo's translations. On the other side I had the notes taken from interviews. In the center was Seiko's letter to Kunio.

I stared at it so long that my eyes started to blur. I looked up at last when I heard a noise outside my door. It was a knock.

"Who's there?" I called before touching any of my bolts.

"Alec and Rika," came the answer in Rika Fuchida's chirpy voice. I looked at my watch again. Yes, it was only 8:15 A.M. Alec Tampole and Rika Fuchida, together? Coming to my place?

I opened the door cautiously and peered out. "Well, this is a surprise."

"Aren't you going to let us in?" Alec asked.

I looked coldly at him. "I'd rather not. Just wait a minute— I'll get my things and we can sit outside."

"Whoa! Who're you hiding in there? The bloke who punched your lights out?" Alec bellowed.

"Rei-san, are you all right? Your face—" Rika chorused.

"No, I'm not all right. I had an accident at the subway station yesterday." I was shocked to hear what came out of me. I was saying "accident," just as the stationmaster had, all because I wanted to divert attention from myself.

I turned to search for my house keys, since I intended to lock the door while I was outside, and in that time Alec walked straight into the apartment, with Rika behind him.

"Oh, what a nice place, Rei!" Rika said. "The decoration is extraordinary! Alec-san, please learn from Rei how to improve your living room. That is an interesting texture, Rei-san. Is it regular paint?"

"It's glazed," I said, feeling the same. So Rika had been to Alec's apartment. They were together at eight-fifteen in the morning. Yes, they had to be sleeping together, and they obviously didn't care to keep it secret. Alec was in a fresh Chemical Brothers T-shirt, but Rika was wearing the exact outfit from yesterday—the Belldandy T-shirt over jeans. Her hair was no longer in a little-girl topknot but flowed freely down her shoulders. It was damp, as if it had been washed just an hour or so earlier.

How long has it been going on? I wondered as I opened a few windows, knowing that once they were in, there was little point in shoving them out. I was opening the windows as a precaution, recalling how well sound traveled. I'd scream if they made a move to attack me. I still was worried that Alec might have been the one who hit me at Kasumigaseki Station.

Rika settled down on the cushions by the tea table, gazing pointedly at the still-hot teapot. "What kind of tea is that?"

"Darjeeling," I said sourly, and banged down two tea cups from my kitchenette.

"Milk and sugar for me, love," Alec said. His eyes were going over the papers I'd laid out on the table. "Glad to see that you're working hard on the story, Rei. I was a bit worried it was all show and no go."

"If you're so worried, why didn't you volunteer to help with the reporting yesterday?" I shot back.

"Please remember I'm an editor, not a writer. Kind of like I'm a lover, not a fighter," Alec said with a laugh.

"Does Mr. Sanno know how much of a lover boy you are?" I asked pointedly.

"This is Japan. Sexual harassment—*seku hara*, as they call it—is just another form of foreplay. Right, Rika-chan?"

"Shh, Alec-san. Don't talk in a naughty way," Rika said. She had begun leafing through the materials on the table.

"Let's go over to the window seat and have the tea there, so there's no danger of spillage," I said, feeling an overwhelming sense of shame and sorrow for Rika. The position she was in with Alec was intolerable, but to her, it was probably a step up. The next man on her list would probably be Mr. Sanno.

"What is this letter addressed to Kunio?" Rika held aloft the letter that I'd been trying to decide whether to open.

"Well, yes, it is a letter to Kunio. If I get in touch with him, I'll give it to him—"

"Let's open it first." Rika slit open the end of the envelope before I could stop her. "Ah, here . . ." She pulled out a thin piece of stationery. "Oh, well, it's not much. Just a bill."

I lost my temper then. "Who told you that you could open that letter? Put it down this minute!"

"It's for paper and photocopying. Twenty-five thousand yen, billable to Kunio Takahashi and Nicky Larsen from Hattori Copy Shop. Oh, how boring. I thought it would be something exciting. A letter from our murderer!" Rika tossed aside the letter.

"Do you realize you could be breaking the law, opening someone's mail like that?" I asked.

"Who's going to report me?" Rika asked.

Alec snorted. "You're not much of a reporter, are you?"

I took a few deep breaths. "Maybe not. In fact, because you have no faith in me, I may as well turn over all my research to the Tokyo Metropolitan Police."

"Come on, give us a laugh!" Alec offered one of his own. "You and Rika are going to scoop this story, not give it up to the authorities."

"Unless you leave my apartment this instant, I will!"

The phone rang then. Beautiful. For once I wasn't hoping for Kunio or Takeo or Seiko on the line. I picked up and said, "Hello?"

"It's Hata here." My lieutenant friend sounded out of breath. "Sorry I had to call you back. We were doing morning exercises."

"Lieutenant Hata. How good to hear your voice," I said loudly, looking straight at Alec and Rika.

"You're just faking," Alec sneered.

"Do you want to speak to him yourself?" I asked Alec.

"What's going on, Shimura-san? Are you safe?" Lieutenant Hata asked.

"I'm quite safe, Lieutenant. Just a minute, please." I put my hand over the receiver and said to Alec and Rika, "If you don't leave, I'm telling him everything."

Rika and Alec exchanged glances.

"We're going to be late if we don't leave now," Rika said, offering a face-saving excuse.

"Righto. But we'll be speaking soon about the story, won't we, Rei? Ta." Alec didn't bother to close the door on his way out.

"Sorry," I said to Lieutenant Hata. "I had some unwelcome visitors." I sighed gustily.

"I must apologize to you, Shimura-san. You were correct about the identity of the man who was found dead in the river. Maybe you already heard about the identification in the newspaper?"

"Yes indeed," I said.

"What do you want to tell me? I heard you saying something to your guests. Are they gone?"

"Yes, but can you tell me something first? How's the investigation going?"

"We are still examining clues taken from the scene," Lieutenant Hata said. "I would like to hear more from you about why you thought you knew the victim in the first place."

Cagily I answered, "Well, I met Nicky Larsen when I paid a visit to a bar in Shinjuku called Show a Boy."

"You go to places like that?" Lieutenant Hata sounded stunned.

"It was for something I'm writing," I said. "So I saw Nicky on a Saturday night, and then I saw him on Monday morning, the day he was killed. That time I knocked on his apartment door by accident, because I was really looking for a neighbor. I wanted to interview his neighbor for my art and antiques feature in the *Gaijin Times*."

"Yes, yes. I know you write for them. What was the exact time of your meeting? I should really have you down to the station for questioning."

Things were going a bit faster than I'd wanted. I said, "I saw him at ten A.M. Getting back to what I've been trying to tell you, I am working on a project that relates loosely to Nicky and, more principally, his missing neighbor, Kunio Takahashi. I've left messages for Mr. Takahashi everywhere, and the only thing that's come of it is that I was attacked yesterday in Kasumigaseki Station."

"Why didn't you tell me this first?" Lieutenant Hata flared. "My goodness, what happened? Are you all right?"

"Well, I wasn't pickpocketed or groped or anything you'd expect to suffer at a criminal's hands in a train station. I'd just exited the train, and when I was walking up the steps to transfer to another line, a man a few steps ahead of me called my name before hitting me in the face. I fell down a flight of stairs before someone caught me."

"Why is there no police report?" Hata said. "Didn't you tell the stationmaster to call us?"

"The stationmaster said the Metropolitan Police heard the story and decided that it was an accident."

"We must get the testimony of the person on the steps who caught you," Hata said. "I don't suppose you have his name?"

"Her name," I corrected. "Talking to her would be a waste of time, because she said that she was aware of other people on the staircase but hadn't noticed a particular man who hit me."

"I wonder if it was *yakuza*," Hata muttered. "Did he look like a thug?"

"I wish I could tell you what the guy looked like, but I'm thinking he was just a typical man. Dark hair, medium height—I know a million guys like that." Among them, Alec Tampole and Mr. Hattori. I'd have to ask someone who knew Kunio Takahashi about his height.

"What about age? Couldn't you tell from his face?"

"He'd disguised it. He was wearing a little nose-and-mouth mask, the type people wear when they have allergies and colds. But his eyes—it's a blank." I caught myself. "I keep thinking of the color black. . . ."

"You mean, he was an African? Nicky Larsen was friendly with an African dancer."

"That's not it," I said firmly. "I mean, the space where the eyes were was blacked out. I think I've got it now—he was wearing black sunglasses! Just like Sunglass Man in the *anime* coffee shop!"

23

After I'd gotten over the excitement of my recovered memory, it took a while for Lieutenant Hata to get me down to earth, but when he did, I landed with a thud. He reminded me that many people wear sunglasses, and there was no guarantee that I'd encountered the same man twice. He also pointed out that a stocky woman with short hair or a short wig could be mistaken for a man.

"Will you please come in and make a formal report?" Lieutenant Hata asked. "We have a special unit on gang-related crime. I think they'd be most interested in your story."

"What makes you so sure this is a gang-related death?" I asked, remembering how Chiyo had said she had to pay protection money to the *yakuza*, but that it didn't make her one of them.

"That marking on the forehead should make anyone think of a gang," Lieutenant Hata said firmly.

"Anyone but me, I guess. Hey, if you wanted to find a gangster, where would you go?"

"I'd have one of our informants suggest a meeting place. Why?"

"Oh, just curious."

"Shimura-san, if you have any intention of going to the corporate headquarters of someone in the crime field, let me warn you that it is a terrible idea. You don't know what you're getting involved in at all."

"So you're saying that it's better to meet on neutral territory?"

"No! It's best not to meet at all. Now, when can I count on you to come to the station?"

I didn't want to go in. It was one thing to get him concerned about the attack on me, but it was quite another to have him looking through all the data I'd gathered for the *Gaijin Times* article. I wanted him to find the killer, but I had to get the article written in the next few days. I'd give him as much information as possible without relinquishing my files. I realized now that I should be making photocopies, just in case.

"I'll come tomorrow," I said, thinking about the copies. "First I've got a business appointment."

After he hung up, I packed up all my notes and trotted around the corner to Family Mart, the convenience store my friend Mr. Waka ran. He wasn't there—a sullen young man I guessed must be a new hire was. He told me the photocopier was out of order and made no further offers of help.

I went out on the street again, thinking that photocopying would be a good reason to go to Hattori Copy Shop to talk to Seiko again. However, even though she'd been so helpful to me, it was too risky to let her see how much information I'd gathered. Instead, I decided to do my photocopying at 7-Eleven. I made two sets of copies—one to keep hidden under the false bottom of the *tansu* chest in my apartment, and another to use for my work. The originals I put on my bookshelf, ready for the police if they demanded them.

I was feeling pretty pleased with myself by the time I made it back to the apartment. It was after 10 A.M., so Seiko would be at the shop. I dialed the number, and Seiko picked up on the first ring.

"I still want to ask you some things," I said in a rush. "Also, I've got a copy of *Showa Story* that you left in the bar the first time we talked. Do you want it back?"

"No, I have plenty of copies," she said in a whisper. "How are you feeling? Did you get home safely from the hospital?"

"I'm out and doing fine. I'd like to talk to you again. Do you remember I was asking you about Rika Fuchida right before they took me away to the hospital?"

Instead of answering my question, she said, "Um, that's going to be difficult. I have to work a lot of extra hours here because of Comiko this weekend."

"Oh, you're going to the convention?"

"Yes. Will I see you there?"

"Definitely. Bye, then." I hung up, thinking. Then I telephoned Takeo at the country house.

"Oh, hello, Rei." He sounded out of breath. "I'm halfway into installing the new bath. How are you?"

"Mmm, okay." I didn't want to worry him with the story about the train station, but I supposed I'd have to tell him when he saw my face and body. "I don't want to keep you at a time like this, but I'm going to make a slightly brazen request. I was wondering if I could come visit you. I know you're busy, but I promise not to get in your way."

"Of course. I'll pick you up at the train station when you get in—I'm not going to allow a miscommunication to happen this time, all right?"

"Okay. I figured your home would be the perfect base for going to the *manga* convention. It might mean long days there, but I found out that Seiko Hattori's going, so I can interview her there as well."

"I thought she didn't want to talk to you," Takeo said. "Didn't she run out on you at the bar?"

"Since then we've met once, and we spoke on the phone just before I called you. She's turning out to be a good source. I can follow up on her, and also on the gangster angle."

"What gangster angle?" There was an edge to Takeo's voice.

"I would like to have a serious conversation with someone in the organized crime field about Nicky's death. Was the mark on Nicky's forehead a gang tattoo? I'd like the opinion of an expert."

"And where do you think you'll find such an expert gangster?"

"A relaxed social setting—the beach near your house. If I handle the situation respectfully, I'll be fine."

"Listen, I'm trying to help you in every way I can, but there is no way I can arrange such an introduction! My family is not friendly with the *yakuza*. We've suffered in the past for it."

I was suddenly interested to know more about that, but I didn't want to get him off track. I tried again. "Look, I'm going to have to find one of these fellows. I have the theory that chatting with one when he's relaxing with a beer and in the mood to talk to girls would be more efficient than knocking on an office door in some sleazy building."

"It's still dangerous. If you try to interview a criminal, will you at least promise to conduct the interviews within my line of vision? I just want to make sure that you're all right."

I nodded. "Why don't you sit at a table nearby? Just don't stare at us."

"We can do it tomorrow." Takeo sounded resigned. "I need to finish up some things in the house. And when you're not doing your interviews, you can spend some time writing at the house."

It sounded like a good plan. The only thing that might be a problem was Hayama's distance from the *Gaijin Times*. I was still disturbed about Rika, though, and her possible role in the bad things that had been happening. It might be better for me to be out of touch.

24

Putting together my luggage for the short stay in Hayama was not an easy task. I figured that I needed all my notes, my laptop computer, and plenty of other odds and ends relating to the animation story. I hadn't been in the mood to pack my bikini, but I supposed that I needed to wear one, if my goal was to approach gangsters on the beach. Making things worse, when I'd taken my morning shower, I had discovered that my bikini line was growing back. So much for Miss Kumiko's painful and expensive waxing. I experimented with a tube of mysterious Japanese depilatory cream that had been lingering in my bathroom cabinet for about a year, and was able to wipe it off just in time to dash out and make the subway connection that would take me to Tokyo Station, where I would pick up the last JR train of the hour to Zushi Station. I moved so fast through the stations that I didn't have time to dwell on the memory of my last time in a train station, when I'd been pushed.

During the hour-long ride, I realized that I hadn't done a very good job wiping off the cream. It was supposed to smell like lemons, but it smelled more noxious than that. People sitting near me kept casting evil glances at me, even after I opened the window. I was getting a depilatory-induced headache by the time I'd gotten off the train and saw Takeo waiting in his Range Rover.

"What happened to you?" he asked from the rolled-down window.

"Well, someone hit me in the train station yesterday. That's part of the reason I wanted to spend some time here." The other part—wanting to avoid Lieutenant Hata's inquiry into my journalism project—I left unsaid.

Takeo jumped out of the car and ran around to open my door. "Take it easy, please! And tell me everything."

I did, and when I was through, he shook his head. "I'm glad you called me. But I would have picked you up in Tokyo if I'd known about this train station attack. How do you know someone didn't follow you from the station out here?"

"I don't." I sighed heavily. "But I like to think that attack was supposed to be a one-time warning."

"Oops, let's roll up the windows. There's a strange chemical smell," Takeo said, shifting into drive. "Probably some work being done in the neighborhood."

Was I stupid or what to worry about my bikini line when there was a bruise marring my face? What was the whole point of beauty rituals at a time like this?

It helps me calm down, I reminded myself. I looked out the window, trying to relax and observe. Zushi Station was surrounded by narrow streets lined with small shops selling household and beach goods. There were a few signs welcoming *manga* convention-goers, too. Young people with spiked hair received curious glances, as well as smiles, from apron-clad ladies sweeping the pavement.

"Why don't you roll down the windows again? I think we're away from the fumes," I said to Takeo after a few blocks. "It's really nice of you to take me to your place. I hope that I'll be able to use the time well. I did some writing on the train, and that only made me realize how far I have to go."

"The further you go, the more dangerous your situation gets. The only comfort to me is that whoever looks at your notes won't be able to understand a thing. Your handwriting is impossible!" We were at another of the interminable stops, and Takeo had taken a quick glance at the notebook I'd carried off the train. The road was narrow, and there was a truck ahead trying to make a right turn against a flood of oncoming traffic.

"I'll switch to using a laptop when I'm at your house," I said. "Right now, I'm still trying to decide whether to keep it somewhat of an art story or turn it completely into a crime story. There's been so much violence that it seems silly to harp on Kunio's depictions of Showa-period decadence."

"Could you do the art commentary in a shorter form—ask some hotshot in the art world to look at comic books and give his opinion?"

"I suppose so. The thing is, I wanted to say so myself, in my own words. I had this crazy dream that I had discovered Kunio and could expose him to the greater world. But it turns out that he doesn't really need exposure. The artist who does the regular *Mars Girl* comic book wanted to hire Kunio. He ignored her."

"Do you really think Kunio's still alive?" Takeo gave me a sideways look.

"Do you think he's been killed?"

"Why else would he be so hard to find?" Takeo sounded impatient, and I wondered if it was because of the traffic or my own slowness to realize the obvious. Of course, I'd thought that Kunio might be dead. But I didn't want to. From the moment I saw his exquisite drawings, I'd started building him into a fantasy figure. All the women who spoke of his gorgeous appearance and charm just added fuel to the fire. First I'd wanted to discover him; after Nicky died, I'd wanted to save him. Now Takeo was stating the obvious, and I didn't want to believe it.

"The afternoon that I said good-bye to Nicky, I called the Show a Boy dance club," I said to Takeo. "A man answered the telephone. When he heard my name, he asked if I wasn't the reporter trying to locate Kunio. I said yes, I certainly was, and he told me that he had heard that Kunio was uninterested in participating in the article. I think the man speaking might have been Kunio himself."

"Why not another one of the dancers?" Takeo asked.

I shook my head. "The dancers are all foreigners. The accent, pace, and choice of words the speaker used were quintessentially Japanese."

"But Kunio doesn't work there. He painted the walls, and he left. Why do you think there's a link?"

I couldn't come up with a good answer.

We picked up speed as we headed on the newer, wider roads to Hayama. I stretched pleasurably, almost forgetting the aches from my subway station fall. For the next day or two, I could balance research on gangsters and animation with thoughtful conversations with Takeo. I liked talking to him about my work. He asked hard questions. I also appreciated that he encouraged me to keep going with the story, rather than to stop. At first, that encouragement had made me almost resentful, but now I knew that I needed it.

"You've stopped writing," Takeo said when he caught me smiling at him.

"I was just thinking about how helpful you are to me," I said.

"It's not such a sacrifice to spend a few days with you. After all, I'm an unemployed guy."

Was there a hint of sadness behind Takeo's light banter? I looked at him closely, but I couldn't see anything in his face. He looked as handsome and relaxed as ever, but his words reminded me that I wasn't the only person who would need special tending over the next few days.

25

The first thing I noticed as we swung into the pebbled drive-way was the new roof. Wave-shaped dark blue tiles covered the roof in neat rows. There were no more gaps on the roof with weeds shooting out of them. I congratulated Takeo on the roof, and he modestly ducked his head.

"There were three of us working on the project. And I feel kind of bad that I had to get rid of so many of the old tiles. The new ones look pretty, but I just hate to create garbage."

As I got out of the car, I saw that he had in fact stacked the old, worn tiles in a large pile behind the house.

"Can they be recycled?" I asked.

"Certainly not for use on a roof. But maybe in pieces—if someone needs weight to hold something down. The broken edges, however, are sharp. They're not safe to touch."

I bent to examine a jagged piece. "If you could smash these up more finely, they could go to an artist for use in a mosaic."

"That's a clever idea." Takeo walked around the pile. "I was thinking of redoing the wall that shields the house from the street. Maybe I could make some kind of pattern with the blue. Blue and gray."

"A very Japanese color combination," I said, tucking a piece of tile in a handkerchief and putting it in the outer pocket of my backpack. I would try to find a harmonious fabric and design some slipcovers for the house's garden chairs.

There was an urn brimming with pampas grass and a few sunflowers next to the door, giving me the feeling that a woman was home. Takeo's mother was deceased, and his sister, Natsumi, and I didn't get along very well, due to some events of the previous spring. However, the flowers weren't from the garden. I'd seen them somewhere.

"Are these flowers from the side of the road? Near Animagine?"

"That's right. I did a little roadside scavenging."

"I'm glad you still are arranging flowers," I said.

"I like to arrange with found materials," he said. "It made me sick the other day when I found out that our ikebana school has just made a contract with a greenhouse in Singapore that uses an incredible cocktail of chemicals to give their orchids a special sheen. I won't touch the plants, even with gloves on, and I don't think the laborers tending them should have to either. My father said we needed orchids, and that was the end of it. I shot off to the country after that."

"Did you tell your father about me?" I asked.

"No. I said that I'd be working on the house."

So he hadn't been brave enough to mention me, most likely because his father would have said no to the idea of us spending time together under the family roof. I remembered Takeo's fear of gossip about us after his old schoolmate had seen us in Animagine. The Kayamas were big carp swimming in a tiny pond. They had to protect their reputation.

"Let's go inside," Takeo said. We stepped in and he immediately switched on a new air conditioner. It started with a gentle hum—Japanese air conditioners are much quieter than their big, bulky American counterparts—and I looked around. The mold that had frosted the rough walls had been scrubbed off, along with the cobwebs and dead insects. An intense grassy smell came from the new, yellow-green tatami mats covering the floors. The house had been thoroughly cleaned and looked much more attractive. I could see that painting needed to be done here and there, but Takeo had made great progress.

"I'm thinking about doing away with some of the walls. There are too many useless small rooms. I want to see the garden all the way from the kitchen." Takeo walked briskly through the house, sliding open doors here and there, showing me the walls that had been repainted in pale colors taken from nature—stones, moss, robin's-egg blue. The feeling of openness was furthered by the fresh paper screens slid to the side of each window, offering views of the sea and gardens.

As I made the circuit, I saw how beautifully Takeo had painted the walls. I also saw how neatly historic-looking tile had been fitted into the old bathroom floors, and how the fine old furniture gleamed from refinishing.

We were going to have to move furniture back into place, an enjoyable prospect for me, because Takeo said he wanted my ideas on how to rearrange things. The one room that was designed to stay permanently empty was a small reception room near the front of the house. Inside it was a gilded antique Buddhist altar that displayed a faded color photograph of a beautiful woman. Set on a plate in front of the picture was a small crystal goblet with a golden liquid. I could smell plums, but there were none in sight.

"Is this your mother's altar?" I asked.

"Yes," Takeo said. "By the way, I put your bags in the same room as last time. Do you want to rest for a few minutes while I make lunch?"

"You're making lunch?" I asked.

"Yes. While I've been out here on my own, I've experimented a little."

I decided to take a shower, scrubbing off the last of the depilatory, and put on my bathing suit, covered by a T-shirt in preparation for my trek to the beach. I applied some cover stick over the bruise shadowing my jaw as well as the ones on my arms and legs. Then I sat on a rock in the Zen garden, letting the sun dry my hair, while Takeo prepared a meal in the kitchen. It was unusual for a Japanese man who wasn't a chef by trade to cook for a woman. Because he seemed intent and a little bit worried in the kitchen, I'd decided not to hang around watching. I hadn't told Takeo, but I was in pain. Not only did I have a headache, but I had a bruised tailbone that felt worse than it had after the attack the previous day.

If I was lucky, I had remembered to bring ibuprofen in my backpack. I tried to go directly from the garden to the sliding windows that led to the moss-green bedroom where Takeo had said we would be sleeping. The new tatami floor was already covered by tidy stacks of home design and gardening magazines. A double bed was set up on a low, lacquered platform with a couple of folded sheets laid out on top, waiting to be made up.

I found that Takeo had neatly unpacked my luggage, including toiletries. He'd arranged my deodorant, hairbrush, moisturizer, and makeup on top of his *tansu* chest. The ibuprofen was still in my backpack, but as I took it out a funny realization hit me: the Valium was missing. I wondered if Takeo had removed it. He wasn't the type who took anything outside of the occasional glass of beer or sake. I wondered whether he had flushed the tablets down the toilet because he wanted me to go holistic.

I took the ibuprofen and went off to the kitchen, seeking answers.

26

Takeo's kitchen renovation was halfway there. He was going to keep some old, charming elements—the weathered cork flooring and a huge kitchen *tansu* that held dozens of blue-and-white dishes. He had a new gas range with a full-size oven, and he'd told me that he was going to buy a German dishwasher. It was a cook's kitchen, and ordinarily I would have looked around it with pleasure, but I was stunned to see that while I'd been out of the house, company had arrived.

Takeo was leaning on the counter, having what looked like a very emotional conversation with a young woman. She had her back to me—a slim, golden back that was bare except for the ribbon straps of a halter. A sleek black pageboy ended at the nape of her neck. I couldn't see her face, but I imagined it was pretty. All of a sudden, I wished that I hadn't been straight out of the shower with half-dry hair and a thigh-length T-shirt worn over my bikini.

"You've got to get her out!" the woman said. "Father will flip if he finds out that she's here."

I recognized the voice as that of Takeo's twin sister, Natsumi. So Takeo didn't have a secret girlfriend. I supposed that I should have been relieved, but the problem was that Natsumi and I didn't get along. She was threatened by the idea of her brother marrying, I guessed because of how it would impact on her power within the family. Not that Takeo had ever asked me to marry him, but she'd brought up that topic with me a few months ago.

"I'm already disinherited. What could be worse than that?" Takeo said angrily over the sound of rushing water at the sink.

"I don't want to run the school," Natsumi whined in a tone that made her sound eight, not twenty-eight. "You could get your position back so easily if you'd just make up with him. This isn't the way to do it."

"Wasabi, please."

I was thinking about ducking out, but it was too late. Natsumi had turned around in the direction of the refrigerator to get the ingredient her brother wanted, and she'd spotted me in the doorway.

"How long have you been standing there?" she demanded.

I regarded Natsumi, who was so well put together that she always made me feel unkempt. That day Natsumi was sporting finely plucked eyebrows and bright scarlet lipstick that gave her the look of a 1950s film star. Below her tiny halter top, she wore a pair of striped bicycle shorts. Her thighs were the width of my forearms. Natsumi had always been thin, but now she was verging on anorexic.

"I've just been standing here a minute," I said. "The part I overheard is that you want me to go home."

Takeo almost dropped his bamboo strainer full of noodles. In fact, he had to lunge to catch some soba in his hand before it reached the floor.

"Don't worry," Takeo said after he had slid the noodles into a bowl. "My sister's not going to ruin our time here. I have at least as much bad evidence about her behavior as she has about mine."

I grew up without siblings, something about which I'd complained to my parents all throughout my childhood. But as an adult, I'd had reason to change my mind. Arguments between blood relations seemed so much sharper and nastier than those between unrelated people. I felt myself begin to sweat just watching the brother and sister who had once been together in the womb face off like mortal enemies.

"I'm staying here for a few days. I've got a friend coming in tonight. I need privacy!" Natsumi sat down on a bamboo stool, crossing her slim legs.

"You're not even supposed to be in Japan." Takeo was vigorously mixing the noodles with sauce. "You're supposed to be having meetings with the flower supplier in Singapore."

"I cannot experience the harsh sun of Singapore with pale skin. I need a few days here to work up a base so that I don't burn while there."

"You're saying you postponed a meeting based on vanity?" Takeo asked.

I was thinking that Natsumi's tan plan meant that she would probably be on the beach that afternoon while I was attempting to chat up gangsters. Great. I could only imagine her charging into our conversation and ruining things. I opened the fridge and picked up a bottle of Evian. I was still carrying around my painkilling tablet to wash down with a cool drink.

"That's my personal water bottle!" Natsumi objected.

"Sorry." I put it back and went to the new stainless-steel sink to start filling a glass. Japanese tap water wasn't especially delicious, but it wasn't poisonous.

"Why apologize, Rei?" Takeo sounded angry. "She's the rude one. Not you."

I was trying to see things from Natsumi's vantage. What if I were the daughter of the house and had come home to spend a few quiet days, only to run smack into a girl whose personality bothered me? It would be depressing, all right.

"If she stays, there are certain conditions," Natsumi grumbled to her brother.

"I'm here. You can tell me the conditions," I said.

"I need to sleep in the peach-colored room that's closest to the bathroom in the hall. There are no other finished rooms, so you'll probably want to check into a hotel."

"No matter. I'm staying in your brother's room, anyway." I smiled, trumping her at her game.

"You can't do that! Not in our mother's house!" Natsumi screeched.

"*Our* house," Takeo corrected. "Where is your friend going to sleep tonight?"

"I was going to put him in the green room—"

Takeo shook his head. "I don't believe that. Besides, you know it's my room."

"You're ruining my weekend here. You might as well make it even worse by not believing what I say."

I felt a little bad for Natsumi, so I said, "Let's start over, shall we? Hi. Would you like to eat lunch with us?"

She shook her head. "Soy makes me retain water. I brought my own health food, which I'll eat later. I'm going to be in my room. If anyone calls, make sure you bring me the telephone." Natsumi grabbed her bottle of mineral water and swung out of the kitchen.

"I'm sorry about her," Takeo said when we sat down at last to eat the chilled noodles. The soy sauce dressing had the surprise addition of ground peanuts and tasted delicious; I couldn't get enough of it.

"I've been trying to think about what your sister's going through," I said. "I'm sure that I've just spoiled what she was hoping would be her private time."

"I sometimes wonder whether Natsumi would have been different if our mother had lived. She had no kind or gentle women taking care of her, you know."

Takeo's mother had died when he and Natsumi were very young. They'd grown up in a Tokyo penthouse surrounded by sycophantic servants, with a father who was frequently absent. When Takeo and I had met, I'd realized how deeply he felt the loss of his mother. Natsumi and I hadn't gotten along from the start, so I didn't know how she felt about not having a mother. But I imagined that she too must have sadness.

"Who knows?" I said, spearing some more noodles in the delicious sauce. "Natsumi is a very feminine woman, but the way that she makes her feelings about things so clear—isn't that more typical of male behavior than of female behavior in Japan? Maybe she learned that behavior from your father. Or you."

Takeo had been picking at his food, and he put his chopsticks down. "I hope not from me. I mean, I'm all in favor of free expression, but it shouldn't hurt others."

"Is that the reason why you didn't confront your father about the orchids from Singapore?" I asked. "Did you think it would hurt his feelings?"

"It's hard to explain," Takeo said. "It's just—I know him so well. There's no point in fighting for anything when he's in charge. It's easier to sit on the sidelines." Takeo took a swallow of cold barley tea. "Renovating this house has been a great pleasure for me. I dream sometimes of hiding out here for the rest of my life. I don't know if you'd be interested in that, though."

I flushed, and it wasn't from the wasabi paste hitting my nose. Was Takeo trying to get serious? If so, there was something I still needed to clear up: the missing Valium.

"There's something I want to ask you. I can't find something that I packed. I wondered if you'd seen it."

"What is it?" Takeo asked matter-of-factly.

"A container of Valium tablets."

A look of horror crossed his face. "Rei, I had no idea you were on tranquilizers. Is life that difficult?"

"No," I said. "The doctor at St. Luke's prescribed them as a muscle relaxant. I didn't take any yet, but I did have them in my backpack, and I noticed now that they're gone."

Takeo shook his head. "I unpacked your luggage because I wanted you to feel settled, but I didn't go into your backpack. I hate to think that my sister did."

I felt relieved, though. "If she starts acting very relaxed and kind to me, we'll know she took it. And that won't be so bad."

"The thought of her on drugs is truly frightening," Takeo said. "I can't sit around here waiting and wondering. What do you think about going to the beach and finding a gangster? Somehow that seems less dangerous."

"All right. Let's go," I said, sounding more cheerful than I felt.

27

I took off my sunglasses and placed them on the round table in front of me to discreetly check my reflection. My MAC lipstick had a subtle sheen, my bruise was well covered by makeup, and my hair was perfectly slicked back with Takeo's Super Hard Gel. I was wearing my trusty sports bikini because I'd heard that gangsters liked foreign brands. The Speedo emblem was on both top and bottom—you couldn't miss it. The emblems were about the only extraordinary things I had going for me, since my bosom was as small as a typical Japanese woman's, and my waist and hips were a fraction thicker.

Takeo, who was wearing stylish black bathing trunks with a decidedly ratty Greenpeace T-shirt, was seated about thirty feet away at the bar, sipping occasionally at a banana milk shake as he worked on a written translation of the *Showa Story* comic. His bird-watching binoculars were at his side, so he could make periodic checks to see if his sister was on the beach.

To make myself look casually decadent, I had ordered something that looked like a tequila sunrise but had no alcohol. It tasted like the strawberry lip gloss I used to wear in junior high school. Actually, it was junior high all over again: I was completely awkward, hiding behind a status brand, trying to act bolder than I was. Why had I thought that I could make contact with the next table over, where two curly-permed men were deep into conversation, smoking their way through a pack of Mild Sevens? The men had glanced up when I'd seated myself, then looked away without interest. That made me decide for sure that they were my prey. I'd even glanced over at Takeo, who had raised his eyebrows, which I took to mean that I'd made a likely gangster identification.

Engage in a normal conversation, I reminded myself. *Think about how casually the conversation started last time with Rika's friends.* But Rika had introduced us. Japanese society ran on introductions.

I caught sight of Takeo out of the corner of my eye. He was motioning for me to put on my sunglasses. I remembered that back at the house, he'd said I should try to come off like a gangster's little sister. It was hard enough to know what to do because I wasn't a sister to anyone.

I put on the sunglasses and searched my backpack for something to catch their attention. I was carrying the *Mars Girl* comic book that I'd been given at Dayo Publishing. I spread it out in front of me and pretended to read. I giggled aloud, trying to make them look up, but they didn't. This went on for about ten minutes. At this rate, they were liable to leave before I got my courage up to deliver an opening line.

A particularly harsh trail of smoke was making its way to my nostrils. How I longed to move. I jumped up and went to the bar to order another mocktail.

"I can't do it," I whispered to Takeo without looking at him.

"It's a shame," he whispered back. "I asked the bartender about those two, and he told me not to bother them. I think that means they're exactly what you think."

I nodded miserably and took my drink back to the table. As I moved, I ran over the various possibilities. I could employ the spilled-drink trick, but since they were dressed head to toe in Nike warm-up clothing, that gimmick might make them angry. I could ask for a cigarette, but I'd embarrass myself coughing to death. All I knew how to do were the good-girl things, the polite introductions that every student of Japanese learned.

Hmmm, I thought. Maybe I had something there.

I sat down, crossing my legs so that no one could see how thick my thighs were from running. I looked directly at the man sitting closest to me and called out.

"It's been a long time!" When the two men regarded me blankly, I said, "You're Tanaka-san's friends. I'm Reiko!" I had started to say my real name, then added a suffix for a little bit of safety.

"Tanaka-san knows you?" one of the men grunted.

"Certainly. We're very close." I beamed. Everyone in Japan knew a Tanaka-san. Tanaka was one of the most common family names.

The two men exchanged glances. I could read, clear as the drinks specials on the billboard, that they were in an etiquette conundrum. The men had to acknowledge me as a friend of Tanaka-san's, because if Tanaka-san heard that they'd been unfriendly to me, he might let them know. The man closest to me, who had been sipping a beer, had a tattoo of a dragon on his biceps. Dragon Man. The other man had a prominent gold tooth.

"Um, good to see you again," Dragon Man said. "What's that pink thing you're drinking? Wouldn't you rather have a beer?"

This was a good step, sharing drinks. I was almost in. I turned to watch the men signal the bartender for another glass, and in that movement I saw Takeo slam a hand over his own drink. He was worried they might put something in my drink.

Trying to be cautious yet decadent-seeming, I said, "I'm more of a hard-liquor girl. Could I invite you guys for a tequila sunrise?"

They exchanged glances. Had I said something that could be misconstrued?

"You're not Japanese, are you?" Gold Tooth asked in an almost kindly manner.

"Of course I'm Japanese, but I have spent some years in the States—didn't Tanaka-san tell you?"

"No," Dragon Man said, exchanging another significant glance with his friend.

"It's a little bit hard for me here," I said. "I can't get a regular job." *Just like you*, I added silently.

"So what do you do?" Gold Tooth looked at my body and smiled. I got the message—he was hinting that I was a bar hostess, or worse.

"I do a little of this and that," I said. "I also am trying to educate myself about Japan. Do you read *manga?*" I held up my comic book.

"I did when I was a kid. But our work is pretty hard. We don't have time to read anything during the day. When we're free, it's better to relax at the beach, feasting our eyes on the waves and pretty women." Gold Tooth grinned.

"People have said that there's a lot of hidden symbolism in the simple cartoons." I felt my pulse race a little faster, and I opened the comic book to a page that showed the front of Mars Girl's tunic, which bore the symbol of Mars that had been on Nicky's forehead. "The planet Mars, for example. I heard a TV reporter say that it's a symbol of a business family."

"You must be from Mars! I'm going to take a crap." Dragon Man stood up and stalked off.

Gold Tooth beamed at me. "Now, where were we?"

"I feel a little embarrassed. Did I say something that made your friend angry?" All of a sudden, I realized how dangerous the waters were that I was treading.

"We aren't used to girls talking to us. You look like you'd fit better with that guy at the bar. He's reading a comic book, too."

I looked over my shoulder, feigning surprise at the sight of Takeo. "Well, I'm sure he wouldn't know about the, um, business aspect of things."

"No, heh heh heh!" Gold Tooth's hand grasped my thigh firmly. I looked down and saw that he had an intact pinky, although it did bear a diamond-studded ring. "I shall tell you some stories."

I wondered if Takeo could see what was happening from his vantage point at the bar. No, because there was a plaid tablecloth that hung low enough to mask things. My impulse was to slap the man's hand away, but that would kill the conversation. I let the hand stay.

I raised my eyebrows at the man. "So, what do you think? Off the record, of course."

"You listen to records? CDs also?"

I guessed that my Western metaphor just didn't translate. "I'll keep it a secret."

"Of course. We'll keep everything that happens between us very, very private. Let's go, *neh*? I'll pay your drinks bill."

Things were going from bad to worse much faster than I'd imagined, thanks to my euphemistic language. But I couldn't stop now. I would have to use euphemism to get me out of a tight situation.

"*Ojisan*," I said to him, deliberately using the term that meant "grandfather," even though he was probably only twenty years older than I, "please. I come to you only with a question about business, a question to which you may not even have the answer."

"You want to talk business." His smile faded. "Ah, that's why Tanaka-san sent you. You're trying to get in, aren't you? I know girls these days are trying all kinds of things."

"No, I come on my own. I want to know if this symbol is known in your business."

He laughed gently. "Of course not. We have a symbol that fits our work much better than some planet, or is it a pancake?"

"I'm afraid . . . I'm afraid I don't know your symbol."

"But it's Tanaka-san's business. He's our supervisor." Finally Gold Tooth looked a little suspicious.

"Why don't you draw it for me?" I pulled out a pen that I'd stashed in my tight-fitting bikini top.

Gold Tooth goggled at that move, but it must have worked because he set pen to napkin immediately. He made a simple drawing of a cat holding a kitten between her teeth.

"That looks like . . . the symbol for a well-known package delivery service."

"That's right! We deliver packages six days a week. Today is our day off."

I stared at him. "You mean . . . package delivery is your line of work?"

"It's a tough job, eh?" He laughed.

"You work for a regular company, then."

"Of course! We make good money. In fact, my friend and I have a rental house just down the beach. I'd like to show you."

"No, thank you. I'm a little bit busy," I said, giving his hand a little pat before I removed it. Where his hand had gripped me, a thin film of sweat remained. I wanted to cleanse myself.

"Why so cold?" Gold Tooth demanded.

"Um, would you believe me if I confessed this was a case of mistaken identity?"

"Sure. Reiko-san, I will be on the beach all day if you change your mind about taking a little rest with me. You are too confused. You do not know what is good for you."

"Well, like I said, I've got to take a quick dip before leaving. *Sayonara!*" I went back to my table and placed a thousand-yen note under my empty glass. Then, trying to look casual, I headed straight for the ocean. The sand was hot, so I ran to the water, thinking over and over again what an idiot I was to mistake deliverymen for criminals.

I walked into the water with pleasure; Hayama's bay was much warmer than the Pacific I'd grown up with, as well as much calmer. There was no lifeguard here, nor were there any buoys marking off a safe swimming area. It was too placid for all that. Wasn't Lake Hayama the nickname foreigners gave it?

I splashed with pleasure once I reached thigh level and could wash off Gold Tooth's lascivious handprints. I stretched onto my side and sidestroked into deeper water, then flipped onto my back. From time to time, a wave would come and I would ride it. This was as far as I wanted to go when it came to surfing.

I wondered if Takeo would join me. He had worn swimming trunks. Maybe he was staying back because he didn't want Gold Tooth and his colleague to know that we were connected. After all, he was not close enough to have heard Gold Tooth confess to being a deliveryman.

Ha. Takeo had talked up the beach as being ridden with gangsters; probably they were all just deliverymen and stereo salesmen, working-class guys trying to look good. I'd been such a fool to descend on those two men. I was only glad that Takeo's sister hadn't been around to witness the humiliating scene.

I kicked gently—my ankle seemed to be tangled in a thick frond of seaweed. When a few kicks didn't release it, I bobbed up to the surface to tread water and see if I could untangle myself. But my relaxed movement did no good. The hold on my ankle tightened. My body sank under the water.

28

I blubbered for help, making no sound and taking in a mouth-ful of water instead. I wasn't a great swimmer, but I'd thought at least I had enough skill to tread water. Somehow that move had gone wrong; with my panicked kicking, I'd gotten a sear-ing cramp in my foot. This was how people drowned. I opened my eyes in the murky water and couldn't see any-thing. My head actually grazed the sandy bed; the water couldn't be more than six feet deep. What a stupid place to drown.

I no longer thought that I'd been caught by seaweed—what was touching me had a hook, almost like an umbrella handle. Suddenly I flashed back to James Bond movies and criminals who had hooks for arms. *Oh, God*, I thought. Maybe it was the Sunglass Man, come back.

A human arm grazed my body. *Please let it be another swim-mer come to my rescue, and not the Sunglass Man shoving me to the bottom of the sea.*

Two strong arms hauled me up suddenly, and my face was out of the water, with my feet on the ground. The place where we were was shallow: not six feet, as I'd first thought, but only four and a half feet. At present, my feet were firmly on the sandy bottom and my head was above water. I coughed, not caring that my nose was running in front of a stranger, because I was so glad to be alive.

I wiped my eyes and opened them, looking straight into the face of a middle-aged man I'd never seen before. At least, I thought so. I pulled out the memory of the ephemeral Sunglass Man. He'd seemed younger than this fellow. I wasn't sure.

I coughed violently, whipping my head around so that I could search for swimmers near enough to call to for help. Ten feet away were a couple of teenagers shooting each other with water guns. They had been having so much fun, they'd missed the fact that I'd almost drowned. I knew now that seaweed had not pulled me down—rather, it had been the curved rubber pipe of a snorkel. Now that the job was done, the man calmly slipped his snorkel in the side of his mouth.

"How are you?" he asked conversationally. It was like hearing someone talk with a cigar in his mouth.

"Fine," I replied automatically. I looked at him. He had flat, unhandsome features, narrow eyes, a chicken pox scar on his forehead. He was balding. This was no Kunio Takahashi, that was for sure.

He raised a hand over his eyes as a shield against the sun and looked straight at me. His gaze was chilling. "You asked the wrong fellows about business," he said. "I can tell you what you need to know."

He really was *yakuza*. Even though the hand over his eyes had all the fingers intact, I suddenly knew. The fact that he still had his pinky finger meant that he hadn't been punished for making any mistakes.

I said, still spitting out some water, "I don't think so. You're more interested in hurting me than helping me."

"I was simply trying to get your attention. At the bar you didn't notice me." The man spoke politely, with a faint accent from the Kansai region. He sounded very different from the working-class joes I'd mistaken for gangsters.

"You almost killed me," I said.

"No," he said. "My superiors have no interest in harming you."

"Who hit me at the train station?"

"Not us. I repeat that I am here to help."

I coughed out the last bit of water in my lungs and said, "I think that your help is designed to steer me away from the truth."

"I give you my word that my organization had nothing to do with the death of Nicky Larsen," the gangster continued in his unemotional tone. "If such an operation had been ordered, it would have been done correctly. The body would not have washed up on the shore of the Sumida River for a fisherman to discover."

I could not fathom that I was having such a conversation with a balding man in the middle of Hayama Bay. I saw a wave coming—not huge, but big enough to move me away from this creep. As the wave came, I pointed my body in a straight line for the shore. The wave carried me twenty feet closer to shore. I touched ground and saw that the gangster had body-surfed alongside me. There was no escape.

"You were saying," I said, pretending that I was completely calm and hadn't tried to run away, "that when your organization works, bodies simply disappear. I wonder if that's what happened to Nicky's friend Kunio Takahashi."

"Takahashi-san is a gifted man," the gangster said. "In my boss's opinion, he could someday be regarded as one of the nation's living treasures. We wouldn't want to lose him."

"What do you mean, lose him? Is he . . . one of you?" I asked.

"No. I was speaking out of respect for his work. He has many years of great artistic work ahead. But he is a poor young man without connections. We would certainly protect him if we could find him."

Ah, here was the reason for making contact. Looking straight into his eyes, I said, "I don't know where he is."

"I know," the gangster said sounding weary. "I was at Bojo the evening you were talking with those college kids about your search to find Kunio Takahashi. I sensed that you were holding something back from them, so I borrowed the little book you were carrying to check your information. Nothing there but addresses of your relatives and friends." He eyed me, and I got the underlying message: *I know who to hurt if you don't cooperate.*

"I'd appreciate having the address book back," I said.

"Of course. If it's all right with you, I will return it to you later. I did not carry it into the water."

"I want to ask you something. Were you watching me in the *anime* coffee shop?"

"No. What happened? If someone is bothering you, perhaps I can help."

"You must be the craziest *yakuza* on the beach." There—I'd used the word, and he seemed to smile at it. This man really was getting on my nerves. At times, he was distinctly threatening; at others, almost fatherly. I guess that's why organized-crime groups were sometimes called families.

"I'm a forty-five-year-old typical Japanese." The man raised his hands in a feigned gesture of helplessness. "I coach my son's baseball team, I give money to a home for the aged, and I clean my neighborhood graveyard once a month. I ride in a Cadillac for work, but at home all I have is a Subaru Justy. We don't all live like the guys in the movies."

"I'm not interested in your lifestyle," I said. "I want to know if there's another organized-crime group that is responsible for Nicky Larsen's death."

"No," he said flatly. "We made inquiries. That was not a

professional job. That circle on Larsen's forehead was the *Mars Girl* symbol. Nothing more."

Out of the corner of my eye, I could see someone tall and slim wading out to us. I thought I recognized the shaggy hair, now wet and flat and plastered over much of his face.

"Your boyfriend's swimming out here. I hope he's not the nervous type," the gangster said to me.

"Not really," I said, my pulse starting to race.

"Be careful what you say to him about our encounter. I wouldn't want him to believe that someone who came to help you actually harmed you instead."

"It's not what I tell Takeo that you should be worried about. It's what I tell the readers of the *Gaijin Times*."

A smile creased the gangster's face. "We're expecting some mention. That's another reason why I'm here. You wanted information. We request that you share our message that we are not responsible for that pathetic little murder. Your magazine is small, but if you report my words, the news will be picked up and carried in all the Japanese papers."

"How can I report your claim when I don't know who you are?"

"They call me the Fish. I don't have time to tell you more, and as you said, you aren't interested in my lifestyle. Ask your police lieutenant about the Fish, if you like. I'm well known." The man gave me a slight bow. Then he pulled his snorkel mask over his eyes and paddled off.

There was a slight stinging feeling on my upper thigh—a jellyfish sting, maybe. I ignored it and stared after the Fish, calmly moving through the waters, attracting no attention, a shark in the midst of unknowing bathers.

There was a great splashing sound as Takeo reached me.

"You're okay!" he said, breathing hard. "I saw through my binoculars that you were struggling for a bit, but fortunately someone was out there to help you. Who was that good Samaritan?"

"I never learned his actual name." What else could I say?

"Frankly, I'm surprised you went in that deep. You told me last time that you aren't a great swimmer."

I looked at Takeo. He hadn't realized that the man who'd saved me was the one who'd jerked me under the water. Something about the memory of the Fish's cold eyes told me not to tell him, at least not yet. I smiled faintly and said, "I was only in four and a half feet of water. My problem was a cramped foot. I'm afraid it made me panic."

"I see. Let's walk in, then, quite slowly. Whatever made you run into the water like that, anyway? I thought you would tell me what your plans were after the interview."

"I got a little overheated. And I didn't want the guys in the bar to see me go straight to you—they were a little suspicious that we might be together," I said.

"Oh, no! I can see why you did that. I would have come out after you immediately, but my sister showed up. When I saw that you were in jeopardy, I had to throw her off with an excuse about needing to cool off."

We walked out onto the sand, and Takeo picked up his binoculars, safely wrapped in a towel on the sand. He put them to his eyes and scanned the beach.

"Those thugs you were talking to earlier are still at the bar. We should go straight back to the house, but let's walk some distance apart, so they don't know we're together. When we're home, I'd like to hear what they said."

"Okay," I agreed. I did want to walk alone, so I could go over in my mind how much I could tell him. I wanted to be honest, but there was no use in giving him more information than he needed. After having met the Fish, I was fairly certain that *yakuza* had not killed Nicky. That still didn't explain the Fish's interest in Kunio Takahashi. There was something there, some connection.

29

An hour later, I had washed off the salt water and changed into a favorite sundress, long and fairly modest except for the side slits. I was sipping a glass of chilled barley tea. I should have been feeling mellow, but I wasn't. I was still trying to decide how much to tell Takeo.

My first and most natural inclination was to tell him everything: to tell him that the two men I'd spoken to in the bar were just deliverymen, but my conversation with them had been overheard by a gangster who pulled me underwater and then brought me to the surface, stating for the record that organized crime had had nothing to do with Nicky Larsen's death.

The second idea I had was to let Takeo think that the two men I'd talked to in the bar had told me the same thing. I could communicate the truth while not mentioning the Fish, per his instructions.

I'd had a strange encounter, which I'd survived. I didn't think I'd see the Fish again. I doubted I'd ever be able to recognize him with dry hair and a business suit. As far as I was concerned, the Fish was a shark who had circled me briefly and then departed forever.

The Fish was gone, and I was safely recuperating in the Kayamas' beautiful garden of moss and stones. The house was high enough that one could see the water, and the sides of the garden that edged other people's property were guarded by ancient, sculptured bushes. The fact that one could sit here and see and hear nothing of others seemed like the ultimate luxury.

My meditation in the silent garden was jarred by the sound of Natsumi Kayama's voice. I could see her through the window. She was looking rail-thin in a green one-piece suit, standing in front of her brother and demanding something. Money. She wanted to borrow fifteen thousand yen because the Korean barbecue restaurant where she was taking her friends did not accept credit cards.

"Remember, you still owe me forty thousand," Takeo said. "From two weekends ago. You said it was a Russian restaurant that didn't accept credit cards."

"I'll pay you back when I get to the cash machine and . . . oh, and I'll pick up some of those croissants you like to have for breakfast tomorrow."

"At a Korean barbecue restaurant?"

"No! I'll make a side trip to that silly place you like."

"Thanks. Come back early tonight, okay?"

"Don't tell me what to do. I'm two minutes older." Natsumi laughed cheerfully as she left. When Takeo came out, carrying his own glass of tea, he smiled at me.

"We have a nice, long evening ahead of us," he murmured.

"But you told her to come home early."

"I said it to make her annoyed enough to stay out really late. That's how my sister operates."

"Ah. Reverse psychology, my father would say."

Takeo pulled a teak chair next to the rock where I was sitting. He straddled it and leaned forward.

"You haven't told me much about your father."

"He's a psychiatrist with academic appointments and a busy side practice. I was lucky to see him one or two hours a day while I was growing up. Those hours were precious to me. I love him very much."

"We don't say love in my family."

"That's a shame." I reached out and squeezed his hand. "Well, I think that your father nevertheless has shown his respect and affection for you by giving you carte blanche with this house."

"What do you mean?" Takeo looked quizzical.

"Well, he owns the house. But I think . . . this house is all you. The way you've changed it. The way it's so open and bright."

"It's not his house." Takeo grinned at me.

"Isn't he the owner?"

"No. The house came from my mother's side, and it technically belongs to Natsumi and me. My father owns the other summer house in Hakone, the one that he likes better. It's more secluded."

"But you haven't done anything with the house until this summer?"

"That's right. This is the first opportunity I've had. First I was too young; then I was working too hard. Now I'm just a dilettante."

"Now I understand why you care about the house so much."

"No," Takeo said. "A house is just a dwelling. You're the one I care about."

Takeo's mouth touched mine, not lightly, as had been his recent habit, but with serious pressure. It felt good to be kissing like this in a garden overlooking the sea. The cicadas covered the sound of our breathing. It was all so heady.

Takeo ran his fingers over a bruise on my arm. "How much do you hurt?"

"I'm bruised but not broken," I said staunchly, taking Takeo's hand and kissing each finger. His hand was clean but rough. I imagined these fingers sliding down my body, and shivered with pleasure.

We didn't say much to each other after that. We linked hands and went inside, first to the bathroom for the essential cleansing rituals, and then into Takeo's room. He had made up his futon with a sheet so fresh that I could still see the ironing marks on it; I was touched by that, and also by the fact that he had an unopened pack of condoms hidden in an antique lacquered sweets box by the futon.

Takeo put his hand in my hair, gently pinning me to the pillow so that I couldn't move. He kissed my cheek and then my throat. When he opened my robe, he was unable to get the sash off. I was too inflamed to fuss with the tiny knot, so I just left it on.

By the time the old grandfather clock in the front hall chimed seven, we were finished. It had been less than half an hour. I was relaxed but not completely fulfilled. I'd been thinking about how close the Fish was to me—whether he knew where I was at that moment, and what I'd just done.

"What are you thinking about?" he asked, stroking the hair away from my face.

"Not much," I lied.

Takeo slid out of bed and put on his robe while facing me. He had a beautiful body—lean but not skinny. I felt a small flutter of desire, but I knew it couldn't go anywhere, not with my growing sense of dread.

"After we wash, let's call out for some sushi," Takeo said. "I'm starved."

"I am, too," I said softly, but doubted that he caught my meaning.

That night, Natsumi probably would have been pleased to see me tossing and turning next to Takeo. It hadn't seemed natural to fall asleep in each other's arms. I lay awake, listening to the tree frogs outside. After hours I heard the sound of a creaking door.

"Natsumi," Takeo said. "Finally."

I hadn't known that he couldn't sleep, either. He'd been utterly silent.

"Are you getting up to talk to her?" I asked.

"I don't think so. I'm just glad to know she made it home. I worry, you know."

Out in the hall, a man's voice spoke instead. "Where are they?"

I reached across the space for Takeo, but he wasn't there. He was already tripping over my backpack on the way to the door.

"Don't go!" I whispered. "It could be dangerous. Let's go out the window to safety."

"This way?" The man's slurred voice was oddly familiar.

"It's my house. I tell you that you can go wherever you like, in whichever room."

Takeo and I both let out our breath at the same time. The answering voice was female and whiny.

"She's brought someone home!" Takeo sounded horrified.

I sat up. "She said it was a friend."

Takeo put a cautionary hand on my arm but didn't say anything.

"You're beautiful. *Très belle*," came the voice, and Natsumi's answering giggle.

"Marcellus!" I whispered to Takeo. When he looked at me blankly, I added, "It sounds like the dancer from Senegal. Let me go out and talk to him. It's important, for my article."

"Why can't it wait until tomorrow . . . when you're dressed?" Takeo regarded my lace teddy with a dubious expression.

"He'll be gone by then," I said. "This is obviously a one-night stand. One-night stands don't linger for breakfast and conversation."

"How about a bath?" Natsumi's voice sounded thick as she spoke to Marcellus. "I'd like to scrub your back."

"The wood around the bath isn't sealed yet," Takeo muttered. "If they get it wet, it'll ruin everything."

So that was what would get him moving: the thought of his precious home renovations being ruined. I hugged my knees to my chest and watched him grab the robe that I'd tried to put on myself earlier.

"Stay here, Rei," Takeo said just before he headed out the door.

I didn't answer, because I had no intention of obeying. Instead I slipped into shorts and a T-shirt and opened the sliding window to the garden. My plan was to wait in front of the house. Marcellus would probably slip out once he was done. It was strange to think of someone I'd considered a trustworthy friend hooking up with Natsumi Kayama. I didn't like it.

The garden air was deliciously cool, and the cicadas that had croaked an early evening chorus were now in full operatic mode. The insects were almost loud enough to cover the sound of revelry on the road beyond the house, but not quite. Motorcycles roared down the lane, one after the other. *Bousouzoku*, dreaded motorcycle tribes of young toughs, drove their noisy way through many Japanese cities. It didn't surprise me that a bunch of *bousouzoku* had come to the beach. I looked at my watch, which read 3:32. My guess was that the beach bar had closed and the *bousouzoku* were heading home.

It was hard to hear what was happening inside the house with so much noise outside. I waited on the stone landing outside the front door, swatting at the mosquitoes circling me, their unexpected midnight snack. The outdoor light was on, making me all the more visible to the bloodthirsty instincts.

A loud bang startled me. Was it a motorcycle backfiring? I listened to the throbbing motorcycle engines, wondering whether in fact the gate leading to the Kayama estate was closed. But it sounded almost as if some of the motorcycles had entered the drive. I walked down the drive, striding as confidently as I could, intent on appearing like the lady of the house. As I passed the bank of hydrangea bushes that hugged the bend in the stone road, I caught the glare of headlights. My worst fears were realized. Natsumi had left the gate open upon her return, and a line of motorcycles was roaring in, spraying the precious river pebbles every which way.

The drivers wore helmets with face shields, so I couldn't see them as I faced them, and that made it all the worse. I wasn't standing in their path, but in the middle of the hydrangeas. They wouldn't run off the road into bushes, I reasoned. They wouldn't want to scratch their big, shiny cycles.

The first driver roared up to the front of the house and executed a sharp turn, heading toward the gate. Two more followed him, but a third motorcyclist turned the other way, roaring across the lawn toward the moss garden.

Takeo had told me how long it took to grow moss, and how even a human footstep could hurt it beyond belief. Should I defend the moss garden? As I struggled to get up the courage, the motorcycle rider hurled a brown package into the center of the velvety green.

30

Could it be an explosive? I jumped out of my hiding place and sprinted toward the house. I'd have to enter through the front to avoid the moss garden with its package. I didn't even know whether Natsumi had left the front door unlocked or if I could reach it before the motorcycle gang. As I ran past the parked line of motorcycles, someone called to me, rather drunkenly, "Hey, big sister!"

I faked a smile and ran all the faster. I was getting close to the stone steps leading to the front door. I was ten feet away from Takeo's front door when it slid open. A huge dark figure clad only in a shower cap and towel stepped out.

"Marcellus, watch out!" I called in English.

But Marcellus stood firm with his legs planted widely on the front step. Mirrored sunglasses shielded his eyes, and in fact, they made him look pretty scary. He was a powerfully built man, with the kind of biceps and pectorals that come from heavy lifting.

"What the 'eck is goin' on?" Marcellus bellowed in his stagy accent, a perfect blending of France-via-Senegal-via-California.

The first rider in line shouted something to his minions and revved his engine ominously. This was going to be a disaster. Ten men in leather and helmets against one man in a towel.

But to my shock, the first motorcycle rider drove forward, executed a wheelie turn, and roared back down the driveway to the gate. The other motorcyclists made similar turns, and within two minutes, all had left, spraying pebbles everywhere and leaving a horrible smell of gasoline exhaust.

I tottered up the steps to Marcellus. "I don't know how you knew what to say, but it worked. Thank God."

"Everywhere I go in this country, men are afraid of me. I just have to show my face." He sounded sad, and I reached out to squeeze his hand.

"Where have you been?" Takeo came out of the entrance hall holding a teapot. He was still clad in a bathrobe over pajama pants. He looked like somebody's father, and he was frowning at the sight of me holding Marcellus's hand.

"There's no time for tea," I said to Takeo. "There might be an explosive in the moss garden. We've got to evacuate."

"Are you sure? I'll turn on the garden lights and see what's there." Takeo went back into the house with the teapot and carefully placed it on a trivet, making me seethe with impatience. Then he played around with a panel of light switches in the entryway. I looked out the main door and, lo and behold, soft lights went on all over the garden, including the mossy patch where the motorcyclist had tossed the unknown object.

"Now all I have to do is get a good, safe view. I can do that from the roof." He took his bird-watching binoculars from the entryway table. "This will be handy. Rei, why don't you stand by with the cordless telephone in case we need to call the police?"

"You can't call the police! Father will hear about it from the neighbors." Natsumi, dressed in a sheer pink baby-doll nightie, had come into the entry hall, rubbing her eyes as if she had been asleep for ages and not just waltzed home with Marcellus twenty minutes prior. The nighttime raid had metamorphosed into a rather bizarre pajama party.

Takeo stuck his feet in some rubber gardening boots and tromped around to the side of the house overlooking the moss garden. The aluminum ladder had been folded and left lying on some stones; together we extended it so the top reached the house's tiled roof, about twenty-five feet above the ground. I was glad it wasn't a two-story house. Takeo climbed as confidently as the firemen doing their exhibition ladder tricks at my neighborhood festival each year, but I was still nervous.

"I've got something that looks like a brown envelope. Let me focus, and I'll tell you what it looks like." Takeo tinkered with the binoculars and said after a few seconds, "I can see it clearly. It's a small package that's stapled closed."

"A package? How silly to get everyone out of bed for it. Rei, just go and pick it up if you're so worried," Natsumi ordered.

"There still might be danger. I'll check it for you," Marcellus volunteered, hips swaying as he set off. You could take the man out of the dance club, but you couldn't take the dance club out of the man.

"Don't get hurt," Natsumi called tenderly after him. She didn't give a damn if my hand was blown off, but she didn't want the stranger she'd picked up to suffer.

"So, has Marcellus told you about his job?" I asked her, keeping my expression bland.

"He did not need to say anything. It doesn't matter one bit, because I'm not looking for a provider, like some I can think of."

If she knew how awkward things were for Takeo and me, she'd be elated. I ignored her smirk and kept my eyes on the dark garden. Marcellus had slipped out of my view, and that made me anxious. I wondered what might be in the package. A poison gas capsule. A snake. I thought of a few more horrible possibilities.

But within a few seconds Marcellus was back, holding the package carefully in both of his hands. He was studying it, so engrossed that he bumped into my favorite rock. As Marcellus pitched forward, his tiny towel slipped, too.

Natsumi screamed at me, "Don't look at what you shouldn't!"

"I've seen it before," I snapped at Natsumi, and her face fell. Too late I thought of Takeo on the roof, taking in every word. I glanced up at him, and he glowered.

"No problem, no problem," Marcellus said, rising and retying his towel without any embarrassment.

Takeo practically slid down the ladder, he was moving so fast. "Let me look at the package. There's still a chance of danger."

Marcellus waved the document at me and said, "It's for you. Your name is on the envelope!"

"How do you even know her name?" Natsumi demanded.

"You explain, if you like," I said to Marcellus. He didn't.

"I think we should call the bomb squad before you open it," Takeo said.

"Why such a change in attitude?" I asked.

"There are probably half a dozen bomb safety experts within a two-minute drive. With the emperor's villa practically next door, there is always a team on hand, with dogs, in the event of any disturbance."

I looked at the envelope, which Marcellus had placed on the house's doorstep. The thickness of it suggested there was a small book inside. I thought about the things that were supposed to give evidence of a letter bomb—oil leaking from a corner, smudges of gunpowder—and didn't see them.

True, my name was not written by hand, but made up of pasted-on letters that had been cut from a magazine. The *S* and *a* used in my surname, Shimura, looked familiar.

"Will you bring a copy of *Showa Story* to me?" I asked Takeo.

"Okay, but please think more about the bomb squad," he said.

When he came out, I realized that my suspicion had proved correct. The *S* and *a* had been cut out of a *Showa Story* masthead.

"It's extremely doubtful that cartoonists would know how to make a bomb," I said, pointing out the lettering to Takeo. Marcellus and Natsumi weren't around to hear; they had drifted away to argue in the moss garden.

"So you're going to open it." Takeo sighed heavily. "Can I at least suggest this as a safety precaution?" He handed me a pair of gardening gloves and a small, sicklelike instrument that he normally used for weeding. I put on the gloves and used the sickle to tear open the envelope edge.

I recognized the worn green cover immediately. It was my address book.

Takeo stared at it. "That looks familiar. I feel as if I've seen it somewhere."

"Yes. It's my address book."

"The one I was supposed to retrieve from Bojo?"

"That's right." I paged through the book, stopping at page one, where my information was listed—name, fax number, address—in case it was lost. With all that, the Fish had chosen to have the book brought in a spectacular fashion to Takeo's house. He was flipping his tail at me, or something.

"I wonder if Marcellus should see this," I mused.

"Why? Of all the people in the world to confide in, why are you choosing Natsumi's fling?"

"Marcellus has a connection. He danced in the same bar as Nicky."

"That friend of Natsumi's is . . . a dancer?" Takeo looked completely confused.

I nodded.

Takeo exhaled. "Oh. Now I understand why you said you'd seen his, um, body."

"Exactly." I was relieved that I didn't have to defend myself. "When I went looking for the *Showa Story* office, that address

turned out to be a ladies-only nightclub. Marcellus was performing."

"I shouldn't care about such things." Takeo sounded pen-
sive. "But somehow, I'd rather my sister's boyfriend be a
house painter or taxi driver than a person who takes off his
clothing in front of others."

"The pay for dancers is good," I pointed out. "I think it's
actually more than you or I earn. But the conditions aren't
pleasant." I thought about Chiyo's dragon-lady nails tapping
the bar impatiently and her shouting at Nicky to clean up
spilled drinks. And later, Chiyo's lack of worry about Nicky's
disappearance—just a quick, angry assumption that he had
gone AWOL to work at another bar.

We settled down at the low walnut tea table in the living
room. As I continued to page through the book, a photograph
fell out. It was of Takeo's Range Rover, easily identified by the
license plates.

"So that's how the motorcycle gang got in tonight," I said.
"They'd spied on you earlier, and figured out the code."

"When I drove back from the tile shop to the house last
Saturday, some men were standing alongside the road with a
variety of cameras. They were dressed in black leather—I
remember thinking that they were probably a magazine crew
from the city."

I pondered the photograph until Marcellus and Natsumi
trooped into the room. They were holding hands and had
obviously made up, given that Natsumi was giggling.
Marcellus was wearing the cotton *yukata* that I'd worn earlier
and left hanging in the bathroom.

"And when you saw those bad men . . . they ran right
away!" Natsumi exclaimed to Marcellus. "Why do you think
that was?"

"There is a terror of people from different cultures,"
Marcellus said.

"I have no terror. Only delight." Natsumi's face coquettishly vanished for a moment behind her smooth curtain of hair. She shook her hair back and smiled up at Marcellus, and I looked at Takeo.

He seemed tense, and I wondered if it was because of more than the fact his sister was about to go to bed with a male dancer. Finding out that he'd been stalked by gangsters must have been at least part of the problem. I wondered if I should have told him about the Fish. But I didn't want to bring that up now, not in front of Marcellus and Natsumi. I had a few questions for them first.

31

"Where were you last Saturday?" I addressed my question to Natsumi, but to my surprise, Marcellus answered.

"I was dancing at the club. It's my usual Saturday night plan. I'm here tonight only because I have one evening per week free."

"That's when we met. Last Saturday night." Natsumi's eyes glittered.

So Marcellus and Natsumi had a new, but pre-existing relationship. They'd probably made plans for a weekend beach rendezvous, and Takeo's showing up with me had almost foiled their plan. This was interesting information on its own, but I had other business to straighten out first.

"Natsumi, last Saturday, were you visiting here in Hayama? Did you see any men in black leather?"

Natsumi answered, "No. As I said earlier, this is my first trip to the country in ages. I'm going to my room now. It's very late."

"I can't speak for Rei, but I'm not going to bed," Takeo said coldly. "In case you hadn't noticed, our property was invaded. It's my duty to stay awake and see nobody comes back."

"I'll stay up with you," I said.

"How paranoid you are!" Natsumi rolled her eyes. "Now they've delivered their envelope, they're done. Isn't that what you told me, Marcellus-chan?"

I stared at Marcellus, who was looking uncomfortable in his tiny robe. He said in a small voice that did not at all befit his physique, "I don't know about these men in particular, but I think that's how gangsters work. I have witnessed some rather dramatic deliveries of letters and such in my work."

"I'd like to hear about that," Takeo said. "Could you sit down for just a second and tell us about it?"

Marcellus looked even more nervous. "Will you tell me what was in the envelope first?"

"I'm afraid it's confidential," Takeo said.

"My address book," I said at the same time.

Takeo sighed heavily.

I said to him, "Marcellus was brave enough to pick up the package. He deserves to know what's in it."

"So you are saying that the motorcycle gang delivered something that belongs to you, Rei?" Marcellus asked.

"Aren't you coming to the room?" Natsumi asked pointedly.

"Later, *chérie*. I want to learn the reason for this trouble."

"Well, I'm too tired for all this! I'm going to be relaxing in the bedroom," Natsumi announced.

When Marcellus didn't respond, she made an elaborate sighing sound almost identical to Takeo's before slamming out of the room. You could tell, for once, that they were twins.

Takeo opened the doors of an antique paulownia cabinet. He pulled out a bottle of sake and three small glasses.

"No alcohol for me." Marcellus screwed up his handsome, beaky nose. "Alcohol dehydrates. It is terrible for my skin."

"I'll take it," I said. I needed something to aid me in unwinding after the fright of the motorcycle gangsters. I went to the kitchen to get a glass of mineral water for Marcellus and ice cubes for Takeo's and my glasses. Sake was usually served warm, but I'd developed a taste for it over ice, especially in the summer heat.

Sipping the powerful, cool fluid, I asked Marcellus, "Would you tell me about the gangsters you've seen at the bar? Did they look like everyday toughs, or were they more . . . regular?" I asked, thinking of the Fish.

"The tough-looking ones come by to collect money every month, but it was not that way in the beginning. A middle-aged gentleman in a suit was the first one to come."

"What time of day? Were the dancers around?" I asked.

"Nicky wasn't there, if that's what you are thinking. It was early one afternoon. I had duty at the door that day, so I saw him go in. I was curious what business a straight-looking salaryman would have with the place—actually, I suspected that he might be a husband of one of our patrons. An angry husband." Marcellus smiled ruefully. "I was wrong. What I overheard was just business talk."

"Can you remember the conversation?" Takeo asked.

"Just what I heard, and to be honest, understanding men's Japanese is more difficult for me than women's."

"What do you mean?" Takeo said. "You seem to understand me."

"Regular Japanese men, in everyday conversation, speak more roughly," I explained to Takeo. "They use verb forms that foreigners don't learn right away in language classes."

"I agree, Rei-san. And for me, it is very difficult because while we are in the bar, we are encouraged to speak very politely to women, and that becomes our standard form of Japanese. Anyway, I was listening as carefully as I could, and what I believe the man was talking about was taxes. He said that Chiyo's business made money that she didn't report to the government."

"Is that true?" I asked.

"Well, we boys are allowed to keep the tips the ladies give us. And there's a back room where, well, sometimes very private things happen. We give Chiyo half of what the girls give us. I don't think she'd declare that money to the government . . . how would she explain it?"

"I see the problem." I paused. "Nicky liked working in the back room, didn't he?"

Marcellus raised his eyebrows. "Very much so. He was very happy that he could get paid for pleasure. I refused to do it. Chiyo said that was okay with her. She understood."

"Let's get back to the gangsters," Takeo said tersely. The conversation's abrupt veering into matters of male sexuality was probably too much for him.

"What more can I say?" Marcellus sighed heavily. "Chiyo made an agreement to pay him. I think that many people in the floating world pay these fees."

The floating world. I hadn't heard that expression in a while. It was a historic term used to talk about the business of courtesans, their customers, and the middlemen who put them together. I supposed that Marcellus and other hosts and hostesses were the closest thing left to courtesans.

"Lots of people in Japan have had problems with *yakuza*," Takeo said. "We've had to turn them away from the Kayama School."

"Are you talking about the school where your sister will become the chief executive officer?" Marcellus asked.

"You haven't wasted time finding out what she's worth, have you?" Takeo sounded as if his worst fears had come to bear fruit.

"She told me right away," Marcellus said. "In fact, it was a group of lady teachers from your family's flower school who came for a celebration last Saturday."

"What trouble have the Kayamas had with organized crime?" I asked, trying to get back on track.

"During my grandfather's and father's time, the *yakuza* bosses have come calling, trying to start a 'partnership,' as they called it, infusing money into the school in exchange for a share of the profits. Even when times were very hard, right after the Second World War, my family refused the help. As punishment, they kidnapped one of my great-aunts."

"How terrible," I said.

"My grandfather refused to pay the ransom. He would have paid if the ransom had been just cash. But the *yakuza* asked again for status as a business partner. So he couldn't. And my great-aunt suffered."

I couldn't bring myself to ask Takeo what happened. He took a sip of sake and said, "The *yakuza* raped her. The family arranged for her to take a cure in Switzerland, but there was a problem with her transit there during wartime, and she died during the trip. Some of my relatives say it was an accident, but my father thinks she committed suicide."

"Revenge," Marcellus murmured. "Perhaps our Nicky was killed in retaliation for something Chiyo-san did?"

"Yes, maybe she stopped paying them protection money, and the *yakuza* sent her a message by killing a dancer!" I was so excited that I knocked my sake glass sideways.

Takeo caught it and said, "Hold on. You've always had the theory that the killing was related to the comic book group. If you lose that, you've lost your story."

I thought that Takeo had a point. If there was no comic connection, there was no money coming in for me from the *Gaijin Times*. Did that matter, though, in the context of the terrible things that had happened? The sinister motorcyclists might have been given the simple job of delivering photos, but by coming onto Kayama land, they had invaded a place I thought would be safe. Similarly, the story Takeo had told about his great-aunt had also stolen something precious from me. For so long, I'd studied Japanese antiques and old-fashioned culture;

this was the reason that I'd admired the *Showa Story* series. Now the comic book was illustrating rape in graphic detail, and I'd learned that Takeo's grandfather had kept his school pure at a terrible human cost.

"It is the truth that matters," Marcellus said softly. "Not any story."

"You're right," Takeo and I both said in unison, but the damage had been done. I'd selfishly voiced my desire to write something that would earn me money, and that had scared Marcellus into standing up, belting his *yukata* a little tighter, and storming off down the hall to Natsumi's room.

I ran after him and grabbed the sleeve of his robe. He stopped.

"What?" He sounded exasperated.

"Why are you sleeping with Natsumi?" I asked.

"You'll put it in your article." Marcellus pulled away.

"No, I promise I won't. I just need to know, as your friend."

"The same reason you're with the brother, *chérie*. Economic survival."

I flushed. "That's not true!"

"Isn't it?" Marcellus sighed. "Well, how lucky you are. The fact is, if I make dates with women, my salary doubles. But after a night like this one, I may just stick to my regular profession."

"Good night," I said softly, and he walked off. I'd thought he had gone in to sleep with her, but a few minutes later, there was a gliding sound. I figured out he'd made good on his word about returning to his regular profession.

"There's something you left out," Takeo said as we settled down on his futon. It was 6 A.M., and we both doubted the *bousouzoku* would come back at such an early hour.

"I can barely think at this point. Can we talk about it tomorrow?" I asked, yawning.

"It *is* tomorrow. I want to know more about the gangster

who spoke to you. The one who said he wasn't involved in Nicky's death."

They say they aren't involved, but with the performance we witnessed tonight, who knows?"

"Now you say *they*, but before you said *he*. I'm confused. You see, you were talking earlier to two men in the bar, two men who I assumed were the gangsters who provided this information. Now you're talking about one man. Was he even at that table?"

"I was told not to say anything to you directly right now."

"You are keeping something from me!" Takeo exclaimed.

"I think . . . the idea was that you would get hotheaded and seek revenge. I was in a semidangerous situation, you see."

Takeo stared at me. "You mean to say that when you were struggling in the water, it had something to do with the *yakuza*?"

"Yes," I confessed. "A gangster pulled me underwater, but that was just to get my attention. After he stood me up, we talked for a few minutes. It ended with him saying that he'd return my address book, which he'd taken from the bar. I had no idea he'd send it to your house with *bousouzoku*."

"I looked through my binoculars." Takeo sounded frustrated. "All I saw was you having a conversation with a completely ordinary-looking man. I mean, I thought he might be trying to make a date with you, but I didn't suspect him of anything else."

"He's a family man. He was strictly business. He knew what information that I was after, and he wanted to make clear that he had nothing to do with Nicky's death. He even said I could quote him in the article."

"But not to tell me?"

"No. I guess he didn't want a scene on the beach."

"How sensitive," Takeo said, grimacing. "Why don't you think he killed Nicky? He sounds like the most qualified person to do it, if you ask me."

I shook my head. "I believe him. He told me he was disgusted with the lack of professionalism in that execution. He would have done it differently."

"This is getting scary, Rei."

"I agree." I paused. "So does this mean we stay up longer?"

"You sleep," Takeo said. "You've got to be at the convention in two hours. I don't."

32

I dragged myself from the futon at ten to eight that morning. To my surprise, Natsumi was awake and eating croissants with her brother. As I'd thought, Marcellus had not stayed the night, but left shortly after he was done talking with us. Natsumi told us both that this was the last time she'd allow us to speak to any of her boyfriends, because obviously we were saying bad things about her that made them want to run.

Takeo raked his hand through his hair and sighed; after a night without sleep, he looked like death warmed over.

I drank a small cup of strong coffee that Takeo had made, then left to take the bus to Zushi, since I insisted that Takeo was too tired to drive me. It was only a fifteen-minute ride to the shining Zushi Convention Center, which bore the engraved phrase ESTABLISHED FOR YOU IN 1999. The center had a glossy edge, but the casually dressed crowd—in blue jeans and T-shirts and character costumes—made the place seem considerably more casual. Entering the packed hall, I felt as if I were slightly drunk. The colorful, costumed conventioneers seemed to have come straight out of a Technicolor dream. I was waiting behind three people dressed up as hedgehogs—popular characters in some comic series, I guessed—and calculated it might take half an hour to reach the cashier, and then another hour to reach the registration desk.

A middle-aged man with a scowl who looked oddly familiar strolled past to the right. I saw him pass by my direction two minutes later with a program and registration packet. He'd gotten everything he needed without standing in line, and that was enough to set me off.

"Excuse me," I called out to him. "Is there a reason you were able to receive your materials while the rest of us have to wait in line?"

"I'm with the press. " He tugged at a plastic identification card hanging on a chain around his neck.

"Oh." I said, belatedly recognizing him from the tabloid TV program *News to You*. He was twenty feet past me by the time I'd finished speaking, during which time I reasoned that since I was on assignment for the *Gaijin Times,* I was every bit as much of a journalist as he was. I smoothed my jeans, as if that could make them look a bit more presentable, and headed off to the roped-off zone from where he'd appeared.

I had to show my Rei Shimura Antiques business card, accompanied by explanations about my moonlighting job, to a young Japanese man padded to look like a character in a sumo wrestling series. There were three other staffers behind him, similarly dressed in bizarre costumes, who seemed occupied with poring over the program, deciding which booth to hit first.

"Any cameras?" the sumo wrestler asked me.

"Of course."

"May I see?"

"Sure." I pulled out my trusty Polaroid. The wrestler swept it out of my hands and into what looked like a small safe.

"Cameras are banned from this convention." He gave me a plastic claim check that I stared at in disbelief. "You may retrieve your camera before going home, and please don't forget about it! Any equipment left here after the convention closes will be given to charity."

"But our magazine photographer is coming! Toshi Ueda is his name—"

"Oh, yes," an extraterrestrial helper said. "He came, and when we offered to confiscate his camera, he decided to leave the convention."

So I was all alone. This story was self-immolating. Feeling quite panicky, I said, "This convention is supposed to celebrate the visual arts. How can I do that without a camera?"

His voice turned chilly. "Have you ever attended one of our conventions before?"

"No, and I'm really hoping to bring it to the attention of our readers."

"We don't need publicity. If you had been here two years ago, you would have heard how some terrible people took photos of our innocent fans and used computer technology to combine those pictures with pornographic images. Since then, cameras have been forbidden."

"If you care so much about your fans, you really shouldn't let them wait in line so long," I chided. "You could have a couple more of your workers taking admissions instead of reading catalogs."

"Which publication did you say you worked for again?" The young man rose, and I realized that maybe it wasn't padding underneath his kimono. He was as hefty as any American bar bouncer.

"Ah, thank you very much." I darted off with my program, leaving him to deal with a reporter for the *Hiragana Times*. Good God, I was behaving irrationally. I wasn't sure whether to chalk it up to lack of sleep.

The convention hall was shaped like an L and filled with a jumble of brightly colored *manga* displays. Music blared from speakers overhead, music that came from the animated television shows that the amateur artists used as their inspiration. What a strange world, I marveled, where one could see a grown man dressed like a diapered baby bowing to a shiny silver robot! It really was a shame that no cameras were allowed. I dragged my eyes away from the distractions and began searching for the *Showa Story* table. It should be at the bend of the L, according to the number assigned in the program.

When I saw an attractive young woman in a blue leotard with a flowing silver cape decorated with the planet Mars, I decided it would be clever to tail her—perhaps she was headed for the *Showa Story* table. As I traveled deeper into the convention hall, the crowds grew so thick that I couldn't even see the tables; all that was visible were flashes of colorful posters hanging behind their tables.

Mars Girl stopped frequently to look at the comic books on various tables. She was shopping around, when I had hoped she would make a beeline to the *Showa Story* table. I realized that we'd turned the corner in the L and completely missed the area where the *Showa Story* table was supposed to be.

Maybe she wasn't stopping there because she had already seen it. I decided to make an overture. I approached her left ear, which was decorated with a delicate pearl stud earring. How funny: a conventional good-girl earring on an animation fan. Well, it did look as if many of the fans were middle-class young women. I spoke softly into her ear. "Excuse me, have you been to the *Showa Story* table yet?"

She jerked her head away and attempted to dive into the crowd. Normally I wouldn't have gone after her, but I'd seen her face.

Heavy makeup couldn't disguise the fact that the Mars Girl I'd been chasing was Rika.

33

"Oh, great! You're here, too!" Rika started to prattle but stopped when I grabbed her upper arm hard.

"This convention was my assignment. Why are you here? Is Alec here also?"

"No, he is not here. I'm sorry that you're jealous of our love, Rei-san."

"Jealous?" I caught my breath. "No. What I feel is embarrassment for you. Did he force you into it? You really could complain."

"I started the thing," Rika said coolly. "And he doesn't know I'm here. I decided at the very last minute to come and help you out."

"At the very last minute . . . dressed like that?" I gestured toward her regalia.

"Costumes are on sale in the next room—do you want one? I've been here for two hours already, so I've gotten the layout. I've even done some interviews." She briefly pulled her Palm Pilot out of a handbag she had strapped across her body underneath the cape.

"Did you know that Toshi had to leave because the Comiko organizers don't allow photographers?"

"I didn't know," Rika said. "Oh, my goodness, now I remember something. Some people costumed like hedgehogs were trying to take a camera away from a young man in blue jeans. I didn't look closely, but now I think about it, the boy had a ponytail, just like our Toshi."

"This convention is turning out to be a real headache," I grumbled. I knew that my headache was the result of my nighttime activities. I wasn't going to tell Rika how poorly I felt. I didn't believe that her appearance at the convention was spur-of-the-moment. The question was whether she just wanted to take over reporting the story, or if she had another, secret agenda.

"So you've been to the *Showa Story* table already?" I asked.

"Yes. I've got plenty of stuff."

"Where is it?"

"Right here." She patted her Palm Pilot.

"Oh, you're talking about where you're storing your notes. I was asking about the location of the table."

"Oh, I haven't been there yet. It's supposed to be somewhere in the middle." She waved her hand vaguely.

"You didn't try to find it?"

"I was on my way, actually. It's just that my time has been taken up at the costume booth. I did a lot of interviews there with people who call themselves *cos-play*. Nicky was in *cos-play* when he died."

Again I didn't quite believe her. I nodded and said, "Well, I'll look some more for the table. If I get close enough to the wall, I may get a glimpse of it." I plunged into the throng, Rika continuing to hover at my side.

"You must be careful, Rei-san. Careful for your health."

"The poster ahead, six to the right—doesn't that look like Mars Girl?"

"No, it's from the *Space Boy* series. Another series, sorry."

We probably walked only fifty feet, but because of the flurries of girls in our path, it seemed longer. I thought I blended

well with the crowd, since more than half of the fans were
young women—high-school- and college-age. Then I remembered that I wasn't in college anymore. Rika was the one who
fit in.

I cast a resentful look over my shoulder, and she smiled
back at me.

"We'll find them, Rei-san. Don't be nervous."

I checked my program one final time. The *Showa Story* booth
was supposed to be between the tables devoted to *Rainbow
Moon* and *Hedgehog*. I knew I'd passed the hedgehogs. I told
Rika, and we reversed direction and got back to the two tables
in question. The table between them was filled with mounds
of both comic books.

"Isn't *Showa Story* supposed to be here?" I asked.

"Cancellation," a hedgehog of ambiguous gender said
cheerfully. "We're using the space for extra storage. Kunio told
us it was okay."

"So you see, I didn't need to find the table at all!" Rika
sounded almost delighted. "We'll go back to field reporting."

"Good idea," I said quickly. "Why don't we meet up in an
hour by the press table?"

I waved her off, and when she was out of earshot I leaned in
toward the hedgehog.

"What's Kunio doing at the convention if he isn't going to
have the table?"

"I didn't ask that," the hedgehog answered. "I must say, it
was a nice surprise to get the extra space. Have you read
Hedgehog? We're spoofing *Doraemon*. Change of animal but all
the same fun."

"How long ago did he talk to you?"

"Just half an hour ago. He said the tragedy with Nicky had
led him to cancel the table, and he was pretty annoyed the
convention organizers wouldn't give him his money back."

"Is he in a Mars Girl costume?"

"No, he is wearing an old Japanese Imperial Navy uniform." I must have looked shocked, because Hedgehog added, "He said there's a character in one of the stories . . . an officer who sends Mars Girl to a house of ill repute."

"I know that story," I said faintly.

"If you need to speak to Kunio-san, you can surely ask Seiko Hattori where he is. She's running around dressed up like a dog."

"Excuse me, do you have any volume two for sale?" A customer cut into our conversation, and the hedgehog immediately turned away from me.

"We certainly do. Each copy is six hundred yen, but if you buy four, it goes down to five hundred yen apiece."

I'd heard what I needed to know. I stumbled back into the maelstrom of animation fans. I wondered if any of the interviews Rika had done were with the Showa Story circle members. I doubted it. She had probably spent the time trying on costumes.

I checked my program to find the location of the costume shop, and made my way to it through the ninjas and rabbits and schoolgirls. A couple of clothing racks were crammed with costumes. A lot of them looked previously worn, especially the school uniforms, which had rather staggering prices.

"Fetishists want those," the costume shop's manager told me. She wasn't in costume, just black leggings and a T-shirt.

"Do you take credit cards?" I hoped that I would be able to charge whichever costume I chose to the *Gaijin Times*.

"Cash only. Mmm, which series do you like?"

"I just want something to cover me up. The face, definitely," I said.

The manager pursed her lips. "I'd prefer if you chose a costume for different reasons. Choose a series that you like. That's what most people do."

I pasted on a phony smile. "I like *Showa Story*, but there's already a Mars Girl walking around and I don't want to look the same."

"Is that so?"

"Yes, you sold her the costume."

The manager shook her head. "No, that cannot be. I only brought one Mars Girl costume and it hasn't sold yet."

I looked at the costume: a scoop-necked blue unitard. Rika had been wearing a turtleneck costume in the same color. Both costumes had silver capes.

In a way, I was sorry to have discovered that Rika had lied to me about the level of planning that had gone into her appearance at the convention. I'd suspected her, sure. But now I knew for certain that she was deceptive.

"Well, what do you think?" the manager asked, waving the costume in my face.

"Is there a—a mask or something?" I was desperate for cover.

"The men who dress up as Mars Girl have to apply special makeup, sure, but since you are a lady, you don't have a problem! There is no need for a mask," the woman said cheerfully.

"I think I'd rather be a cat." A fuzzy blue cat costume on the rack included a head.

The woman gave a long look at me and shook her head. At last she said, "You don't really like cats."

"How do you know that?" I was irate. What kind of a convention was this—animated psychics?

"There's no crossover between *Kittie Pie* fans and *Showa Story*. *Showa Story* is a violent, kinky series. *Kittie Pie* is very sweet. You cannot enjoy both types of comic. In my experience with *doujinshi* people, I have never seen it."

"Well," I said, switching to English, "I'm a foreigner. We are open-minded."

The woman looked at me hard as if to ascertain I was the real thing, and I took a look at the price tag for the Kittie Pie costume. It was about $150. It might not really be worth fighting to buy such an expensive piece of fluffy acrylic that I'd never wear again.

"Take the Mars Girl costume," the woman repeated. "It's half the price of the Kittie Pie outfit, and you'll be safe in it."

"What do you mean, safe?" A chill ran down my back. Did she know the whole story?

"It's a safe buy. It will fit you, and if you really want to change your look, I can give you a discount coupon for hair and makeup at Power Princess Spa. They've got a booth here, you know. How about it?" the woman coaxed. "You can try it on behind the curtain."

"Okay." I disappeared behind a gaudy lamé curtain. I didn't have time to dither about—I wanted to get in drag as fast as possible. Did it count as drag if I was masquerading as a same-sex alien?

The unitard was so tight you could practically see through to the rice balls I'd eaten for breakfast. The cape barely brushed over my clearly visible panty lines. I was a walking fashion violation, down to my grimy pair of Asics running shoes.

"*Suteki!*" the costume saleswoman said, telling me I was cute, when I stepped out.

I shrugged, not believing her. The only thing I could hope for was salvation through makeup.

It was just my luck that of the two makeup and hair artists working, one was Miss Kumiko.

"Shimura-san, waxing is not possible today." She looked disapproving when she saw me.

"Actually, I just need makeup." Embarrassed that a roving group of Pocket Monsters had overheard, I handed her the discount coupon showing what I wanted.

"Oh. By the way, how was the beauty treatment conducted at our Hibiya salon? Are you still free of excess hair?" Miss Kumiko said loudly.

"Fine. But I'm really in the market for artificial hair. Can we talk about that?"

Grudgingly Miss Kumiko rented me a lavender wig that swooshed all the way to my waist. She painted my face an unearthly shade of pink that camouflaged my bruise completely. When the garish eyeliner and a rosebud mouth were drawn on, I didn't look like myself anymore. I looked like Mars Girl. No, I realized with a shudder, I looked a lot like dead Nicky dressed up as Mars Girl. My American nose and cheekbones were more akin to his than I'd thought.

I paid 2,500 yen to Miss Kumiko and made a second entrance into the main hall. Things seemed different now that I was in drag. Strangers smiled as if we were friends. One young man and two women friends in Mars Girl outfits stopped to chat. The man complimented me on my shoes, which made me laugh. I asked if they'd seen Seiko in her dog costume or Kunio in his vintage Japanese military costume.

"Well, there's a guy dressed in a blue uniform in the next room," the young man said. "I think I saw him examining the different *doujinshi* tables."

"Was he very good-looking?" I asked.

The young man grinned. "I don't know—he's not my type. I guess you could say so."

That was good enough for me. I wove my way back into the other room, searching desperately for a glimpse of uniform that wasn't schoolgirl or schoolboy.

At last I saw a well-built man's back covered by a pressed navy blue jacket. Beneath it were matching pants and shiny black shoes. On the head, I saw an officer's hat trimmed with braid. This view from the back didn't look exactly like the military uniforms drawn in *Showa Story*, but then again, the Mars Girl costume I was wearing wasn't perfect.

As I drew closer, it was clear that the uniformed man was chatting with a fan dressed in a Mars Girl uniform. I couldn't make out the conversation, but waited for it to end, which it did with the man slipping the girl a business card. *Very smooth, Kunio,* I thought.

The man turned around, and I saw in an instant that I'd been wrong. The man wasn't Kunio. He was Lieutenant Hata, and the blue uniform that I'd assumed was military turned out to be police.

34

Lieutenant Hata nodded at me, and his eyes eagerly scoped my costume. I realized then that he couldn't see through my makeup to the old Rei Shimura he'd been trying to pin down for a police interview.

I nodded back, and moved on quickly.

"Um, miss," he called after me. "Could I speak to you a moment? I'm looking for someone who might be a friend of yours."

"Oh?" I said noncommittally. The fewer Japanese words I spoke, the more I'd come off like a native.

"She's called Rei Shimura. A Japanese-American."

"Can't hear through this wig," I said loudly, nodding at him again before plunging into the crowd. I was shaking as I moved through the room. What a close call. It was terrifying to realize that Lieutenant Hata was looking specifically for me— did this mean I was now a suspect? Even if he just wanted to take me into custody for questioning about the others I'd interviewed, it could last for days. The police had a right to hold people for questioning for up to ten days.

I slunk down the hall, glad for the huge crowds, as well as the fact that there were more Mars Girls around for Lieutenant

Hata to detain. As I neared the press check-in table, I saw Rika standing there patiently, her Palm Pilot tucked against her flat stomach like a talisman of fertility.

"Hilarious!" she squealed when she caught sight of my costume.

I didn't respond to her left-handed compliment. I asked, "Did you find Kunio?"

"No, but I think I found some of his fans. Two fans dressed just like us, as Mars Girl, but they refused to do an interview. Maybe it's because they're members of the circle," she added darkly.

"Doubtful," I said. "The only living members of the circle are wearing dog and military costumes. Which brings up a question I have about your costume. You didn't buy it here. You purchased it earlier. You'd planned to come to this convention from the very beginning, hadn't you?"

Rika's face flushed. "Alec suggested it would be a good idea."

"So he's the one you're loyal to. Tell me, how far would you go for him?"

Rika didn't move. She'd turned into a perfect statue.

"It's very interesting how you turned up here, just as you turned up at my apartment the day after I'd been attacked."

The statue's lips moved. "What do you mean, attacked? You said that you'd had an accident."

I stared at her and said, "I'm on to you."

"What nonsense is that, Rei-san? You are not on me, you are across from me. If my English is becoming better than yours, clearly you are confused. Please take a rest somewhere. I'll help you."

Anyone listening to the conversation would think that Rika was engaging in typical Japanese oversolicitousness.

"There's too much to do," I said angrily. "We should split up and keep working. We've got no photos, no interviews with the artists, nothing. This is just a big washout."

"Very well," Rika said, and gave an angry little half bow before stalking off.

The fight with Rika—if you could call my heated accusations and her strained responses a fight—had infused me with a strange energy. I slammed down a Pocari Sweat and began to cruise the halls. I tried to think like an insider. Why might the members of a *doujinshi* circle come to an *manga* convention if not to sell their own comics?

They might have come to find someone. The thought came to me as I watched, ten feet away from me, a young man in jeans bow to another young man and then hand him a business card. Conventions were places where people convened from far-flung locations.

Perhaps, given the circle's financial crisis, Kunio and Seiko were looking for someone to infuse cash into their operation. Or, since Nicky had died, they were looking for someone to replace him.

I went back to the *Hedgehog* table. When I smiled at the talkative hedgehog who had helped me earlier and drew only a blank, I guessed that he had not recognized me in the Mars Girl costume.

"Excuse me, but I'm Rei Shimura. I'm the one who asked you about *Showa Story* earlier," I began.

"Oh, you do make up nicely!" His laugh sounded delighted. "So you found Kunio-san?"

"No. But I've been thinking. . . ." I paused, not sure how to phrase it. "Do any really important people come to this convention?"

"Oh, yes. Our fans are the most important people on earth!"

"Um, besides them. Are there businesspeople attending this convention? Persons who might help fund production of a *doujinshi* series?"

Hedgehog scratched his appropriately bristly chin. *"Eh to . . .* I understand what you're asking. The type of people who might discover a *doujinshi* and help the artists make money."

"Yes. Who would that be?"

"Well, we are doing it on our own. We have some part-time jobs that help pay for paper and so on. Other circles might have their comics printed for free, but then, of course, they give their profits straight to the printer to cover the cost."

"I see." Seiko's father owned Hattori Copy Shop. There was a great deal of leeway she could have had in getting the printing done at a reasonable cost. That is, if her father had been helpful to the group. He had sent a bill for printing to Kunio Takahashi—it didn't look like a free arrangement anymore.

"I don't know if there are any printers here today. To tell the truth, I don't think they seek out amateur *manga* artists like this. We're more likely to lose money than make it."

I was reminded again of the voice on the telephone that had told me that Kunio wasn't interested in making money. But Nicky had told me that Kunio had debts to pay.

"How much did this table cost you?" I asked Hedgehog.

"Mmm. Ten thousand yen for the whole weekend. If we're lucky, we'll make it up in sales. But in the past, we have taken a loss."

"You're here because of your love of the art," I said.

"We don't love art. We love *manga.*"

"I really appreciate the time you've given me. I'd like to buy one of your comics," I said.

"Great! I'd recommend you start with the first in the series. Would you like my autograph?"

"Very much so."

I opened my backpack and took out a thousand-yen note to pay for the magazine. When I was handed back four hundred yen, I said, "Can you give me a receipt? I think I can claim this as a business expense."

"Sorry, but I can't. We're not like a regular shop or anything. We don't pay taxes to the government."

I'd forgotten what Hiroko, the managing editor at Dayo Publishing, had said about *doujinshi*. She'd mentioned, with a slight air of resentment, how her company had to pay taxes on their profits from the magazines sold. The amateurs could keep everything.

I took the magazine from the hedgehog and wandered off, thinking about what he'd told me. Nicky had been the business manager for the circle. I wondered if, in some way, tax issues might have led to his death.

Now I had to decide where to venture next. I didn't think I'd get much out of sitting in a dark room watching *anime* films, and I thought there was no point in going to the costume contest, since I could see pretty wild costumes going right by me. I decided to go the main stage, where an event called Freestyle Draw Room was taking place. An emcee, a twenty-something boy with a harsh blond dye job, was speaking earnestly into the microphone about the competition at hand. The audience would suggest popular *manga* characters, and the artists onstage would be given two minutes to draw an impression. The audience would vote for originality and accuracy, two concepts that seemed to me to be antithetical.

When the call for the first character came, a young woman dressed in a school uniform was picked to choose the theme.

"Um, well, how about Sailor Moon?" she ventured.

I expected to hear groans of boredom from the hundreds of *anime* fans sitting cross-legged around her, but there was only polite applause. So Sailor Moon it was. The three artists sketched, and out of the wide strokes of calligraphy pen, marker, or pencil, the familiar saucer-eyed schoolgirl heroine began to take shape. Everyone drew Sailor Moon's braids and face in a similar manner—here was accuracy in play. Originality was to be seen in Sailor Moon's actions. One artist drew her with an assault weapon pointed at the audience; another depicted her with her skirt blowing up; the third drew her standing at an easel, drawing a picture of herself.

Even though the artist who drew the sketching Sailor Moon hadn't quite finished the illustration when two minutes were up, he received the most applause. I didn't agree—I thought the sketch of the gun-toting schoolgirl was the best, even though the theme disgusted me.

The artists autographed and ripped off their work from the easels. A few people rushed forward to claim the rejected art. Collectors wanted everything—even unpublished *manga*.

I watched a few more cartoon characters get their two minutes in the spotlight. Two of the three artists kept winning. The artist who kept drawing each character with weapons in hand did not. Her thin shoulders sagged with desperation, and she drew more slowly.

Watching the art contest was making me tense, so I stood up to leave. All around me, people were spread out with colorful comics around them. The colorful patchwork they made reminded me of beachgoers with their towels spread out over the sand at Isshiki Beach.

Applause meant that someone had won again. Now the emcee was calling on another audience member to suggest a theme.

"You, you," a woman sitting near me said, suddenly pointing at me.

Oh, God. The fact that I was standing made them think I had a suggestion. *What the hell.* "Mars Girl," I said.

"She said Mars Girl!" the girl near me shouted toward the stage.

"How about it?" the emcee said to the artists. "Can your talents take on the universe's deadliest girl alien?"

Now I had to stay. I moved back closer to the front so I could see the artists' work better. I was rooting for the girl who kept losing, but it didn't look as if things were going to change—her Mars Girl was skewering herself with a long, sharp bayonet. An uncomfortable, violent, sloppily drawn image. The artist who liked sexual themes drew Mars Girl pulling on a pair of stockings, and the third artist, who had won the very first round with Sailor Moon, depicted a beaming Mars Girl holding up two fingers in the peace sign.

This camera-mugging Mars Girl won—why on earth did people think the work was good? Sure, it was executed precisely, but the themes were always so corny. The artist was a tall, thin young man who was dressed like a salaryman. Maybe this was the kind of *doujinshi* artist who would someday be hired by a mainstream publisher, I thought as hands stretched out for the finished picture he was tossing off the stage.

Wait a minute. Here was art I could use to illustrate the convention that wouldn't let us take photographs. I surged forward, trying to make it to the stage at the same time I was identifying the fans taking hold of the pictures. I would have to bribe the fans to let me have the pictures.

A young man who had stood up from the group was dressed in a tailored white jacket and trousers gone yellow with age. His profile revealed an elegant jaw, but his eyes were masked by wrap-around sunglasses. He had gone straight to the young woman who had drawn the ill-fated picture with a bayonet. As if to better see her picture, the man took off his sunglasses and left them casually dangling from one hand. He took the sketch of Mars Girl disemboweling herself with the other.

I could see the artist's expression. She looked rapturous. A flush bloomed on her cheeks, and she blinked rapidly. She didn't say anything, but her lips parted, as if for a kiss.

With a reaction like that, she had to be looking at Kunio Takahashi.

35

The conversation lasted only a moment, and by the time the emcee was calling out for new draw-on-demand requests, Kunio had slipped his glasses back on and was striding toward the room's exit.

I draped myself casually against the set of doors that shielded the exit. He would need to ask me to step aside. Contact would happen.

As he advanced in my direction, he unrolled the picture and began looking it over. It's hard for me to walk and read a map at the same time, but Kunio took everything—literally—in his stride. I thought I saw his nostrils flare slightly while he studied the picture, and I wondered if that meant he disliked it.

We were about six feet away from each other. Kunio took off his glasses, as if to get a better look at my costume. I examined his face, the high, sculpted cheekbones and dark eyes with velvety lashes that looked as if they'd seen a few coats of mascara. A perfect, side-parted red-brown bang swooped over one of his eyes.

I recalled how gorgeous all the girls had said he was. To me, though, he was an androgynous mannequin. A boy straight out of the comic books.

Kunio offered me a charming smile and a half bow. I readied myself for some kind of compliment on my costume. He looked like a flatterer. He had probably flattered the artist who gave him the picture.

"Excuse me," he said in a soft voice. I didn't move. He tried again. "Um, sorry. I need to get by."

"Why did you take that sketch?" I asked. His conversational style was less charming than I'd expected.

"I like Mars Girl." He moved closer to the door, as if trying to coax me to move away from it.

"I guess you're collecting all forms of Mars Girl now that your *doujinshi* is finished."

Kunio blinked his perfect eyes and examined me more closely.

"You don't recognize me," I said.

"Did we drink tea together once or something?" He was using a Japanese euphemism for dating.

"Sorry, that's not it."

"Your teeth look American," he said.

"That should be a clue." I was almost enjoying myself.

He put his dark glasses back on. "Come on, who are you?"

People in the hallway were banging on the other side of the door, wanting to get in. But I kept it barred, not wanting to end my talk with Kunio. "My name is Rei Shimura," I said at last. "I've left some messages for you to call me."

"Oh!" He bit his luscious lower lip. "You look different today."

You look different today. If he'd only heard me on the phone, he wouldn't have known what I'd looked like that day. I put two and two together. He had to be Sunglass Man, who had stalked me in the *anime* coffee shop the afternoon Nicky died. And maybe pushed me in the train station, too. Now that he'd concealed himself behind his dark glasses, his expression was unreadable.

"How did you learn so much about Japanese history? Comfort women, organized crime, all that?"

"Nicky studied Japanese history in America. He told us those stories. I wasn't sure if half of them were true, but they made good comics," Kunio said. "So he's the one you should have concentrated on. Not me."

"But you have an artistic gift," I said. "I loved your illustrations in the comics, and your mural at Show a Boy. I thought that I could organize a gallery show for you. You could create provocative paintings based on the best illustrations you've done in the comics."

"You talk about provocative painting. That sounds like bull. All I want to do is make comic books."

"A comic book gives you just a few inches of space to exercise your creativity. A painting, such as the mural you made, shows the breadth of what you can do. In fact, I believe that mural was promising, but just a hint of the good things that are to come from you."

"It was a stretch. Drawing at that different scale was fun, but . . ." He shook his head. "How many times will I be given a blank wall like that to work on? In a city as crowded as Tokyo?"

"You could work on canvas," I suggested.

"Who can buy materials like that? I have no money."

"But you're ahead financially now that Nicky's dead."

"What?"

"You borrowed money from him."

"I repaid him."

"Not before he died," I said. "I know. I was at the apartment building where you live, and he complained to me."

Kunio was still for a minute. Suddenly his arm flashed out and pushed the door open. He squeezed through the anime fans waiting on the other side of the door.

"Hey," I called, trying to catch up with him. But the crowd

that had amassed while I kept the door shut had surged forward. I was like a surfer on top of a fast-rising wave.

"Stop the man in white," I shouted. I'd been so stupid to reveal my identity to Kunio. Why had I done it? I'd wanted to get a reaction. Well, he'd come through with one, and it wasn't what I'd wished for.

My calls for help had attracted attention.

"Ooh, it's a role-playing game!" someone shrieked.

"Mars Girl, may we join you?" my hedgehog friend called out.

"Yes, yes!" I said wildly, trying to keep Kunio in my line of vision. "Just catch the man in white."

Now the wave had turned into a riptide. I was carried along in the collective energy of a group of ninja warriors, Sailor Moons, and Pocket Monsters surging behind the slim figure in white hurrying down the hall. In the midst of the multicolored throng, I thought I caught a flash of blue. Yes, a man in his thirties wearing a police uniform had joined the crush. It was Lieutenant Hata.

"Police," he boomed. "All people must stop running. Stop running now!"

The crowd obediently halted, which in turn caused a massive collision. It was like standing in the middle of a packed subway car that had suddenly come to a halt. I was pushed back and forth, and someone grabbed at my Mars Girl wig. A girl toppled on me; I lost time brushing myself off and engaging in mutual apology. All the fans were getting sheepishly to their feet and grumbling about the unfair censorship of a great role-playing game.

"It's a shame you couldn't lead the game in here, Shimura-san," the hedgehog mourned. "Let's try again outside, say, in a couple of hours? How about on the beach?"

Lieutenant Hata's loud voice cut into our conversation. "Shimura-san, so you're here! Were you responsible for inciting this riot?"

"I didn't mean to," I said, feeling desperate. God, was inciting a riot punishable by jail time? "I was only trying to catch up with Kunio Takahashi."

"You were?" There was genuine surprise in his voice, and perhaps a hint of envy.

"A riot is not what we want. The comic book freaks promised they'd be calm, *neh?* This is a violation of that agreement!" A middle-aged man on Lieutenant Hata's heels threw in his own two yen's worth. I guessed he represented the convention hall.

"It's not the group that's at fault, though I must say they behaved without thinking," the lieutenant said to him. In a louder voice he added to the crowd, "All right, everyone, pick yourselves up and go back to what you were doing. But please don't ever run in this hall. Even in the case of emergency, proceed quietly to the nearest exit."

"After exiting, convention-goers cannot come back in," the manager said. "And you, young miss, must exit immediately."

Everyone was looking at me. I looked back and caught a glimpse of Rika behind someone. She looked horrified, and I wondered if it was because she was really worried for me, or because now she knew our news story had totally collapsed.

"You must go," the manager repeated.

Lieutenant Hata cleared his throat. "I'm sorry to say, Shimura-san, that by law he can decide that."

"But I—I'm in costume. I've got to get my real clothes back."

"No time for that. We must restore order." The sumo wrestlers who had served as the convention security had appeared. They looked even more menacing this time around.

I thought I caught a flash of sympathy in Lieutenant Hata's eyes, but he only said, "Actually, it is the prerogative of the building's management to refuse admission. I'll walk out with you. In fact, I've got those questions I want to ask you—"

"Forget about it," I said furiously, gathering my convention bag tightly against my blue unitard. I began my solitary walk toward the exit sign.

A high voice came from behind me. "Rei-san, I'll retrieve your clothing for you. Where did you leave it? Please don't be anxious." It was Rika, following me, but then that was the usual course of events.

"Do you think I believe you'd do anything in my interest? Anyway, I'm not worried about my clothes," I snapped at her.

"But you said—oh!" Her eyes widened. "You were making an excuse to stay in."

I was almost to the steel exit door. In a stony voice, I said, "Now that I'm going, the story is in your hands. Take it."

"Don't say that!" Rika cried. "We work together. You are the *sempai*, and I am the *kohai*."

She was using classical terms, calling me the superior and herself the inferior.

"You'll stay and finish up, won't you?" I asked bitterly.

"I'll try."

The sumo wrestler who had been tailing us held the exit door open. There was nothing for me to do but go through it.

36

It was the weekend, which meant Hayama and Zushi were clogged with traffic. I waited with a crowd at the bus stop, feeling the sweat trickle under my costume. I felt as if I'd been wrapped in foil.

There were a few conventioneers at the bus stop who didn't give me a second glance, but I could tell that the coolly dressed beachgoers were intrigued. Surfers poked their friends and whispered about whether I'd made my outfit out of a tanning blanket. I stared into the road, willing the bus to come. At last one came, but it was headed in the wrong direction: toward Zushi Station, not the emperor's palace.

I decided to walk. This way I could keep scanning the landscape for Kunio Takahashi, who probably was on the loose from the convention. But I saw no young man dressed in a white military uniform, just people on motorcycles or in cars. What had happened to the Japan where people were known for walking for miles?

The heat seemed to increase exponentially underneath my tight nylon outfit. Within a few minutes, I went from feeling damp to completely soaked. Now my outfit was truly obscene.

Probably no bus driver would want me to board his vehicle.
My best bet was to walk all the way to Takeo's house.

I was so hot and thirsty that I stopped at a vending machine
to buy a Pocari Sweat. I drank it down in less than a minute.
The machine had a little hole in it where you were supposed to
throw the empty can, but it was all filled up. Too many thirsty
people.

I continued my walk, looking for a place where I could
throw away the can. There was an actual wastebasket on the
corner ahead. It looked fairly stuffed, but I could perch the can
on top of it. As I drew closer, I saw something hairy on top. It
looked fairly unappealing; as I launched my can into the
wastebasket, I saw that the hairy object was a dog's head. Not
a real one, but one made of acrylic fur with holes for eyes. It
was a dog's head mask.

A dog's head. I remembered Seiko Hattori's supposed dog
costume. Had she recently walked by? If so, why had she discarded the head of her costume?

It was an odd place where the head had been dropped:
about a quarter mile from the convention hall, but just a
stone's throw from a beach entrance. This was part of Isshiki
Beach, but not the end that was close to Takeo's house. I didn't
know it at all. I looked at the dog's head, and I listened to the
waves hitting the rocks, just across the street. I supposed that a
person heading to the beach might abandon a heavy mask.

I waited for a break in traffic and crossed the street.

"Look at the freak!"

I heard the giggles after I set foot in the sand. Young people
lying on their towels were openly gaping at me. Maybe I
should have thrown away the wig I was wearing; I hadn't
done it because it was a rental. Somehow I'd try to return it
and get my money back.

"It's a convention of them," a mother massaging sunblock into her baby's shoulders murmured to her husband. "So many today."

I turned to address them. "Have you seen a dog? I mean, a person dressed like a dog?"

The woman clapped her hand over her mouth, as if to hide her embarrassment.

The man spoke sharply. "We don't know your kind. This beach is for families, *neh?*"

I could have argued that they didn't need to know my kind, all they had to do was tell me whether they'd seen someone dressed as a dog, but there was no point.

How I longed for Takeo's bird-watching binoculars so I could scan the beach at a glance. I trudged through the sand, my head whipping in all directions. I truly felt like an alien from outer space.

I walked the whole section of unfamiliar beach without luck and decided that I might as well continue on my route to Takeo's house via the water. At least, if I walked by the water's edge, I couldn't hear all the snickers of the people lying in the sand. I unlaced my Asics and threw them in the convention tote bag; now, as I walked in the shallow water, at least my feet were pleasantly cool. I was almost to the section where the Bojo bar was located. I didn't want to go too close, lest I encounter the Fish.

A man was standing in the water ahead of me; there was something familiar about the profile. He was wearing an undershirt and a pair of white trousers. He slowly circled, turning toward the string of bars in the sand, as if he was looking for someone. From the smooth movements, I recognized him. Once again, Kunio Takahashi.

He'd recognize me in a flash in the creepy Mars Girl outfit. I sat down quickly on the sand, unzipping the unitard. Underneath it, I was wearing a black Jockey bra and underpants.

Well, it almost looked like my Speedo bikini. I washed the makeup off my face in the shallow waters and then picked out the sharp fragment of tile that I'd been carrying in my backpack and gripped it in my hand, just in case.

As I started walking toward Kunio, I remembered how I'd once had nightmares about appearing in my underwear in a public place. Yet here I was getting far less attention than when I'd been wearing the Mars Girl costume. I was twenty feet from Kunio now, and he hadn't noticed me. If he saw me and decided to run, I'd follow. He might be faster in the beginning, but I doubted that he'd have as much stamina as I did. Besides, I was in sporty underwear, and he wasn't. He'd be vastly uncomfortable if he got into motion.

I was about ten feet away from Kunio when he finally noticed me. He put his hands on his hips and stared me down.

"Another tacky Rei Shimura costume. Who are you playing this time?"

"Myself," I said. "I'm the same woman you watched in the *anime* coffee shop, and whom you punched in the train station. I don't think you're going to get the better of me this time."

"I was in the coffee shop, but not in any train station, okay? Not that you'll believe it—you think I killed him. Is that why you're carrying that weapon in your hand?"

I looked at the tile, and I handed it to him. "No, I don't believe you could have. Now I'm thinking that you first spotted me when I was at your apartment building, and it was you who shut the door to your apartment so I couldn't keep looking around. You were worried, so you followed me around all day. Because of that, you couldn't have killed Nicky. If you were in the coffee shop when I was, you didn't commit the murder."

"Do you think . . . the police would believe it?"

"Maybe. Especially if you helped them find the killer," I said.

His eyes were darting around the beach.

"You know who killed Nicky," I said. "Is she here?"

"She was," he said in a low voice.

"It makes perfect sense," I said. "How exactly did you tip off Chiyo about *Showa Story*?"

Kunio stubbed his toe in the sand. "It was a mistake. When I asked for her help, I told her that I couldn't afford a post office box because we had to give all the profits to the printer. I guess she told them then."

"You mean she told the *yakuza*?" I said. The sound of waves masked the word from others.

"That's who's after us, right? I was getting these strange fan letters from a man who called himself the Fish. It was really giving me a stomachache, reading all this stuff about me being a living national treasure. He wanted me to draw *manga* glorifying the gangster tradition. Can you imagine how that made me feel?"

"The Fish didn't kill Nicky. He wouldn't do anything to hurt your series. He wanted to keep reaping profits."

"How?"

"The *yakuza* must have been taxing Seiko Hattori's father—because he printed your *manga* and kept the profits. They like to get a handout from illicit businesses. It used to be that *yakuza* mostly hit up businesses in the floating world. But now, even a copy shop printing *doujinshi* can come under scrutiny."

"I could have quit a year ago." Kunio sounded mournful. "This artist at Dayo Publishing wanted to hire me. But I was proud. I wanted to do my own work."

"I have one question for you," I said. "Nicky and Seiko—I just can't understand. Why did he have a romantic relationship? He could have had anyone."

"You mean someone who's got a better body than Seiko?"

"No." I blushed, and suddenly I remembered I was having a conversation standing in my underwear. "In fact, Nicky told me he felt sorry for me. That I couldn't possibly get anyone in Japan."

Kunio smiled a world-weary smile. "Have you noticed the sex in *Showa Story*?"

"There was quite a lot of it in the later issues."

"Yeah. Nicky came up with the stories. I just illustrated."

"Oh?"

"He was seriously kinky. And not many girls would have done the things he liked to do in private. Seiko loved him more than life itself. She'd do anything, he said."

"Oh," I said again. "I wonder how much her father knew."

"He didn't know she was sexually involved with Nicky," Kunio said. "If he knew, he'd have been very angry. Most fathers want their daughters to stay pure. I know Seiko was not pure, but she was fragile."

Fragile wasn't the word I'd pick. Seiko was so sturdily built. She'd been reading an erotic comic when I saw her on the bus. She didn't strike me as a shrinking violet.

"I saw a dog's head mask in the trash outside this beach. Why did Seiko throw away her precious costume?"

"She didn't say. She left about fifteen minutes ago, after telling me that she was sorry and wanted to say good-bye."

"Where is she going?" I asked, completely confused.

"I don't know. She didn't mention that. She paged me at the convention, and when I called her back, we made this plan to meet here. I assume it was convenient for her."

"Why would it be more convenient to meet here than at the convention?" I shook my head and stared into the waves. "Which way did she go when she left you?"

Kunio scratched his chin. "Well, we were sitting on the sand. From one of the little stands, she ordered both of us ice cream and glasses of lemonade. She said that she wanted me to have a tart memory, because the time we spent working on *Showa Story* was the most bittersweet time of her life. Then she just stood up and left, taking her lemonade. I couldn't leave because I had to find the cash to pay the bill. I didn't have quite enough, but the waitress let me off. I was pretty embarrassed that this happened when both of us were wearing costumes. It gives *manga* fans . . . well, a bad image in the mainstream."

"I know what you mean." I was continuing to look along the shoreline. Two hundred feet ahead I noticed a yellowish pile of something. It made me feel strangely worried.

I looked at Kunio. "Tell me, are you a good swimmer?"

He shook his head. "Not at all. I grew up in the mountains. No chance to learn."

"Call an ambulance. I might be going in."

"Going in where?"

"The water. I think that Seiko might have gone in."

Normally I would stretch and start off rather slowly when I ran; this time, I went full blast. As I drew closer to the pile, it began looking like a fur coat. No, it was an acrylic dog costume. A dog collar and shoes were neatly laid beside the clothes, along with an empty drinking glass and a small vial. It was an empty container that had a Valium prescription and my name on it. Seiko must have taken the drugs from my backpack during the brief time that I'd gone to the bathroom at St. Luke's and my cousin had left her to deal with his emergency-room concerns.

I began shaking then, because I knew that my first thought was right: Seiko had probably committed suicide.

I scanned the ocean, noticing about a thousand heads with straight, shiny black hair. I was looking for a head that wasn't close to anyone else's, a head that was taking a lonely trajectory out to sea, or struggling far past the buoys.

I ran through the water, because I knew my feet would carry me faster than my arms. When the water hit waist level, I slowed down. I got on my right side and sidestroked, cursing myself for never having learned the crawl correctly. I stopped to tread water for a minute and decide whether I had the strength to go on.

I thought I could see a black speck in the distance, a moving black speck. Could that be Seiko? She was out far beyond the safe swimming area marked with buoys. If there had been a lifeguard, he might have noticed her. But on this beach, there were no lifeguards.

I turned my attention to the people around me. There were some guys on Jet-Skis, a couple necking in an inner tube, and a couple of elementary-school boys battling over a boogie board.

I looked at the board. It reminded me of the kickboards I'd used in school—great for someone who needs to go far but doesn't like to put her head in the water.

I waved at the children, affecting the cheerful tone of a teacher. "Hello, children. Did you hear about the free ice cream on the beach?"

"Ice cream?" Being in Japan, the kids were not instantly suspicious of strangers.

"My friend, Mr. Kunio Takahashi, the man dressed in white standing in the shallow water, says that he is buying free ice cream for anyone who needs it. The catch is, I'll need to borrow your boogie board while you're on shore." They'd find out later how short on cash Takeo was. Perhaps the police would get involved, which was what I'd need after I got out of the water.

"It's my boogie board!" one of the boys shouted.

"Yes, yes, I'll take good care of it." I already had it under one arm and was launching off. In less than a minute, the boys' shouting receded, and all I heard was my kicking. I was moving faster than I'd thought possible, wired on adrenaline. It was so different from swimming in a pool. Every couple of minutes, a wave roared in and pushed me backward twenty feet. I reminded myself that the waves were pushing Seiko back, too. Maybe that was why she wasn't so far ahead.

I estimated that the gap between us was about fifty feet. She was swimming a slow breast stroke, and when her head and shoulders came up, I could see her shoulder-length hair.

I waited for a moment of calm before I called out to her. "Seiko, wait!"

She stopped and cast a glance over her shoulder. She was treading water. Her hands barely broke the surface of the water. She seemed very tired.

I didn't know the expression for "treading water" in Japanese, so I said, "Keep moving! I'm coming to help you."

I couldn't see her facial expression, but her movements became more agitated. She turned with a big splash and started swimming farther out.

As I floated and kicked, I thought about how the sequence of events must have gone. Kunio had let drop to Chiyo that his profits were going to the Hattori Copy Shop. Chiyo in turn told the Fish, who hit the father up for a "tax." Seiko knew about that, and she was trying to end her life as her own punishment for causing the problem.

Seiko was splashing only intermittently now. I paddled as fast as I could; if she went under, I'd be useless at retrieving her.

I wondered whether her slow movements were genuinely a show of weakness. Seiko was a sturdily built young woman who had overpowered a well-muscled young man. She was a much better swimmer than I. The only reason I had been able to close the distance between us was because I had the support of a boogie board. I was getting nearer, but another wave was headed my way. A big one. I watched it swell.

Seiko wasn't aware of the coming wave. When it hit her, her naked body was picked up like a cheap plastic doll and spat out into the air. I couldn't watch anymore; I made my body into a straight line so the wave would roll over me. The sound was deafening.

When the wave was gone, I raised my head and saw a hand in the water about twenty feet from me. I paddled over as quickly as I could, and let go of the board to try to haul up the body that matched the hand.

The body was Seiko. I'd imagined that if I caught her, she'd fight me, but she was limp as a noodle. Fortunately, she wasn't dead. She was coughing as if she'd swallowed a ton of water, but her eyes were closed. The Valium must have taken effect.

Now it was up to me to get her to safety. The outlook was bad: I was a weak swimmer bringing in a woman incapable of movement, and perhaps in need of mouth-to-mouth resuscitation. The one thing I had to help me was the boogie board.

Treading water, I managed to slide the board under her chest. She now hung over the board like a collapsed drunk at a table. There was no room for me on the board, but I could keep one hand on its side and kick, slowly moving us both toward the shore. The danger would be waves—I didn't know if we could both successfully hang on and ride.

We were still in water deeper than five feet, but I could see people swimming around. I took a hand off Seiko to wave for help. Nobody noticed. When I got closer, I would yell.

Just then, though, a familiar roar sounded behind me. A wave. I peeked over my shoulder and saw that it was a big one. Seiko was lined up well on the board, but she didn't have a firm grip on it. I awkwardly clambered on, making a tight hold with my own hands so she was sandwiched between me and the board. This was a move that skinny kids under ten could do with ease; it was decidedly awkward for women our size.

Seiko must have come to, because she moaned just as the wave shot up behind us. All I was conscious of was holding on to the board, which the wave threatened to rip away, along with Seiko's body.

The next thing I knew, Seiko's body and the board were gone. When my body came to rest, my nose was in sand. We'd been flung so far that we were in shallow waters. I shakily stood up in the thigh-deep water. Seiko and the board were still together, floating a few feet away. We were just a few footsteps to safety. I bent over and, with my hands, pulled the floating girl to the beach.

37

After the water had been pounded out of Seiko's lungs, she was too zonked from Valium to talk to anyone. In fact, she fell asleep. All the rescue people and police and *manga* fans who had materialized were disappointed. As they crowded in around us on the sand, talking on their radios, I saw a balding man standing at a distance in bathing trunks.

I looked straight at the Fish. He flashed me the peace sign and slowly moved off toward the road. I saw a Cadillac with long fins waiting. He got in the back, and the car moved off. I wondered how much he'd seen of the events at the beach—whether he'd watched me flail out in the water with Seiko and decide justice would be served if she or I, or both of us, died.

Lieutenant Hata told me to go home, get some rest, and meet him at the hospital the next morning.

We went in together, and the sun was shining brightly through the window on her wan figure lying in bed. There was supposedly a law in Japan about every hospital room having windows designed so that patients would experience sun to uplift their spirits. But Seiko wasn't smiling. When she saw me, she covered her face with her hands.

"I'm so sorry," she said.

Snapping on a tape recorder, Lieutenant Hata said, "Sorry about what, exactly?"

"Sorry for the trouble I caused you, Rei-san. I was with my father in the train station when he hit you on the staircase. I caught you because I didn't expect you to fall that way, and I thought you might die. But I knew, I knew the whole time what happened."

"So your father killed Nicky Larsen?" I asked.

"No, no! I did it. I—I had to."

"He made you?" I asked, incredulous.

"Let her speak freely," Lieutenant Hata whispered to me, and Seiko did. The words poured out. Chiyo had accidentally let the Fish and his group know that a *doujinshi* artist was using her business as a mailing address. The slip had occurred because someone had left *Showa Story* mail lying on the bar, and the Fish asked about it, sensing a new source of income. He'd first asked Kunio for the money; Kunio had protested that any money they made went to their printer, to cover his costs. Then the Fish changed tactics and demanded money from Mr. Hattori.

Mr. Hattori became very frightened and sent a bill to Kunio, trying to prove that he wasn't bankrolling or making money from *Showa Story*. He also yanked Seiko out of school and told her to shut down the circle. Kunio, being Japanese, had understood the threat immediately; he'd left his apartment for a while because he didn't want the *yakuza* to come after him. But Nicky, with his all-American ideas of capitalism, had been unwilling to desist. His plan was to translate all the existing issues of *Showa Story* and sell the series on the U.S. market. He wanted to do more Japanese issues as well, and even said that he would draw the comics if Kunio wouldn't.

"So you were in a very difficult situation," Lieutenant Hata said at the end of Seiko's recital.

"Yes. If the *yakuza* became involved in my father's business, his life would be ruined. My mother's life would be, too! If only Nicky had just been willing to stop, the way Kunio had been. But Nicky was a typical foreigner. Handsome and charming, but he didn't understand how to fit in with others. He cared only for himself."

As Seiko finished speaking, I thought about whether her description of foreigners applied to me. Did Takeo see me this way? Was my problem at the *Gaijin Times* my fault?

"What happened on Monday, the day that Nicky Larsen died?" Lieutenant Hata.

"I went to my father's shop to work and told him that I needed free time between one and three that day." Seiko spoke in a rush, and I sensed she wanted to unload her sad experience for good. "I told him that I would like to attend a presentation on new photocopying equipment in Akihabara. He thought it was a good idea."

"You went to meet Nicky for the matinee," I said.

"That's right. My family has a car, which I drove to his apartment. Nicky had always wanted to, um, do it inside the car. I think that is an American tradition. Is that true, Rei-san?"

I blushed. "I think in movies and such it is, but probably not in real life. It's quite—risky."

"Nicky loved risk. I didn't." Seiko cried softly for a minute. "He liked to do this thing where he would stop breathing for a few seconds at the time of . . . you know, the time of the most pleasure."

"What exactly happened during your last time with Nicky?" Lieutenant Hata continued the questions.

"He asked me to draw a stocking tightly around his throat. We'd done it about ten times before. He was enjoying the time in the car so much, he insisted I use one of my stockings."

"Where was the car parked when this was going on?"

"By a vacant warehouse near the river. I knew the place had gone out of business, because we used to pick up goods there, and now it's closed. So I thought it would be a safe spot to make love." She cried again. "We did, and when it was time for him, he signaled me with his hand. I pulled the stocking, and everything flashed before my eyes: the problems with my father and the *yakuza*, how stubborn Nicky was. I knew the problems would all go away if Nicky stopped breathing."

She paused and stared out of the window for a long time. Then she looked directly at me.

"I was thinking about what it would be like to keep pulling on the stocking. I didn't realize until a minute later that I'd really done it. His eyes were wide open, but they didn't see anymore. And he was not breathing."

"Oh, my God." I put my face in my hands, unable to look at her.

"I ran out of the car and into the warehouse, which was unlocked, thinking maybe there was a telephone, I could call the ambulance for help. But of course there was no telephone; it was closed. I went back to the car, and the body was there. I started thinking about how now I was a murderer, that my father could trade me to the *yakuza* as an—an employee!—and they would stop asking him for money."

"Did you do that?"

"Oh, no. When I was calm, I took a tarpaulin from the trash outside the warehouse and brought it to the car. I wrapped it around Nicky—that way I could drag him to the river's edge, and there I threw him. I drove back to the copy shop. My father asked where was the literature from the Akihabara photocopying demonstration. I said I'd forgotten it. He said, 'You've been with that American, haven't you? I can tell.' Then he hit me; that was the black eye that you saw. After he hit me, I told him he'd never need to worry about Nicky again, and he said, 'It's a good thing you're finally listening to me.'" Seiko paused. "Pretty soon after that, it was reported on television that Nicky had died. I think my father guessed that something might have happened in the car, because he had it cleaned the next day. But he never asked me any questions. I think he believes I did it to save our family."

It almost seemed like an accident, I thought. Manslaughter, with a cover-up. Curious about one thing, I asked Seiko, "Why did you make the *Mars Girl* marking on his forehead?"

"I didn't do that. He did it himself. He liked to draw on both of us during those moments. I washed my forehead off in the river. Oh, I should have just drowned myself then. I'm going to be put to death, aren't I?"

"Capital punishment is usually only exercised in situations of premeditated murder," Lieutenant Hata said. "Of course, I can't speak for the judge who will hear your case. But I will tell him that you were forthcoming with the story."

I left the hospital that afternoon and never saw Seiko Hattori again. She was transferred to a police-controlled sanitarium. The word was the government wanted to try her for manslaughter, not murder.

Curiously, Seiko became something of a cult heroine. The fact that she'd suffered abuse from her father for a relationship with a foreign boy made the Seiko-Nicky story one of star-crossed lovers. I hadn't tried to play it up that way in my article for the *Gaijin Times*—I'd just written furiously for three days. My article came in on time, but I told Mr. Sanno that he would get it only if Alec and Rika had no editorial responsibility. I just didn't trust them.

Rika and Alec stormed about it—in fact, I heard from Karen that they broke up, and when Rika's internship ended, she was not asked to reapply. Rather typically, Alec got to keep his job; I wondered if Rika would think twice about sleeping with someone in a Japanese office next time.

In the end, Norton Jones, the boring, slightly pompous business editor, edited my story. He asked me to clarify a few points, and he rewrote my lead, but otherwise, the story was just as I would have told it. Nicky and Seiko were the cover story of the next month's issue, and with Kunio Takahashi's permission, sections of his best work for *Showa Story* were included. Mr. Sanno decided to print a complete Japanese translation of my article, to run side by side with the English version, so for the first time anyone could remember, Japanese people bought the magazine. When the issue sold two hundred thousand copies, Mr. Sanno declared he'd discovered a winning formula. Japanese people liked being able to read what foreigners were saying about them—especially if it was conveniently translated. Frequent Japanese-English translations, in addition to *manga*, were going to make the *Gaijin Times* a hot new publication.

A week after the article was published, Kunio called me. He had decided, in light of all the fabulous publicity that had resulted, that he wanted me to represent his artwork. He'd decided that this was a golden moment.

I told him that I hated gold unless it was antique and gilding the edge of a screen. I was going back to selling antiques—no more dabbling in writing about modern art or artists. It was a dangerous distraction.

When I told Takeo the story of that conversation, he hugged me and said, "Does this mean you care for wood? For paper? The simple things that make up a simple Japanese house?"

"Well, of course," I said, kissing him. "My life's work is furnishing houses."

"Now that this house is fixed up, I'm thinking of doing another. The real estate market is depressed enough that I could actually buy an old house, then fix it up and sell it."

I shook my head. "There'll never be another house like this one. And it's in your family! How can you think of such a thing?"

"I'm not saying I'd give up this one," he said. "In any case, I couldn't. Not with Natsumi's half ownership."

"Oh, right." I frowned.

"In any case, I'll be bringing up the matter of buying more houses with my father when he comes for dinner tonight."

"You didn't invite him knowing I'd be here, did you?"

"Of course I did. He was most impressed with your article, he said—particularly the way you managed to keep our family name and house out of it."

"Well, I didn't see the point of bringing up anything that happened on your grounds, because I'd hate for it to become a tourist spot." I'd have to see Takeo's father that night. Did this mean I had to cook? Feeling completely frazzled, I asked, "What does your father like to eat?"

"Relax. I've ordered a platter of sashimi from the best place in town. It will be delivered half an hour after we're finished."

"Finished what?" I asked.

Takeo began to shimmy out of his shorts, and I could guess the rest.